Lo
like

Alm
vicin
stable

U
fire,
of u
stam
the
ther
to ca
Lo

Other books in the Women of the West series

BLUE FIRE
by Emma Harrington

Published by
PAGEANT BOOKS

WOMEN OF THE WEST

SILVER EYES

LAUREL COLLINS

17726

PAGEANT BOOKS

PAGEANT BOOKS
225 Park Avenue South
New York, New York 10003

Cover artwork by Franco Accornero

Printed in the U.S.A.

First Pageant Books printing: October, 1988

10 9 8 7 6 5 4 3 2 1

For my father,
J. T. Lemieux,
my first hero and a true Southern gentleman,
who raised his children to believe
that civility, gallantry, and honor
still have a place in the world today.

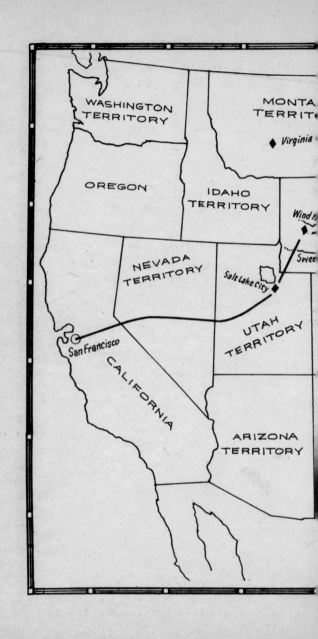

"The graceful white bird came to me, and I saw my dreams reflected in the silver of her eyes."

SILVER EYES

Prologue

✦✦✦✦

January 17, 1866—Madison County school authorities announced today their requirements for one-dozen young women of good moral character, each of whom would be willing to take up the position of schoolmistress in one of that Western county's several thriving communities. To be considered for employment, one must be at least sixteen years of age, must have successfully completed an approved course of study, and must pledge to remain unmarried for three years. Interested applicants should contact: Mr. N. P. Langford, Virginia City, Montana Territory.

Lorena Mackenzie read over the advertisement one more time, barely able to contain her excitement, then folded it neatly within

1

the letter she'd received just three days earlier. It was from Mr. Langford himself, informing her that her application had been accepted. She was exceptionally well qualified in all respects, Mr. Langford had written. And she would have no trouble meeting the last requirement, she told herself. Marriage was the last thing on earth that she wanted, for it was precisely what she was escaping.

Twelve dollars a month and board was not a fortune by any means. Lorena had spent larger sums during a single shopping excursion to New York City, but she would be traveling west, which sent her spirits soaring. Finally she would see for herself all the wondrous sights about which her father had written to her. And after all, the profession she'd chosen was a respectable one. It was a way out of her dilemma, a way to make her own way in the world so that she'd never again have to be beholden to her uncle.

For most of her eighteen years Lorena Mackenzie had lived a pampered existence on her mother's family estate in the Hudson River Valley. Her mother had died when she was only a small child, and her father had left her in the care of her uncle, Harrison Gilmore, while he pursued his dreams of finding his own fortune in California gold. Not too many years later, though, Lorena received word that he, too, was dead; and now her uncle, who ruled his household with an iron hand, was upsetting her comfortable world by planning to marry her off to his stepson, Henry Edgington.

But this time he'd not have his way, Lorena said to herself as she sat down at her writing desk and took up a sheet of paper. This time she would win.

Taking care not to reveal her plans, she had already sent two trunks of her belongings on ahead to the depot in St. Joseph. Now, by taking whatever else she could manage to carry on her own and slipping away this very night, she could be gone before her uncle had any clue that she intended to defy him.

As Lorena tucked her precious letter away in the pages of a book she'd been reading, she did not notice the advertisement slip out. It fluttered down like a leaf to the floor and floated beneath her chest of drawers.

Having decided upon her course, Lorena penned a letter to Mr. Langford, informing him that she accepted his terms and would be leaving immediately. Then, careful to avoid the prying eyes of her maid, she packed the remainder of her possessions. Like her father before her, Lorena Mackenzie would follow her dreams westward.

Chapter One

✦ ✦ ✦ ✦

July 1866

BEN THORNE COULD see the encroaching signs of civilization as he rode into Fort Kearney, Nebraska, on a late summer's day. There were more wagons waiting to depart than he'd ever seen before: more farmers and miners chasing the dream, hopes written plainly on their faces. Ben dismounted, tying off his reins on the hitching post, and tried to brush the worst of the trail dust from his buckskin shirt. This was the closest he'd come to civilization in months.

Broken Hand, the Indian accompanying him, grunted in disgust. "More and more white men cross the river. There will be much trouble . . . soon."

Thorne nodded and pulled thoughtfully at

his beard-stubbled chin. "There's no stopping it now," he told his friend.

Thorne looked around curiously at the bustling yard. From out of a door across the compound a young lady appeared. She was a vision in lavender-striped muslin with eyelet lace and a straw bonnet with flowing ribbons. It must be his mind playing tricks, Thorne thought. She seemed a mirage in the desert; no woman could be so beautiful. But as he watched her cross the parade ground, her form did not dissolve into the air like some phantasm. A prairie wind rose up, billowing the soft fabric of her dress and fluttering the wide-brimmed bonnet, tugging at it until finally it slipped down her back and rolled across the open yard like a tumbleweed. The lady gave chase, but in two quick strides Thorne had snatched it up like a prize.

She stopped short before him as he held it out to her. "Thank you, sir," she said, reaching a gloved hand out for it.

She had burnished gold hair that waved into a knot at the nape of her slender neck, and the air around her was sweetened with violets, but it was her eyes that held him transfixed . . . eyes like two pools of silver, so pure that he saw himself reflected.

"My pleasure, ma'am."

Who could she be? he wondered. And what had brought her to this place? She was most definitely Eastern-bred. Likely as not, she was some junior officer's wife, or the daughter of any one of a number of greedy devils sheltering here—who would soon be off on a hunt for gold. Thorne was angry all at once at the selfish fool responsible for her; any half-wit could see that such an exquisite blossom could never survive these climes.

She backed away then, a smile curving her lips, and Thorne rejoined Broken Hand, using the kerchief around his neck to mop his brow.

When they reached the post commander's office, Colonel Palmer was waiting for them. He quickly rose from his seat to extend a hand to Ben.

"Captain Thorne. Good to see you again."

Palmer settled himself behind the desk and gestured to the pair of chairs opposite. "Rest yourselves, gentlemen."

Ben eased into the chair and glanced over at the Indian, Broken Hand, who chose instead to stand in the shadows beside the window.

"I've resigned my commission, sir," Ben informed him. "It's just plain Ben Thorne now . . . and this is my partner, Broken Hand, of the Oglala Sioux tribe. You'll find him quite handy as an interpreter. Colonel Carrington told us you might need a scout to take you up to Fort Reno."

Palmer smiled, leaning back in his chair. "We do, indeed. I've an infantry company a number of civilians heading that way. We could use your assistance."

"Glad to help, sir. When can you be ready to move out?"

"First light of day."

Surprised, Thorne's eyes traveled to the window, unconsciously seeking another glimpse of the Eastern-bred beauty. But she'd disappeared from the parade ground, and he wondered if she'd only been a product of his imagination after all. "Are there many civilians in your party, Colonel?"

"Half a dozen emigrant families will be traveling under our protection as far as Fort Laramie, and three wagons have been set aside for Army wives and children."

Ben's heavy brow furrowed.

"Do you foresee a problem, Captain?" Colonel Palmer asked directly, choosing to call him by his former rank.

"Every wagon that heads north of Fort Laramie is a likely problem, as I see it."

"But the Peace Commission concluded a treaty with the Sioux and Cheyenne," Palmer protested, "we were advised that the matter was settled."

"Those who would fight did not come to the parley at Laramie," Broken Hand said from the corner of the room, speaking for the first time.

Ben nodded in agreement. "My friend here and I were at Fort Laramie in June, Colonel. While it's true enough that there were some peaceable Indians present to accept trinkets and put their mark on the treaty, I can assure you that more by far have decided that they will never sell their hunting grounds along the Bozeman Trail. They will shed blood, if they must, to protect them."

Broken Hand stepped out of the shadows and came to stand behind Thorne's chair. "Red Cloud, great Sioux chief, and Spotted Wolf of the Cheyenne came to this parley, but when the White Chief rode in with many soldiers, all knew the truth. The white man would steal the road before the Indians say yes or no."

"It was an unfortunate piece of luck that Colonel Carrington should arrive with his troops in the midst of the negotiations," Ben added. "It's shown them that we're not to be trusted."

Colonel Palmer rose to his feet, and with his hands clasped behind his back, began to pace a small stretch of the floor. "This is most distressing, of course, but I have my orders. The Bozeman Trail is to be made safe. I shall take my men to Fort Reno, where I am to assume command of the garrison. We will do our best to ensure the safety of the civilians in our care, and may God protect us in our endeavors."

Ben looked briefly at Broken Hand, who was shaking his dark head. Unlike the colonel, neither he nor the Indian was willing to leave their fates in the hands of the Almighty.

There were plenty of God-fearing men who'd headed out on the trail spouting that credo who now were lying in shallow graves up and down the Bloody Bozeman.

Lorena Mackenzie was unaccustomed to dust . . . and heat . . . and hard travel. Yet despite her pampered upbringing, she had adapted surprisingly well during these past weeks to the rigors of cross-country travel, comforting herself with the knowledge that at last she was free of her uncle.

She'd managed everything quite well so far, having arranged to travel along with the Army train to Fort Reno, where she could have a short visit with her old friend Charles Ackerman before continuing on to Montana and her new life.

Charles had been her closest friend throughout her life. His family's estate was near her uncle's home, and as children they'd been playmates, close as brother and sister. He was three years older, yet even when he'd outgrown their games, Charles had always let her tag along behind him and had remained as protective of her as if he were truly her brother.

When he went off to West Point, though, Lorena could not tag along. She was sent to Mrs. Fraser's Academy for Young Ladies where, instead of fitting in, she discovered what it was to be lonely. Charles wrote to her, though, exciting letters about his life at the military academy and the plans he'd made for his career. Then came the war, and while he went off to become a hero, Lorena could only stay behind and read the letters detailing his many adventures. Now, at last, Lorena would have an adventure of her own, one that would allow her to visit Charles, whom she hadn't seen in three years. The Army had sent him to Fort Reno, along the Bozeman Trail in the Dakota Territory, and Lorena would be passing that way en route to Montana.

"There's Indians hereabouts," the girl beside Lorena whispered under her breath, breaking into her thoughts.

Lorena turned to look at her friend. She had met Sarah Rawlins on the train in St. Louis, and immediately decided that she liked the slim young woman with the chestnut curls and ready smile. Sarah was a wide-eyed young Army bride, who saw this trip westward as a great opportunity for adventure. She'd admitted to Lorena that there hadn't been much adventure in her life thus far, growing up as she had on a quiet farm in Ohio. But now that they were twelve days out of Fort Kearney, Lorena saw misgivings in the speculative look on her friend's face. The landscape along the course of the Platte River had hardly been picturesque: bleak sand hills and endless expanses of grassland, the monotony relieved only by an occasional clump of willow and cottonwoods along the shore of the dark waters.

Now they were traveling in a mule-drawn Dougherty wagon, often referred to as an ambulance, since it was commonly used by the Army to transport wounded soldiers. The women shared their rough accommodations with Mrs. Owens, the wife of an infantry captain, and her three young sons, a restless brood who divided their time between wrestling with their litter of pups on the canvas and straw of the wagon bed and making general mischief among the other travelers in the wagon train.

Each morning Sarah and Lorena made themselves as comfortable as they could on a seat fashioned from a folded tent and spent their days looking out of the side of the wagon, where the canvas had been rolled up, at the scenery . . . such as it was. The summer's heat was oppressive; the hot winds carried clouds of fine dust that had been kicked up by the main body of troops and wagonloads of emigrants who preceded them in the line. The alkali dust covered every inch of skin and clothing and made traveling most uncomfortable for the ladies. But their discomfort was small compared to the small rear guard and the teamsters in charge of the baggage wagons, who were forced to travel all day in the dust of the others.

"Look there!" Sarah said, pointing at the

two riders making a wide circle around the wagons. "You see, I told you there were Indians traveling with us."

Lorena drew a handkerchief from her waistband and wiped away the perspiration that beaded her brow. She followed her friend's outstretched arm and studied the pair. One was, indeed, an Indian. Though he wore the tattered remnants of an Army tunic, he was otherwise clad in a breechclout, and she could see his long dark braids and the cluster of eagle feathers that hung from one of them. But it was his companion who attracted most of her attention. He was tall and lean, his features hidden beneath the wide brim of a cavalry officer's campaign hat, his sharp jaw shadowed by the stubble of a beard. He seemed at ease in the saddle, taking his Indian pony across the hard ground at a gallop to circle and draw up beside his friend as they studied the terrain.

"They're scouts for Colonel Palmer," Lorena explained. "I saw the pair of them at Fort Kearney, crossing the parade ground. I don't think that this particular Indian qualifies as a 'savage redskin,' Sarah, and certainly not one that we ought to be worried about."

Lorena felt Sarah shudder beside her, despite the heat. "Just the same, I'll rest easier when we've reached Fort Reno, where my Jed is waiting for me."

Jed was Lieutenant Jedediah Rawlins, 18th U.S. Infantry, and Sarah's husband of two years. During those two years, however, the couple had been together only a few months, for soon after their marriage Jed had enlisted with the 18th and gone to war, distinguishing himself at the Battle of Murfreesboro. Having decided on an Army career, he followed his regiment west into Indian country.

Lorena thought Sarah's story was a highly romantic one, and when she saw Sarah pining after her husband, she wondered if there'd ever be a man who could make her feel that way. But it probably wasn't in her nature, she told herself; she was too practical to pine.

The call for the nooning break went out, and the caravan came to a halt. Lorena had decided earlier that she was going to use the break to pay her respects to the colonel's wife, with whom she'd struck up a polite friendship. She had invited Sarah to come along, but her friend declined, saying she found Mrs. Palmer a dour matron whose only amusement seemed to be sitting in her rocking chair and boring others with her pontificating. Sarah also resented that the colonel's wife traveled in a more luxurious style than the rest of the train. Because of her husband's rank, she had been allowed to appropriate an entire ambulance for herself and her belongings, and she'd brought along her maid to see to her comfort.

So Lorena walked on her own along the line of wagons, which were drawn up now in columns, four abreast, to Mrs. Palmer's wagon, only to be told when she arrived that Mrs. Palmer had taken to her bed, suffering with a megrim. Since the nooning break would continue for a while longer, allowing time for the animals to graze, Lorena slowly headed through the tall prairie grass toward the sand hills, hoping for a better vantage point from which to survey the land.

The ground was uneven and dotted with clumps of grass and the evil-looking prickly pear, and she was glad she'd had the foresight to wear her riding boots as she clambered over the hills. The Army encampment disappeared from sight as she followed a rough path, created by buffalo, into a deep ravine. As she scaled the opposite wall of the ravine, she hoped that she might be treated to the sight of a herd of the shaggy beasts over the next rise. The buffalo had thus far not come within sight of the wagons, though the scouts and several of the cavalrymen had gone out hunting them on several occasions, returning with the meat of the beasts tied to strings of rawhide hanging from their saddles.

Lorena did not see any buffalo today, however. As she reached the crest of the hill, she gazed out over the vast expanse of prairie where she spied only a pair of antelope springing through the tall grass. On her right, cutting through the sands, lay the Platte River, half a mile wide and scarcely two feet deep. Just below was a grove of cottonwoods and low bushes through which a tributary coursed. Feeling an urge to explore further, Lorena made for the grove.

By now the midday heat was intense, rising off of the sand in shimmering waves. She found herself short of breath and suddenly lightheaded from her exercise. Having wandered from camp without a sunbonnet, she was thankful to reach the shade of the cottonwoods and settled herself beneath them, drawing out her handkerchief to sop up the rivulets of perspiration that trailed down her face. A fine, white dust was embedded in every pore and rose in a cloud when she shook out her skirts. Thoroughly exhausted, she rested her head against the trunk of the cottonwood tree, only for a minute. . . .

When she woke, she felt certain that she'd only dozed for an instant and did not think to check the position of the sun. Noticing the spring and the clear, still water of a pool in the thick of the cottonwood trees, she decided to rinse out her handkerchief and perhaps dangle her feet in the cool water. As she sat down on the grassy bank to pull off her heavy riding boots and unroll her stockings, the water was so tempting that she impulsively shed her clothes, opting for a bath.

Chapter Two

✦ ✦ ✦ ✦

RIDING OUT AT the head of the line of march, Ben Thorne scanned the horizon to get his bearings. "Another four hours at best," he told Broken Hand. "We'll reach the Old California Crossing by nightfall."

Just then a young soldier cut in front of the pair and wheeled his horse around, drawing up beside them. "Captain Thorne, sir," he said in an excited tone, "the colonel wants to speak to you right away. One of the young ladies is missing."

"One of the ladies?" Ben repeated.

"She must have wandered away from the camp back there while we were resting," the lad put in.

"Damned foolish Eastern women," Ben said, under his breath, shaking his head as he changed direction and spurred his horse toward the mounted contingent of officers.

Colonel Palmer confirmed the story. "It seems Mrs. Rawlins thought that Miss Mackenzie might be riding with my wife, since she'd gone to visit her, but when she learned that my wife never saw her, she sounded the alarm."

"The ladies must be made aware, Colonel, of the hazards of the prairie," Thorne said, irritation in his voice. "They cannot take the air here, wandering where the whim takes

them. This is not a country meadow for pic-
nicking and pleasure. There are wolves and
venomous snakes in the area, and then, of
course, there are the Sioux, who would not
hesitate to—"

"I certainly hope that no harm has befallen
her," Colonel Palmer cut in.

"I'll go after her," Ben growled.

"When you deal with her, pray remember,
Captain," Colonel Palmer chided, "that Miss
Mackenzie is young . . . and fragile."

"Too fragile for this kind of life," Ben replied curtly as he rode off.

He rode like the devil was at his back,
spurred on by his knowledge of the degrada-
tions likely to befall a white woman unfortunate enough to be captured by a renegade
band of Indians. He covered the distance
they'd traveled that afternoon in half the time,
and when he reached the place they'd stopped
for the noon break, he dismounted and led his
horse by the reins, searching for signs of the
missing woman.

Apprehension crept over him as he considered the possible fates she might have suffered, none of them pleasant. But to his relief,
he could find no sign of disaster. At last he
picked up her trail on a ridge of sand hills and
followed it to a shaded grove. Tying the reins
of his mount to a low-hanging branch, he
crossed under the canopy of leaves on silent,
moccasined feet.

She was there, blissfully splashing in a

deep, spring-fed pool, seemingly unaware of the consternation her disappearance had caused. Ben felt the anger rise in him and took a step forward, intending to lash out at her. At that moment, though, she rose up out of the water, droplets gleaming on her skin, and walked toward the place where her clothes were folded in a neat pile. This was the same woman who'd captured his attention on the parade ground at Fort Kearney, he realized now. He found himself mesmerized by the movements of her graceful, white limbs and the dappled sunlight that played on the soft, round curves of her naked body. His anger ebbed, replaced by a more urgent emotion. He drew a long ragged breath, unable to move as he watched her raise her arms above her head and slip on a chemise that clung to her damp skin, even as she tied the ribbons at her breast.

The heat in the grove was nigh unbearable, and Ben loosened the kerchief from around his throat and buried his face in it, trying to recover his strength.

She must have heard the movement, for she called out, "Who's there?"

Ben looked up slowly, thankful that she had nearly finished dressing. She did not look quite as fragile as she had on the parade ground, in all her frills and furbelows. Still, he found her no less enticing in cambric basque and riding skirt.

He approached her boldly, some of his irritation returning. "It's Ben Thorne, ma'am," he said. "Colonel Palmer sent me to fetch you. The wagons moved out about an hour ago."

Lorena cocked her head, shading her hand to check the position of the sun. "I . . . why, I must have fallen asleep."

He drew nearer, crossing his arms over his chest and lounging against the trunk of a stunted willow tree. "It isn't wise to wander off," he told her, his green eyes studying her in leisurely fashion. "This is a wild, dangerous country. Surely you have been warned?"

"Indeed," she replied, a smile curving on her full lips. Suddenly she drew a small, short-barreled pistol from the folds of her skirts and held it in her outstretched hand. "I'm not so helpless as I look, Mr. Thorne."

Ben threw back his head and laughed. "A Sioux brave would have your scalp before he got in range of that."

Miss Mackenzie was not so amused. Steadying one hand with the other, she got off a shot that whizzed by Ben's head and splintered the tree trunk he'd been leaning against.

The pistol's report had startled him at first, but as soon as he realized what she'd done, he went to her and grabbed her wrist, the frustration of the ride and search causing his ire to boil over. "That was a foolish display! You'd best realize that this is no game, Miss Mackenzie, and the West is no place for a spoiled and pampered child."

With her free hand Lorena slapped his face.

In retaliation, he grabbed for her hair, which hung in a heavy plait down her back. She jerked her head back, and met his smoldering eyes. "The Indians would consider this yellow hair a great prize," he said. "You'd be wise to change your ways if you intend on keeping it for yourself."

They were scarcely a foot apart and Ben could feel the rise and fall of her full breasts as she fought to keep her composure. He did not release her, and she did not pull away. Perhaps it was only curiosity that was holding her there, Ben thought, but the increasing pressure in his loins told him that he must release her soon or lose all control. For the moment, at least, he gazed into her pale eyes, wanting to know so much more of her, cursing himself for already putting them at odds. He loosed her braid and allowed his hand to wander along the satin planes of her back, taking pleasure in the sigh that escaped her parted lips, telling him that she was not immune to him, despite her earlier slap.

Uttering an explosive curse, he let her go and turned away. This was an untenable situation. She was part of the train, entrusted to his care, and he could not allow himself to become entangled with her, even if she did cause his blood to course through his body like a fever. She didn't belong in his world.

When he had released her, Lorena had fallen to her knees. She pocketed the pistol and rubbed her wrist, which ached from his grip. Struggling to hold back the tears of embarrassment and pain that threatened to spill forth, she tried to avoid his sharp eyes, which were cold and green as bottle glass. She had behaved like a child, a foolish child, and earned Ben Thorne's scorn. Though she could not fathom why, it pained her to realize it.

Lorena rode behind Ben as they made their way to rejoin the train, clinging to his waist, pressed shamefully close against him. They did not speak, and though she knew it was wrong, she spent the hours studying him, for she had never been this close to any man.

Ben Thorne was tall and lean, clad in Indian buckskins, with not an ounce of spare flesh on his frame. At one time he might have been conventionally handsome, she thought, but now the elements had etched themselves on his rugged features. His brown hair, which had grown long over his collar, was burnished with gold by the harsh sun, his skin tanned to a warm bronze. Today, as the last time she'd seen him, he sported a day's growth of beard; it shadowed the square line of his jaw and lent a harshness to his expression.

Lorena speculated about him as they silently rode on. Was he born in the wilds, or had he once been a civilized gentleman who for some reason chose this unfettered way of life? Did he have a wife somewhere . . . or children . . . or was his a solitary existence? She surmised that he'd been a soldier. He wore a battered cavalry officer's slouch hat, and she was sure she'd heard some of the men refer to him as "Captain" Thorne.

And was he as unfeeling as he pretended? The war had made so many men cold that it would not be a far stretch of the imagination to believe it so. But there seemed to be a complexity of emotions behind those sharp, green eyes, and a passion that Lorena sensed quite clearly each time she met his gaze. She had to admit that she was disturbed by the response he had evoked within her earlier.

When they'd ridden for what seemed to Lorena to have been at least two hours, the silence became overwhelming. Finally she could stand it no longer. "I never meant to be a bother to anyone," she told him, trying to maintain her dignity. "I am sorry, Mr. Thorne, if I've behaved childishly."

"You're not to blame," he replied. "The very idea of the Army bringing civilized young ladies into hostile territory is, well . . . foolishness, plain and simple. Any husband who would insist on dragging his wife along into the wilds is an irresponsible jackass. You no more belong out here than Chief Red Cloud belongs walking the streets of an Eastern city."

Lorena felt a wave of anger rise within her, which she strove to quell. Her father had gone west when she was only a babe, and from the time she was old enough to read the letters he sent, she had set her mind on one day joining him. Even though he'd died at the hands of a drunken miner, Lorena was following his dream.

Thorne's words had cut too close. Her uncle had always said a lady could never survive in the West, and he'd constantly tried to dissuade her from her plans. Harrison Gilmore fervently believed that the only women suitable for life on the frontier were farm wives, harlots, and Indian squaws. There was no place at all for a civilized lady, a cultured lady, a proper lady. *Lady.* Oh, how Lorena hated that word!

"You know nothing of me or my life, Mr. Thorne," she replied, barely maintaining her calm, "I have no husband, and I was not dragged along. I chose my own path."

"A garden rose uprooted will soon wither and die," he said, sounding more pensive and poetic than she had expected.

"No garden rose. A hardy bloom, rather," she offered, "with roots bound in its small plot, unable to blossom because of choking vegetation. Such a plant must be uprooted and planted anew . . . or die a slow death."

He was silent a moment, pondering her response, then laughed. It was not a pleasant sound, and she bit down on her tongue lest she anger him again with a sharp retort.

Late that afternoon Lorena caught sight of a trio of horsemen in the distance, across the barren prairie. Her heart lifted as she assumed they had reached the rear guard of their wagon train. But as the figures drew nearer, she saw that they were Indians. Thorne had apparently noticed them as well, for without a word he drew his rifle from its case and laid it across the front of his saddle. Though she was apprehensive, Lorena felt a rush of excitement run through her, too, and shivered.

"Rest easy," he told her. "It's only a small hunting party."

It was clear that their paths would cross, and Lorena unconsciously tightened her grip on Thorne, her heart thumping hard against her breast.

"Open that saddlebag," he commanded, and slapped it for emphasis.

She did as he ordered and saw an Army pistol.

"That'll be of more use than the toy you're carrying, if the occasion arises."

"Do you think—" Lorena started, but he cut her off mid-sentence.

"Keep silent. Do nothing, and for God's sake, calm yourself," he directed as they drew nearer the Indian band. "Sioux can smell fear, same as an animal can."

When the Indians came beside them, Lorena drew a long, uneven breath and lowered her eyes, staring into the middle of Thorne's back as he exchanged guttural greetings with them. Only when he'd slipped from the saddle did she turn her attention to the braves, who had now dismounted as well. They were a fierce-looking lot, wearing buckskin breech-clouts and leggings, their shiny black hair hanging in long plaits. Each carried a long bow with a quiver of arrows slung across his back. The central figure seemed to be the leader. He was stout and strong-looking and carried a lance decorated with eagle feathers.

To Lorena their conversation seemed to be a series of unintelligible syllables and hand gestures, which Ben Thorne apparently had no trouble deciphering. When the leader made a gesture toward her, she could not help but flinch. Thorne let go a hearty laugh, and with his rifle still resting on his arm, went to examine the spotted Indian pony, nodding his head in admiration. He spoke to them in a few words of their own tongue, followed by a rapid series of hand signs. The Indian with the lance had fixed his beady black eyes on her, and Lorena wondered how Thorne could remain so cool throughout this ordeal.

It seemed a long while before he returned to her and the horse and drew a small pouch from his saddlebag, which he tossed to the Indian who'd been leering at her. This evoked a favorable response, and at length the trio took to their horses and rode off to the south, disappearing over the rise of undulating grasses.

Ben Thorne remounted and rode on silently. "Well?" Lorena demanded, when she could stand it no more.

He turned around to face her, with one brow raised as if he didn't know what she meant.

"I'm afraid I've not your facility with Indian tongues, Mr. Thorne. What did they want?"

"The one fellow seemed determined on a trade," he began. "His prized war horse for my squaw."

An amused smile curved on his lips as Lorena digested what he had said. Her eyes widened in shock. His squaw! The savage had presumed that she belonged to Thorne and had actually intended to trade for her.

She shook her head in disbelief. "What sort of people are these," she wondered aloud, "who hold women in such low regard?"

"You ought to be flattered, actually," Thorne countered. "It was a valuable animal, by their standards, and an Indian does not barter away such a commodity lightly."

Somehow this did not appease Lorena's anger. "How did you dissuade him in the end?"

"I told him that I did not wish to cheat him, that his pony was worth far more than a woman who could neither cook nor sew and who had no more strength than a child. And then I gave him a plug of tobacco for his pains." Again the sound of his laughter rang out on the open air.

"I suppose I ought to thank you for pointing up those inadequacies in my character," she said sarcastically. "If I weren't such a worthless creature, I might have found myself taking up residence in an Indian tepee."

"Worthless?" he echoed, pulling on his chin. "Don't believe that was one of the words I used, miss. No, I'm sure that it wasn't."

Inwardly Lorena seethed at his evaluation. She wished that she could run off to nurse her wounded pride, but since it wasn't possible, she welcomed the silence that followed.

Though realizing that the United States Army would not have halted its march while Ben Thorne went off in search of an errant civilian, she was still surprised when he informed her that they would not reach the Army train by nightfall and would have to camp along the river.

Her reputation would undoubtedly suffer if it were discovered that she had spent a night alone in the wilderness with Ben Thorne, she thought. That type of indiscretion could cost her the schoolteacher's job waiting for her in Virginia City. Fortunately, though, there were no evil-minded gossips lurking in the tall prairie grass. And it was not Thorne's fault that she'd been foolish, wandered off, and lost track of the time. No, she had no one to blame for her present predicament but herself, and the thought shamed her. Small wonder Thorne should think her a simpering, empty-headed female!

*　　*　　*

There was still an hour or so of daylight left when he decided that they would make camp for the night. He chose a sheltered spot near a bend in the river. After he'd picketed his horse, he spread out an India rubber cloth with the saddle blanket over it and instructed Lorena to wait at the campsite and keep out of trouble while he went down to the water to fish for their dinner. He had only a crude hook and line and some bits of salt pork for bait, but was confident that he would catch something. Lorena, meanwhile, believed there could not possibly be a living creature beneath those swirling, muddy waters, and likely as not, she and Thorne would be dining on dried beef and hardtack tonight.

She had no intention of sitting idle in his absence. In fact, she wanted to prove to this rough man that she was more than a useless bundle of petticoats and ribbons, to somehow restore at least some of her lost pride. From the days she'd spent on the trail thus far, she had learned much. Sarah Rawlins had been instructing her in the rudiments of cooking, an art in which her education was sorely lacking. Now, mumbling to herself that she was no helpless female, she marched off in search of buffalo chips in order to make a fire, wrinkling her nose at the prospect of the chore.

This time she was careful not to wander too far, and in short order she'd set the fire. Using a tin pot and sack of coffee she'd found in

Thorne's saddlebags and some river water, which was passably fair after the mud had settled, she proceeded to brew coffee for them.

The sun was a fiery orange globe settling on the horizon against the western sky when Thorne returned. Lorena was sitting demurely on the saddle blanket. He raised a heavy brow at the sight of the blazing campfire and the enticing aroma of coffee, and she did likewise when she noticed the string of fish he carried.

"Well, I am surprised," he said.

Proud of her accomplishment, but unwilling to let him know how close to the mark he had been earlier, Lorena turned an innocent expression on him. "Why, Mr. Thorne, I did only what any proper young lady would do, I rang down for the cook."

His eyes narrowed as he looked down at her. Her voice was all sweetness, but the eyes . . . ah, those marvelous eyes sparked with a murderous glare. His mouth twisted into a wry smile. "I deserved that, I suppose."

She reached for the string of fish, but he drew them back. "Allow me. We'll call a truce, shall we, Miss. . . ? What do your friends call you, Miss Mackenzie?"

"Lorena," she replied, still eyeing him cautiously.

"Lorena," he repeated aloud. It suited her, and he liked the sound of it. "While I put our supper in the pan to fry, suppose you tell me

—what is it exactly that brings a lady such as yourself so far from the comforts of civilization?''

"I'm on my way to take up a position," she replied with simple pride, "as a schoolteacher in Virginia City, just as soon as I've paid a visit to an old friend at Fort Reno."

Ben's brows lifted. "Virginia City? I'd be willing to wager that before this journey began you'd never been west of St. Louis. Am I right?"

Despite their truce, he could not resist the opportunity to taunt her, Lorena observed ruefully. Her silence gave him his answer.

"Don't misunderstand, Lorena. I'm certain that you're more than qualified. But all things considered, I doubt you'll find the job what you'd expected. The people out here may crave the gentility and refinement you'll bring them, but years of hard living has made them rough, and it'll likely wear you down, too, before you can change them for the better."

"You can't frighten me off so easily, Ben Thorne," Lorena retorted. "I've made my decision and I intend to stand by it."

"Tell me about this friend at Fort Reno," he asked her, trying to make peace by changing the subject. "What's his name?"

"Brevet Major Charles Ackerman."

"The Madman of the Shenandoah?" Ben replied, incredulous.

"It isn't so," came the retort. "Charles is kind and thoughtful, and not half of what has been said about him is true. Of that I am certain, Mr. Thorne."

"But the stories—"

"Those stories were penned by war correspondents looking for an exciting tale. Doubtless they embellished upon actual events."

Thorne stared into the flames of the campfire without replying, as though he did not believe a word of what she'd told him. Lorena was irritated. Why did he insist on taking the opposite point of view on whatever they were discussing? "I assume you went to war with the rest, Captain Thorne. Surely you can see how such tales could be fabricated."

Ben looked up, capturing her eyes with a hard stare. She tried to look away, but he would not release her. "I know how war can change a man," he said, and then after a long silence, "have you seen him since then?"

"No," she admitted, "but he writes to me."

Again Ben turned away, this time concentrating on the meal he was preparing.

"He has not changed," Lorena insisted, and her words hung on the still night air for a very long while.

After dinner and a few strained attempts at polite conversation in which neither of them discovered much more about the other, Lorena retired to her rough bed, under the blankets that Ben had laid out for her. The barking and baying of coyotes in the nearby hills distressed her, for the wild, savage sound reminded her of the Indians they'd met that afternoon. What if they'd doubled back, she wondered, and were out there in the night even now? She tossed fitfully, resisting sleep, and feeling like a child afraid of hobgoblins. She found herself looking to Ben Thorne for comfort. He sat, staring out into the shadows, his rifle close beside him. Apparently he did not intend to sleep that night. Perhaps her fears were not so groundless after all, she thought. But secure in the knowledge that Ben Thorne was her sentinel, she settled down peacefully at last.

Resting himself against his saddle, Ben found that he could not help but watch her as she slept. He did not know quite what to make of this particular young lady, who always regarded him as if poised for battle. What would it be like, he wondered as a wistful mood overtook him, to have those unusual eyes look upon him with tenderness rather than disdain?

She made a deceptive picture now; asleep, she seemed no more than a child, the wispy tendrils of hair that framed her face gleaming like spun gold in the firelight. A slight smile came to him as he recalled how he'd come upon her this afternoon, as she rose like Venus from the waters, and the memory of her soft body pressed close against him filled his senses once more. He had known then and there that he wanted her, more than he'd wanted any woman in a long while, and now he allowed his greedy eyes to wander over her features, imagining a curve of pleasure upon those soft lips, and silver eyes dark with passion. Ben knew full well what folly there was in such imaginings. Lorena Mackenzie was a lady of refinement, not the type to be had for one night's pleasure. Still, he was intoxicated.

But while he studied her fair complexion and the graceful, white hands resting upon the blanket, he went suddenly numb. Other, more painful memories possessed him, memories that he thought he had buried long ago—of another delicate lady, whose soft skin he had seen so cruelly weathered by the elements and whose hands, which had been made for more gentle pursuits, had become callused and work-worn under the labors demanded of her. This was what the West had done to his mother . . . before it finally took her life.

Chapter Three

◆◆◆◆

THOUGH THEY COULD clearly see the billowing clouds of dust raised by the Army train ahead of them, it was late in the morning of the next day before Ben and Lorena finally caught up. Lorena found that she was more than a little disappointed to have come to the end of their adventure. Ben Thorne was more mysterious than ever, and she only knew that he and she came together like fire and water, and this combination fascinated her. She had a thousand questions, but there was no conversing with him; something had made him particularly silent and sullen.

When Ben drew his pony alongside one of the ambulances, Lorena's friend Sarah peered out of the side, where the canvas was drawn up, and let out a joyful cry, waving excitedly. Lorena returned the greeting, and as she slipped from the saddle, she stumbled over her words trying to thank Ben. In return, he caught her hand tightly and met her eyes in a way that left her breathless. "Lorena . . . if you should change your mind—if you decide you want to return home—please know that you may rely upon my help."

And with that he turned his horse and rode away.

*   *   *

When the Army train reached Fort Sedgwick, it had already traveled two hundred miles west from Fort Kearney. Those miles had taken their toll, especially on the ladies, who were sore from the constant jouncing of the ambulance over the rough terrain, their strength drained by the relentless summer heat. The dry winds that swept the prairie had parched and cracked their lips and kicked up clouds of fine dust that clung stubbornly to skin and clothing.

After the hardships of the past few weeks, Sarah and Lorena appreciated that evening's opportunity to dine in relative comfort with the post commander, Captain Neill, and his family. The evening's menu included such unusual entrees as buffalo rump, antelope steak, and prairie chicken—served with biscuits, boiled potatoes, and greens. Regardless of the novelty, it was the tastiest meal any of them had had in weeks.

With several of the officers and their wives in attendance, the company was pleasant and the conversation lively. Lorena found herself seated near the head of the table, with Sarah directly opposite and Colonel and Mrs. Palmer nearby.

"I'm sure I speak for my fellow officers when I say that we are fortunate, indeed, to have so many lovely ladies at our table this evening," Captain Neill commented. "I am pleased to see that none of you has been unduly affected by the rigors of travel."

"We are grateful to you, Captain, for your hospitality," Sarah said in reply. "It is pleasant to return to civilization, if only for a short time."

"You're an Army girl now, Sarah," Mrs. Palmer put in, "and ought not to mind a little adversity."

Lorena watched as her friend's expression darkened. Fearing how Sarah might reply, she tried to redirect the conversation. "How many more miles must we travel before we reach Fort Reno, Colonel Palmer?"

"Two-thirds of the journey is still before us," he told her.

This comment effectively doused whatever lightheartedness might have been in the air, and dinner was concluded in relative silence. Afterward, over coffee and pie, the conversation turned to Army life and war exploits and such. Lorena excused herself and went out onto the wooden porch that ringed the building to get some air. She sat on a split-log bench and stared pensively up at the waxing moon.

"I wondered where you'd got off to," Sarah said when she arrived a few minutes later to join her on the bench.

"I was feeling a bit out of place, I suppose, and came out to look at the stars."

"I know what you mean. I can't help but be envious of those women traveling with their husbands. Here I am, all bathed and perfumed, dressed in one of my finest frocks, and my man is still hundreds of miles away. It's a sad state of affairs, that's what it is." After contemplating her words, Sarah apologized. "Oh, I am sorry, Lorena. That was a selfish thing for me to say."

It was a long while before Lorena responded. "It's all right, Sarah. I'm not the sort who's meant for marriage."

"Nonsense! You've just not met the right man yet, that's all."

"No, truly," Lorena told her. "In order to get this job teaching school, I've had to make a pledge not to marry for three years."

"Hmmph! If you ask me, it's ridiculous to ask someone to make such a promise. You're only teaching school, not taking your vows and entering the convent, for heaven's sake."

"Don't worry about me, Sarah. I can see the logic in it. There are few respectable females of marriageable age out West, you know. A town goes through all the trouble of hiring a new teacher and waiting months for her to arrive, and then when she's finally settled in, she's inundated with marriage proposals from every lonely bachelor in the county. Sooner or later one of the fellows strikes her fancy, and the poor townsfolk have to start the process all over again."

"And you think it won't be the same way with you?"

"I've given my word to ensure it," Lorena explained. "And more importantly, I've sworn to myself that I shan't turn over control of my life to a man, not ever again. Living with my uncle has taught me that much at least.''

"You've all sorts of wild imaginings flitting through your brain tonight," Sarah noted.

Lorena had to admit that it was true. She sat there in the darkness, staring up at the moon for some time yet after Sarah had gone to bed. She was struggling to make sense of the jumbled thoughts that forced themselves upon her and would not let her rest. Perhaps, as Sarah had said, they were only wild imaginings. Her path had seemed so much more clear-cut at the beginning of the journey. But now. . .? Now, despite her confident words and the years of planning to leave her uncle, Lorena found herself afraid of the prospect of a new life and of what the future held.

It was a natural reaction. To her, change of any sort had always brought pain: her mother's death when she was a child, her father leaving her to search for gold in California, Charles going away to school, and then her father's death and her uncle's attempt to force her to marry. All these changes had been unhappy ones.

Lorena sighed as she studied the sky. Maybe she'd been avoiding the truth. Maybe it was not the changes all around her that she feared so much, after all, but the changes occurring within her, and she did not dare think on what, or who, had brought them about. . . .

"Good evening, Miss Mackenzie."

Lorena looked up at Ben Thorne, who smiled at her and sat down. She was not surprised to see him, for it seemed she had conjured him out of the air. She noticed he was dressed in more formal clothing, rather than trail garb. He was clean-shaven, and wore a white linen shirt and dark waistcoat, with a clean kerchief tied about his throat. His trousers, with a gold stripe running their length, were part of an officer's uniform, and he'd traded his moccasins for a pair of highly polished black boots.

"Good evening, Mr. Thorne," she finally replied.

"What is it you find so fascinating about this military post?" he asked. "Most young ladies would rather be inside socializing."

"It's a comfortable haven, a semblance of order in the disorder of the wilderness. . . ."

Again there was a long silence, then Lorena asked abruptly, "What made you resign your commission, Mr. Thorne?"

Once again she had surprised him. Ben had promised himself that he would not seek her out tonight, no matter how much he longed to. But when he'd seen her from Captain Neill's window, sitting on the veranda, bathed in blue shadows and moonlight, his good intentions were tossed aside without a second thought. Now he sat close beside her, breathing her sweet violet scent, trying to keep a clear head while his eyes traveled the golden wave of her unbound hair, over bared white shoulders to the swell of her full breasts above the fall of lace that formed the deep corsage of the coral-colored evening gown. He was so distracted that he could scarcely string together two coherent thoughts, and she was asking questions about his military career!

He drew a long breath and focused his attention instead on the yellow squares of light across the darkened compound, coming from the barracks' windows. "I'd had enough of killing after the war," he explained, "and no matter what the justification, I'll not be a party to the extermination of the Indian race."

"Surely that's not what the Army intends," she said.

"Perhaps not, but that won't change the outcome. The Army doesn't half understand the Indians. They treat them like children, hoping to pacify them with trinkets and treaties." The contempt was plain in his voice. Only months before, he'd watched the government representatives making promises at the Laramie council that they knew they could not keep. "There'll be bloodshed before the year is out, you may depend upon it."

How swiftly his temper had been roused,
Lorena thought. She continued to regard him,
her gentle brow quirked in surprise.

Suddenly he felt the need to apologize for
his vehemence. "Of course," he told her, "I'm
sure that you will not be witness to it."

Lorena stared into her lap, where her
hands lay neatly folded. She gathered her
thoughts, then turned her luminous eyes on
him. "Since our first encounter, Mr. Thorne,
you have taken it as your duty to dissuade
me from traveling west."

She watched as he looked away from her,
his jaw tensed, realizing too late that such a
matter-of-fact approach was sorely lacking in
ladylike tact. "While I do appreciate your
concern," she added, "I assure you I am
tougher than I appear. My father was a stub-
born old Scotsman who made his own way
west in 'forty-nine. He settled in California,
living in the gold camps, and my childhood
was colored with his tales of Western life in
his letters. But for his untimely death, I'd have
joined him there."

Having stated her case, she rose and
turned from him in a rustle of silk skirts,
leaning against the upright post that helped
to support the roof. She'd made her point
in concise fashion, she thought, yet her
hands were trembling. She ought to go inside, she told herself. There was something
in the night air, something infectious, dangerous. . . .

"You've no right, you know, to dictate my life to me," she said, endeavoring to keep a clear head.

Ben drew up beside her, placing his hand over hers, and it immediately touched off a warning signal in her head.

"You're right, of course," he told her in an apologetic tone. "I've no right to pry into your life. No right at all."

Somehow, before she'd realized it, his arm had snaked around her waist and he'd pulled her closer to him. She did not see it happen, but then how could she have been any less than mesmerized by the blaze of emerald fire in his eyes? For an instant she half convinced herself that this was only a dream, that she'd wake to find herself safe and snug beneath her quilt. But in that same instant Ben Thorne caught her up against his hard body and her breath left her in a sudden rush.

Though she would never have dared admit it, she had imagined this moment since their first encounter, and she'd been curious as to how it would feel. And it was curiosity that held her now, and kept her rooted to the spot as his hand slipped into the silken tangle of her hair and he brushed his lips over hers. His kiss was chaste, seeming far too gentle for the man who'd bestowed it. But he'd only been testing the waters, and when next his mouth sought hers, it demanded response. She did not disappoint him, yielding to his urgency as her own desires were awakened.

The night spun around in kaleidoscope fashion as Lorena gave in to her senses. She did not half understand what was happening to her, but like a greedy child, she wanted more. A pleasant warmth coursed through her veins now, suspending thought. Pressed close against him, she was aware only of the increasing tension in his lean frame and of an undeniable sense of anticipation growing within her.

Ben captured her soft, willing mouth yet again, a feeling of triumph overtaking him. Instinct had not misled him; Lorena Mackenzie was all that he'd imagined her to be. He reveled in the feel of her lithe form in his arms, in her labored breathing, which hinted of her desire, and he fought to keep a rein on the rising urgency that threatened to overwhelm him.

With the sound of a soft footfall nearby, Lorena's pale eyes went wide and she drew away from him. Ben looked up over her shoulder to see Broken Hand standing in a solemn pose, like Ben's own conscience, the Indian's black eyes fixed upon him.

Lorena was trembling now, embarrassed at being discovered, and a sob caught in her throat. Before Ben could calm her, she struck out at him, the flat of her hand connecting sharply with his jaw. In the next moment, she ran off into the night.

The Indian approached, and Ben turned from him, grasping the wooden railing as he stared after Lorena. "Don't say a word."

"We should leave the soldiers here," Broken Hand said evenly. "We should ride north of Mauvais Terres, far away from the track of the iron horse and the dusty wagon road."

Ben turned to face him, his voice hard. "We have a contract with Colonel Palmer to lead the Army train to Fort Reno. It's a contract I intend to honor."

Broken Hand regarded him without expression, but Ben still felt accused. "She is not for you, my friend," the Indian said at last.

Ben uttered a curse and began to pace a small stretch of the wooden porch. "Do you think that I don't know it?" he retorted. "I'm not proud of the way I behaved just now. It was a mistake, that's all."

Broken Hand came to stand beside him, and both men focused their attention across the compound to the barracks building where the women were lodged for the night. The Indian acknowledged Ben's words with a nod, but Ben still felt uncomfortable as he met his eyes. "You must take care, my friend," Broken Hand cautioned. "This path you choose leads nowhere."

"There's nothing to this, I tell you," Ben insisted, "nothing. Once we've seen Colonel Palmer and the rest to Fort Reno, we'll ride home to Wind River and be done with it."

Broken Hand regarded his friend silently. Despite Thorne's protestations, the Indian thought there would be no easy end to this. In all of the years he'd known Ben Thorne, he'd never seen him quite so unnerved by another human being . . . man or woman. He knew there was trouble yet to come.

After drawing the necessary supplies for the remainder of their journey from the stores at the fort, the troops made ready to ford the south fork of the Platte River and begin the second leg of the trip.

In anticipation, wagons were double-teamed and loads lightened. Still, the Platte, with its varying depths, its quicksand bed, and unpredictable currents, would be a challenge.

As the train reached the river, soldiers on foot alternately waded and swam, helping the wagons get across. Lorena could not bear to watch as their wagon teetered on the bank and then plunged into the swirling waters, immersed to the axletrees. Inside their ambulance, Lorena and Sarah clung to the sides as water seeped through the floor, soaking the hems of their skirts. Their companion whispered prayers and clung to her three young sons, who were staring out of the rolled canvas at the commotion all around them, eyes wide.

Lorena kept her eyes squeezed shut, unable to watch. More than one soldier had succumbed to the swift currents, carried away like so much flotsam, only to regain his footing in shallower water downstream. It was a harrowing process, and for most of the crossing Lorena sat very still, lips pressed tightly together as she listened to the sounds carried on the brisk wind: the bawling of the emigrants' cattle, the shouts of the soldiers, and the mules braying in protest as they were whipped on by their teamsters.

At length the Platte was crossed and the caravan began a long trek northwest. After the pleasant respite at Fort Sedgwick, the heat and dust of the following days were particularly hard to take. The entire command moved at a snail's pace and halted each hour for a short rest. The march proved especially grueling for the infantry, and by day's end all of the ambulances and wagons were filled to capacity with those who had been debilitated by the unrelenting heat and wicked terrain. As for herself, Lorena considered the discomfort she suffered no more than the penance she deserved for her behavior at the fort and her attraction to Ben Thorne.

For the next five days she did not stray far from the ambulance. Although the journey was beginning to wear on her, it was encountering Ben Thorne that Lorena feared above all. Within the canvas shell of the am-

bulance that was her cocoon, Lorena spent
the hours rereading letters Charles had sent
her over the years. She had saved them all:
those chronicling his years at West Point,
those following him through the campaigns
of the war, and, of course, his most recent
letters, sent from the desolate outpost in the
Dakota Territory where he'd been assigned.
These last letters were full of loneliness, and
made Lorena feel that her visit would do
him good.

Through the pages, Lorena reacquainted
herself with Charles. Now and again a smile
would touch her lips as she recalled events of
the happy childhood days they'd shared before he went away.

Early on Charles had cast himself in the role
of her protector, though she realized now that
she had always fancied herself his equal. As
children he had let her have her head, then
followed patiently behind, ready to repair
whatever mischief her latest scheme might
have wrought. He'd listened to her opinions,
and no matter how outrageous they'd been,
he'd never laughed. He had been a good
friend as a child, and she was certain that he
had grown into a good man, kind and
considerate—and not at all like the blackguard
Thorne.

On the eve of the sixth day after crossing
the South Platte, the Army train camped
near Pumpkin Creek, in the shadow of
Courthouse Rock, an immense natural for-

mation rising some four hundred feet above the level of the water. This landmark, standing in solitary splendor upon the open plain, had been in view for all of the day's march, and Lorena was pleased to have reached it at last.

Curious, she decided to examine this wonder of nature from a closer vantage point, and so when supper had been eaten and the tin cups and pans washed in the clear water of the creek, she ventured out to explore, at last putting an end to her self-imposed exile.

She briefly thought then that Sarah might wish to join her, but her friend was not to be found in the circle of wagons. Lorena was growing uneasy when she heard a soft sobbing from within one of the baggage wagons. Moving closer cautiously, she came upon Sarah, sitting upon her heels in the bed of the wagon before an open trunk and clutching two broken pieces of porcelain to her breast.

"Sarah, what is it?" she asked softly, pulling herself up into the wagon. She had never seen her friend look so forlorn.

"Oh, Lorena, it's my grandmother's serving platter, broken to bits . . . and just look, the rest have fared no better."

She waved a hand at the open trunk. Within were the shattered remains of a delicate, rose-patterned china service. Sarah's dark eyes were bright with unshed tears, her face washed of color.

Lorena felt ashamed of herself. Throughout the journey Sarah had been the one to keep up their flagging spirits. She'd looked upon the cross-country trek as one great adventure, while Lorena, more serious by nature, had been so involved with her own concerns that she'd never even stopped to think that her friend's resolve might have suffered along the way.

Staring at the trunkful of broken crockery now, Lorena realized how hurt Sarah must be at the loss. It was, more than anything else, a tangible reminder of the home she'd left behind, and here it lay, shattered beyond repair.

She put her arms about her friend. "We can still salvage some of the pieces, I'm sure. Why, that plate looks undamaged, and the sugar bowl has only lost its cover. We'll go through the whole trunk this very minute, you and I, and I'll wager we can scare up enough whole pieces so you'll be able to serve your Jed a fine meal on our very first night at Fort Reno."

Sarah stared at the broken pieces of the platter in her hand before replying. "Thank you for your kindness," she said in an unsteady voice, "but I think I'd like to be alone . . . just for a while." As Lorena looked at her apprehensively, Sarah forced a smile. "I'll be all right, truly, and we can sort through all of this later."

* * *

Reluctantly, she left Sarah to manage on her own, wishing there was more she could have done to lift her friend's spirits. Finding herself alone and no longer eager to explore, she wandered the camp by a circuitous route, through the tangle of wagons and past the tents pitched near a picturesque cottonwood grove, where the soldiers were clustered in groups around their campfires. The desire for solitude carried her on into the wild landscape of the canyon beyond. There, low shrubs clung to outcroppings of sandstone and marl, and the soft hills were cut with deep ravines, cloaked in shadow now as twilight approached.

On a rise a few rods distant, she saw a peculiar sight. It was a circle of rocks, interspersed with whitened buffalo skulls that were stuffed with prairie grass. Within this circle were the charred remains of a campfire. Curious, she approached the arrangement and bent to touch one of the skulls. Somewhere on the plain a coyote sent up a mournful howl. A skittering pebble alerted her to a human presence and sent a shiver of fear through her. In clambering to her feet, she knocked several of the stones out of place, then turned to face the intruder.

Chapter Four

◆◆◆◆

SILHOUETTED AGAINST THE blood-red sky was the Sioux brave, Broken Hand. His arms were folded across his chest and he seemed to be studying her. Even when she met his dark eyes, he did not look away, but only regarded her with what she took to be a puzzled air.

Recovering from her fright, Lorena laid a hand over her heart. "You gave me quite a start," she told him. He did not reply, and after a long silence she continued. "They've sent you after me, haven't they? I suppose I've acquired a reputation as a wanderer now and am not to be trusted out of the sight of camp."

Broken Hand walked around the circle, putting aright those stones that Lorena had displaced. "This is Indian 'medicine,'" he explained. "A holy man has come to this place to pray and to make an offering to *Wakan-Tanka*, the Great Spirit."

"What sort of prayer would he make?"

"For the success of his people in the hunt . . . or in battle."

A chill came over her as Lorena contemplated the second possibility. Surely, though, a hostile Indian band would not be so foolish as to attack an Army train.

"Or perhaps," the Indian went on, "the

holy one faced a choice and was asking for guidance. Perhaps that is what has brought you to this place. Have you a choice to make?"

Broken Hand's sharp eyes were fixed upon her, awaiting her reply. Lorena met his gaze with a quizzical expression, wondering at his odd question. Could he be referring to what he had witnessed between her and his friend, Ben Thorne?

Lorena could feel her heart drumming in her breast. She did not like the accusing look he sent her, as if she were some hard-hearted vixen and Thorne an innocent schoolboy. She wanted to shout that it was not so, that what had happened that night had been a mistake, no more, but she kept a tight rein on her emotions. "My choices have all been made," she assured him in a cool tone.

He did not look convinced. "Even the strongest reed sways in the wind," he told her, and then he disappeared into the lengthening shadows of the canyon.

With the dawn, a towering mass of gray thunderheads had rolled out of the west and now lingered ominously in the morning sky. The command marched all day to the rumble of distant thunder, expecting to be deluged at any moment. But the rains held off until late in the afternoon, as orders were given to make camp. The emigrants and the Army wives kept to the cover of their wagons, but the soldiers had to pitch their tents in the midst of the downpour, and once inside the canvas shelters, made a sorry meal of their Army rations of dried beef and hardtack.

Within the confines of his own tent Ben Thorne sat cross-legged atop a gutta-percha blanket, drawing on the stub of a cheroot that he held in his teeth. He was restless, there was no denying it. Maybe Broken Hand had been right to suggest that they should ride far north of this dusty track of civilization . . . into the Black Hills to hunt where the white man seldom ventured. Or they could head homeward to Wind River, so Ben might see for himself if his father had managed yet to drink himself to death or at last gotten his wish and struck the mother lode.

With an unintelligible grumble Ben unfolded his long legs and quit the tent, tossing his cigar stub into a puddle that had formed just outside. It landed with a hiss. Oblivious to the steady rain that was falling, he began to pace, intent on shaking off the malaise that gripped him.

The gray evening gave way to a night as black as pitch, and the drum rolls of thunder that had rumbled back and again across the open prairie were now punctuated by sharp cracks that reminded Lorena of the leather snap of the teamsters' whips as they drove the mules.

The ladies had gathered together in a circle in the snug shelter of the wagon bed and were engaged in light conversation that they hoped would make them forget the raging storm. The wind had picked up and wound through the camp with a shrill cry, upsetting everything that was not tied down and flapping the canvas, threatening to unroof those within their wagons. From her position, Lorena saw Mrs. Owens's three young sons clinging to the back of the wagon, watching wide-eyed as lightning cut a jagged line across the night sky. Again the thunder crashed and the sky was lit by a brilliant white light, illuminating the spire of Chimney Rock in the distance.

The sandstone monolith was the most celebrated of the natural formations they had come upon thus far, but Lorena and the other travelers had been largely deprived of the view by the heavy clouds that had hung low over the prairie most of the day. Now those who had witnessed the spectacular sight in the split second during which it had been visible were open-mouthed with awe. Lorena fancied that it resembled some eerie Gothic tower stretching upward hundreds of feet into the clouds. But Sarah commented, and rightly so, that it would make an excellent natural lightning rod. The grim thought of the storm wreaking its vengeance upon the slender rock and sending a rain of stone shards down upon them effectively silenced further comment.

The next lightning strike caused the ground to shudder beneath them and startled even the most fearless of the women. The youngest of Mrs. Owens's sons had been clinging to his whimpering pup throughout the commotion, but with this jolt the dog wriggled free and bolted from the ambulance. In panic, the boy bounded after it. Mrs. Owens cried out, and Lorena, who was nearest, went after him. She caught him in only a few strides, lifted him off his feet, and despite his struggling, managed to carry him back into the waiting arms of his mother.

"No! Let me go!" the boy wailed, still flailing his limbs. "I have to go after him. He's scared, and he'll get lost out there in the dark. The wolves will get him, or the coyotes—"

Lorena didn't break stride as she took him back to the wagon, but was touched by the suffering in the boy's small face. "Don't worry, I'll fetch him for you," she offered, hoping this would cheer him. "He's probably only hiding beneath one of the wagons."

After leaving him in the wagon, she headed into the storm. In a matter of seconds the rain had soaked through the thin fabric of her dress and dampened the petticoats beneath. Her sodden skirts brushed the ground and soon grew so heavy that they clung to her thighs and slapped at her calves with each step. But she plodded on nonetheless, around the circle of wagons, calling for the dog until at last she saw a small black head peering from behind one tall, spoked wheel.

"There you are," she said in soothing tones. "Come along now. Let's go back in where it's warm and dry."

Just as she reached for the shivering pup, though, another clap of thunder sounded and the animal slipped out of her grasp and cut a black streak across the grassy field, heading for a ravine. Without pausing to think, Lorena followed, sprinting across the uneven ground, the wind whipping at her skirts. Guided by the eerie blue flashes of lightning, she made her way through the tall grass, away from the shelter of the camp. . . .

Thorne had gone to check the horses, stamping and whinnying in protest of the weather. It would be hard luck, indeed, were they to pull up their pickets and run off. The sturdy Indian ponies that he and Broken Hand rode were calm enough, but he could see the larger cavalry mounts not far away, rearing their great heads in response to each lightning flash.

His eye was drawn then to a running figure, crossing the open field just beyond, and his heart began to hammer double-time. He could tell by the glimpse of white petticoats afforded him as she ran, that it was a woman, and she had long, fair hair which had pulled free of its pins and was now flagging out behind her. He knew it was Lorena, even though he could not clearly see her face. What other woman would be so reckless as to run off into the eye of the storm?

She disappeared into the ravine. Lightning struck perilously near, and Ben raced after her, following the path she'd made over the rough ground. When he'd covered the distance between them, he reached out and caught her by the waist, swinging her around to face him. "Are you aiming to get yourself killed?" he shouted.

"Let me go!" she cried, pulling away from him.

But Ben did not let her go. He could not predict what she would do next. "Not until you tell me what's going on. Where were you headed just now?"

"I don't owe you any explanations, Ben Thorne," she said, still struggling to free herself.

"No, but you're not going anywhere until I get one; so unless you want us both to catch our deaths standing out here in the rain, you'd better start talking."

Lorena glared up at him in defiance, revealing nothing. If she told him she'd been chasing a frightened pup, he'd have only laughed at her.

Ben watched her patiently, staring down upon the features, now freckled with silver raindrops, that had come to haunt his every waking moment: the full, soft mouth and haughty nose, the arched wings of a brow that framed the most unusual gray eyes he'd ever seen. The rain-soaked bodice of her blue-sprigged calico had molded itself to her body, and his eyes lingered. The thoughts that ran through his mind now were not at all honorable.

Honor be damned! He freed one hand to brush away the damp strands of burnished gold hair splayed across her face and backed her up against the red rock wall of the ravine that sheltered them. Nothing was real here in the darkness, with the cleansing rain beating down upon them. It was, he told himself, only a dream. . . .

Lorena knew quite well what he intended. "Please, Ben, no," she begged, the swell of her breasts heaving against him as she struggled to catch her breath.

His mouth covered hers swiftly, before she could protest again, and though she pressed her palms against his chest, intending to push him away, her resistance melted soon enough, soft lips parting under his. As if on their own, her arms wound around his neck and she came full against him. Ben groaned in response. Drunk on the taste of her, his head reeled. Soon, very soon, it would be too late for reason.

"What can I do?" he whispered against her ear. "How can I fight this? You've bewitched me."

At this he bent to press rain-wet kisses along the column of her throat, and one callused hand slipped from her shoulder, edging down her spine at a painfully slow pace to at last caress her thigh through the damp fabric of her skirts. Lorena fought against the pleasant warmth rising in her. Somehow she must gather the strength to resist him, or else be lost forever. She felt the rasp of his beard stubble against the soft nape of her neck, and when his mouth captured hers once more, he drew the very breath from her, leaving her giddy and shaken.

How could he claim to be bewitched? Surely this spell was of his making. Her strength gone, Lorena dropped to her knees and Thorne bent to catch her. Still trapped in the circle of his arms, she turned her face skyward, letting the rain wash over her, hoping it might cleanse her soul. She was bitterly ashamed of her weakness, ashamed to admit that she ached for the touch of this rough-edged Army scout. She knew nothing of Ben Thorne, not what sort of man he was, nor where he came from, nor who his people were. Yet it did not matter. Nothing mattered but that she came alive in his arms as she had never been before.

Ben eased her onto the soft bed of sage-scented grass, with the wind howling a protest. He'd have taken her then and she'd not have resisted, but for a blinding flash of lightning that split the night and lit up the sky as bright as day. Striking to the very core of him, it jolted him back to reality as he saw her delicate visage illuminated. It was, he knew, only a trick of the light that had made him see his mother's serene features appear in place of Lorena's, but effective nonetheless. He drew away, as if he'd been burned.

Lorena Mackenzie was an innocent, and he'd shamelessly played upon the attraction between them to lead her this far. Certainly the guilt of this one night's passion would have stayed with her forever, and he'd have been to blame. She was the sort of woman who needed one man to love, one man to love her. Ben knew he could not be that man. Love was one thing he'd never considered, but whether the force that drew them together could be called love or not did not matter. There could be no future for the two of them, that much he knew. His was a coarse but unfettered life, and he could never ask her to share it, for it would surely destroy her.

And so, reluctantly, he released her and stepped away, leaving her to think that he'd only been trifling with her all along. He saw at once her hurt look as she righted herself and hugged her knees, and he felt a twist like a knife in his gut.

As Thorne drew away, Lorena went from embarrassment to hurt to anger in a matter of seconds. He'd been amusing himself at her expense, she thought. "I hate you, Ben Thorne," she said with deadly calm, and a long silence ensued before she found her voice again. "You told me from the first that I did not belong here. Are you pleased to have been proven right? Without the proprieties of an Eastern drawing room, I am led like a child."

At this the mongrel pup she'd been chasing appeared, barked a greeting, then tugged at her skirts to gain her attention. She scooped him into her arms and buried her face against his dark coat to hide her shame.

Ben was shaken. He wanted to protest that this was not a game he played with every woman he chanced upon. But he remained silent. Better by far that she should hate him, for he had nothing to offer her.

There was a question in her eyes as she regarded him one last time, and he knew he had to crush any hope she might still harbor. With all of the strength he could muster, he turned and walked away.

Chapter Five

♦ ♦ ♦ ♦

THE FOLLOWING DAY the whole of Colonel Palmer's command—infantrymen and officers; emigrants with their bellowing livestock, baggage and supply wagons; officers' wives in their wagons—was herded through the narrow, twisting pass at Scott's Bluff. Exhausted by their efforts, they camped that night at Fort Mitchell, an adobe stockade garrisoned by two companies of the 8th Infantry under Captain Hughes.

Lorena endured a sleepless night. This last encounter with Thorne preyed on her mind, allowing her no peace. How she hated him! Perhaps the truth of it was that she hated her own weakness more. After she'd sworn to herself that she'd never again give control of her life over to a man, Lorena had proven herself to be as malleable as clay in Ben Thorne's hands.

Put your trust in a man and you're sure to be disappointed. It was a lesson Lorena ought to have learned long ago. She'd trusted her father to love her forever, and he'd gone west and left her behind. She'd trusted Charles to be her friend, to stick with her through thick and thin, but adventure had lured him to the war and then to points beyond. She'd trusted her uncle, her own blood kin, to see to her welfare, and he'd tried to marry her off to a man she despised. And yet still she'd reached out for Ben Thorne, thinking he'd be different. What a fool she was!

With the dawn the bugler sounded reveille, and she found herself inexplicably drawn from her bed to the loophole window in the outside wall of the apartment where the ladies were quartered. Peering through the small opening, she saw the distant figures of two riders who'd crossed the Platte and were now heading northward. One was the Indian, Broken Hand, and the other . . . Ben Thorne.

It was later that day before she learned that the scouts would not be going on to Fort Reno with the Army train but had, in their stead, enlisted an old trapper named Gallien to see Colonel Palmer's party on to their destination. She ought to have been relieved that fate had intervened on her behalf, but knowing Ben had gone out of her life, something tugged at her heart.

It was the middle of August 1866 when the Army train passed Fort Laramie and said good-bye to several companies of soldiers destined as replacements there. Another six weeks passed before those who remained reached their destination on the Powder River.

Fort Reno was located on a bluff some hundred-or-so feet above the river, on a barren plain dotted only by sagebrush and cactus.

Had they not been anticipating their reunion with Brevet Major Ackerman and Lieutenant Rawlins, Lorena and Sarah might have been sorely disappointed with the desolation of the country.

In actuality, the accommodations had been much improved by the efforts of the men of Colonel Carrington's command, who had come through only a few months before on their way to build new forts farther north along the Bozeman Trail. The zealous soldiers had, in their short stay, erected several new buildings, enclosed the parade ground, and completed a stone magazine. Still, this fort on the banks of the Powder River was little more than a desolate outpost in a hostile land.

As the Army train drew within sight of the fort, most of those traveling in the ambulances got out to stretch their legs. Lorena, though, found herself suddenly apprehensive at the prospect of seeing Charles again, and so she remained behind, hiding herself in the wagon as she succumbed to her nervousness.

All of the fears that she'd pushed into the back of her mind came to the fore now. What if Ben Thorne had been right? What if Charles were no longer the same kind young man who'd been her friend so many years ago? Lorena had counted on his company and counsel, if only for a few days, before she went on to her new life in Virginia City. What if he'd changed?

"We're nearly there, Lorena. Come and

see," Sarah called up to her as they approached the fort. Then her friend climbed into the wagon bed and noticed Lorena's distress. "What's wrong? Oh, I know the fort isn't much to look at, but it's not that bad, really."

"It isn't that, "Lorena said.

"Well then, what is it? Aren't you happy that you'll soon be seeing your childhood friend?"

"Yes, of course I am. It's only a case of nerves, I suppose. Since the night I ran away . . . everything seems to have happened so fast, and I just haven't had the chance to adjust to it all."

"You never told me that you'd run away, Lorena," Sarah said in a hushed voice.

Lorena decided that talking about the whole mess might help her to relax, and with a deep sigh she set out to tell the whole of her story.

"About six months ago," she began, "my uncle decided to marry me off to his stepson, Henry Edgington."

"What sort of man was he, this Edgington?"

Lorena wrinkled her nose in distaste. "We didn't see much of him at first. He was away at school when his mother married my uncle, and then he went to live in the city. He's a fancy lawyer in New York, and his office is there. Then last summer, at my uncle's request, Edgington came to visit us and suddenly took an interest in me. The two of them may have thought me only a simple-headed girl, but I'm not so naive that I couldn't see what their plan was. My father had made a handsome fortune in California—"

"Gold?" Sarah's eyes widened.

Lorena shook her head. "He found a more lucrative pastime: selling supplies to the miners. When he died, he left all of his fortune to me. The will, though, stipulates that my father's partner in California has control of the money until I reach my majority . . . or until I marry."

"So if you were to marry this Edgington fellow, they'd have control of your fortune," Sarah deduced.

"Exactly."

"What did you do?"

"I told my uncle in no uncertain terms that I should sooner marry the stableboy than such a noxious, preening peacock as Henry Edgington."

"Good for you!" Sarah exclaimed.

"But then my uncle told me that I'd best watch my tongue or such a match could quite easily be arranged, and I knew that he was determined to make my life a misery if he didn't get his own way."

"What a fix!"

"That's the truth of it," Lorena echoed. "I didn't know where to turn, and then I saw an advertisement in the newspaper for schoolteachers. . . ."

*   *   *

Sarah and Lorena clung to one another nervously. They had donned clean frocks and put up their hair in anticipation of this moment, and at last it was nearly upon them. For Mrs. Owens and Mrs. Palmer and others whose husbands had been with them on the march, there was more of a sense of relief that the journey was over at long last, but for the two young ladies who had been on their own, it was an anxious time.

"Put a smile on," Sarah whispered in Lorena's ear. "He'll be the same old Charles, and he'll be so pleased to see you, wait and see if he isn't."

On the parade ground the travelers were met by a contingent of officers, and introductions began all around. A tall blond man with a ruddy complexion appeared out of the ranks and swept Sarah off her feet and into his arms, and it was plain to see that this moment made her forget all the discomforts suffered over the past months.

Lorena scanned the crowd again and again, looking for Charles. Surely he could not have changed so much as to be unrecognizable in only the three years they'd been apart? Tears blurred her vision as she realized that he was not to be found.

Lorena had spent the last days of the journey imagining this moment of reunion, trying to push other thoughts out of her mind. She needed desperately to throw herself into

Charles's arms, to talk with him as they once had. But where was Charles?

At length Sarah noticed Lorena's distress, and dragging her husband by the hand, drew up beside her friend. "This is Lorena Mackenzie," she told Jed. "We have traveled together all these past months, and she has grown dearer to me than a sister."

Lorena put out her hand to him. "I'm pleased to meet you at last," she told him.

"Miss Mackenzie," Jed Rawlins replied as he took up her proffered hand, "this is a pleasure."

"Miss Mackenzie is a good friend of Brevet Major Ackerman. She's traveling to Montana and intends to visit with him for a few days before going on with the next wagon train. Jed," she said, "I'm sure Lorena would appreciate it if you could tell her why her Charles is not here to greet her after our long journey—"

"I did write and tell him I'd be coming," Lorena said.

"Yes, well, miss, the mail delivery in these parts isn't what you'd call dependable. We've been pestered in the last few weeks by a renegade Cheyenne band led by a young chief called Spotted Wolf. . . ."

The ladies' eyes went wide.

"Charles is all right, isn't he?" Lorena asked. She hadn't even considered that he might have been injured . . . or worse.

A chill gripped Lorena. The Army had repeatedly assured the travelers that this part of the country was secure. In fact, she had read that Major General Sherman was encouraging all of his officers to bring their wives and children with them on their assignments in the West. They'd been told time and again that it was safe. But now, after listening to Jed Rawlins, Lorena was not so sure.

Lieutenant Rawlins amended his statement at once. "He's fine. I'm sorry if I frightened you, miss. All of this is nothing serious, you understand. On one occasion some braves ran off the sutler's horses, and two days ago they rode off with some emigrant stock. They're only letting us know they're out there. After this last foray, Brevet Major Ackerman volunteered to lead a company of men after them. I'm sure that he'd never have gone if he knew the Army train was nearly upon us, Miss Mackenzie. We weren't expecting all of you for a few days more at least."

"I see," was all that Lorena could say to this. It was frustrating to realize that she'd have to wait for her reunion with Charles for a while longer yet.

Colonel and Mrs. Palmer offered to take Lorena in for the duration of her visit, and they accepted her as warmly as if she'd been their own daughter.

So Lorena's belongings were brought into the post commander's quarters. There were the two trunks she'd brought from home and one more, which was particularly heavy, being filled with books she'd purchased when her train had stopped in St. Louis. Lorena had heard that there was a dearth of books in most Western towns and that she might arrive to find only one primer, a bible, and a dictionary for her use in instructing the students, and so she'd purchased some on her own.

She'd chosen a number of invaluable texts, such as Mr. Colburn's *Intellectual Arithmetic* and *McGuffey's Third Eclectic Reader*, selections of the works of Sir Walter Scott and Nathanial Hawthorne, and even a few of the current best-sellers, such as Currer Bell's *Jane Eyre*, which Lorena intended to read for herself as soon as she was settled in.

To most, all of this might have seemed a foolhardy expense, especially considering that by running away, Lorena had cut herself off from the allowance her uncle had given her each month. But she was determined not to start out in her new position at a disadvantage.

The following day, while the men were occupied with their duties, Sarah came by to visit Lorena. She was met at the door by Cora, Mrs. Palmer's maid, who was a pleasant-looking girl of seventeen with a generous sprinkling of freckles scattered over her round face and luxuriant red hair that was ever escaping the topknot she wore it in.

"The missus is resting," the girl told her.

Sarah smiled inwardly at her good fortune. "Well, as long as I'm here, perhaps I'll just visit with Miss Mackenzie."

Cora nodded and let Sarah in, leading her back to the tiny room she and Lorena were sharing. Lorena was there, on her knees before her trunk and rummaging through its contents. Despite her pose, she looked very ladylike in her dress of soft green cashmere with its long row of pearl buttons, her honey-blond hair wound in a neat coil at the nape of her neck.

"I don't imagine you're accustomed to such spacious accommodations," Sarah said sarcastically, as she stepped over one trunk and squeezed between the pair of Army cots that took up much of the floor space.

"I don't mind, really," Lorena replied. "There's only the one other bedroom, you know, and when compared with the wagon and tents we've been living in these past weeks, this is luxury."

Sarah settled herself onto one of the cots and wistfully fingered a patterned silk scarf draped over the lid of the trunk Lorena had been ransacking, then, as if to regain her hold on reality, she touched her own rough wool skirt. "I suppose that's true," she said at last. "The whole of the quarters given Jed and me isn't much bigger than this. It's not quite what I'd expected, but we'll make do. Now what are you up to here? It would appear you're digging for buried treasure in that trunk."

"Not treasure, only a pair of practical shoes. I'm sick to death of these old riding boots."

Lorena drew out one blue satin slipper and a high-heeled shoe of soft gray kid. Shaking her head, she tossed them back.

"Don't bother with that now," Sarah told her, her voice brimming with excitement. "Jed tells me that the officers have planned a celebration for Saturday evening . . . to welcome the colonel and the other new arrivals. You ought to spend your time searching in there for something to wear."

"Sarah, I don't know if I could attend—"

"Of course you could, and you shall. You're a guest here and certainly as welcome as anyone. Besides, there's to be dancing, and the gentlemen will require partners. In case you've not noticed, this post is dreadfully short of women."

Lorena looked at her friend, who had given in to a burst of enthusiasm and was now rummaging through the second trunkful of clothing. Sarah was positively radiant; there wasn't a line to mar her delicate features, even after all the rigors of their cross-country journey. Lorena knew at once what it was. How satisfying it must be to know such love as Sarah and Jed shared! And then, as quickly as it had come to her, Lorena banished the thought.

Sarah squealed and drew out a gown made of shimmering white faille, with a skirt layered over in gauze that was gathered up by clusters of tiny pink roses. "You must wear this," she decided. "Charles will take one look at you and ask for your hand, and then you won't have to go off and become a school-marm. You can live right here, and we'll keep each other company and—"

Lorena's mouth dropped open in amazement at the absurd fantasy Sarah was weaving for herself. Had she been hoping for something like this all along? "I couldn't possibly marry Charles," Lorena told her quickly. "He's like a brother to me."

"Well," Sarah said, disappointed for only a moment, "one of the others, then. There are plenty of suitable bachelors hereabouts."

"Listen to me, Sarah," Lorena snapped, losing her patience. "I'm not getting married, not now, not ever!"

Sarah ignored Lorena's outburst and made her try on the gown nonetheless. They soon discovered that since the last time Lorena had worn it, the gauze had torn away on a section of the skirt and the hem had ripped. Sarah offered to help with the mending and proposed they begin at once. The maid, Cora, came in to lend a hand, and they started to work.

While standing atop an empty crate as the two women pinned up the hem of her gown, Lorena heard a commotion from outside that wrested her from her thoughts. Excitement at last! Heedless of the work going on at her feet, she lifted her skirts and ran out of the room to the parlor window, hoping to see riders.

The sounds had wakened Mrs. Palmer, who came in behind her, smoothing her silver hair, and surely enough, out the window they saw that a dusty-looking cavalry troop, with swallow-tailed guidons flying, had just ridden in and drawn up before the post headquarters. Colonel Palmer came out of his office to greet them. The man at their head addressed the commanding officer and then, still on his mount, turned to shout orders to his men.

When he turned her way, Lorena's heart gave a leap. He looked much older in his officer's uniform, and his boyish face was marred by the jagged line of a saber scar running along the cheekbone under his right eye. It gave him a menacing air. He wore a moustache now, too, and it was touched with the same reddish highlights as his auburn hair. But despite all the physical changes, it was most definitely Charles.

"Get away from the window, child," Mrs. Palmer entreated. "You don't want everyone to see your dress before the party, now do you?"

Lorena turned her attention back to the women in the room. "It's Charles! Help me out of this—quickly!" she directed Sarah, who'd already begun unfastening the long row of buttons at the back of the gown.

"Did you see?" Sarah asked her, giving way to excitement once more. "He's captured two of the savages. What a triumphant return! Jed says your Charles is quite the fire-eater, and that during the war they called him the Madman. You never told me that, Lorena."

Lorena could not hide her irritation. "Because it's stuff and nonsense, that's why. Charles is a gentleman mindful of his duty as an officer, but he hasn't a contentious bone in the whole of his body."

Yet even as Lorena was speaking, the parade ground was filling with soldiers who were whistling and cheering at the success of their comrades-in-arms. Lorena stepped out into the bright afternoon sunlight in time to watch Brevet Major Charles Ackerman lead his bay once more around the grounds, one hand raised in acknowledgment of the accolades. At his order the men dismounted, then he did likewise, brushing the dust from his blue tunic.

Lorena ran to him and fairly threw herself into his arms, so relieved was she to see him at last. For the moment all of her doubts were cast aside. "Charles!" she cried. "I hardly expected so grand an entrance."

"Lorena? By God, Lorena, it is you! I don't believe it!"

He pulled her against him with a flourish and his mouth descended on hers in a kiss that left her startled and breathless. She soon realized, though, that he was playing to the crowd, for another cheer went up with their embrace.

"How did you get here? Whatever are you doing out here in the middle of nowhere?" he whispered against her ear, sounding more like his old self.

"Then you didn't get my letter?"

"Letter? Why, no. I've not had a letter from you in almost a year. But then the Sioux have been known to ambush our mail carriers now and again. . . . So tell me, Lorena, what miracle is it that's brought you here?"

"I'm on my way to Virginia City, Charles. I've accepted a teaching position."

"You?" he said, and his familiar laughter rang on the air. "You're going to be a school-marm?"

"Take care, Charles, lest I box your ears right here in front of all your men. And I don't see why you're laughing. I'll be a perfectly wonderful 'schoolmarm.' You know I've always loved children. And I've even brought my own books!"

"You've not got two minutes' patience in the whole of your body, Lorena Mackenzie," he teased.

"It's something I really want to do, Charles," she told him, serious now.

She felt she should explain the whole situation at once, about her uncle and how she'd run away, but he looked so pleased, and she didn't want to spoil things just then. There would be time enough later to make him understand, she decided.

As she crossed the compound on Charles's arm, Lorena was able to rest easy at last. She'd managed to escape from her uncle, and even if that fool Edgington did have a mind to come after her, he'd never guess where she'd gone. Best of all, she told herself, her relationship with her old friend hadn't been tarnished by time.

"It must've been a hellish trip for you—coming out here, Lorena," Charles said.

"I got on well enough," she assured him.

"I should have guessed that you would. I haven't yet met a woman who could match you for your resolve. So here you are, come west at last, just as you'd always said you would."

"I did, didn't I?"

She looked up into his warm brown eyes, and his arm tightened across her back. "You're really here, aren't you?" he said again. "I still can't believe it."

There was a tracing of icy fingers running the length of Lorena's spine, as if someone were giving her the evil eye. She scanned the crowd and her gaze settled upon the two Indian prisoners, hands bound before them with leather thongs, being led across to the guardhouse. The taller of the two was a young brave, clad only in breechclout and leggings, with a number of decorated eagle feathers worked into the plait of his shining black hair. He bore himself with pride, despite the taunts of the soldiers, and he did, indeed, have his dark eyes fixed on Lorena, but for only a moment. Then he turned a baleful glare upon her companion.

Lorena shivered and slipped her arm

through Charles's. She noticed that he'd responded by sending the Indian a black look, filled with no less venom than he had received.

"Who is he?" Lorena whispered.

"Spotted Wolf, a war chief of the northern Cheyenne," Charles replied, making plain his distaste.

"War chief?" she echoed.

This was not the first time that Lorena had been left with the feeling that there was more to the disagreement between the government and the Indians than any of the ladies had been led to believe. More than could be settled with only the words of the Laramie treaty.

It was clearer to her now why the command thought so much of this capture. This was not just a case of a few stolen horses; both sides must be thinking in terms of war.

"What will happen to him?" Lorena wanted to know.

"He and his braves attacked an emigrant train about two weeks ago, north of Crazy Woman's Fork," Charles explained. "They drove off the stock and killed two men in the process. He'll have to stand trial."

"But how do you know he was responsible?"

"Don't be a child, Lorena!" he snapped, and suddenly there was a hard glint in his eye, which was made more malevolent by his twisted scar. "Whether he took the scalps himself or not, *he* is responsible."

Lorena felt as though she'd been smartly slapped, and was surprised at the change that had come over him so abruptly.

His tone softened somewhat as he continued. "I hope that you haven't been taken in by the tripe that the Eastern papers are printing about the 'plight of the poor redskin.' They are a cunning and ruthless people who look upon war as if it were sport. You simply cannot know what an insatiable thirst for blood is in them. I, myself, have seen more than enough of their handiwork in the time I have been here: scalpings, horrible mutilations, atrocities which I dare not mention."

Lorena felt the blood drain from her face. There was something decidedly alarming in his frenzied manner. "I—I'm sorry, Charles," she stammered. "Of course you would know more about these affairs, I only wondered—"

As swiftly as it had appeared, the feverish look was gone. He patted her arm. "Forgive me, Lorena. I've frightened you now, haven't I? And that wasn't my intention at all. You needn't worry about the savages. We are, most of us here, hardened war veterans. We have only to receive the order and we shall trample the entire Sioux and Cheyenne nations like blades of grass beneath our bootheels."

Chapter Six

✦✦✦✦✦

WORD OF SPOTTED WOLF'S capture had already reached Fort Phil Kearny by the time Thorne arrived with the dispatches he'd agreed to carry to Colonel Carrington. The news was well-received by the soldiers, who had themselves endured a summer of strike-and-run attacks and other types of harassment by Indians. Only a week before, after the latest in a series of raids against emigrant trains on the Bozeman Trail, a small force out of Fort Reno under the command of Brevet Major Charles Ackerman had set out in pursuit of the raiders, bent on retribution. Their leader was a man possessed, it was said, who'd kept up the chase even after the Indians had abandoned their stolen herd. The major was only satisfied with the capture of the warrior chief himself.

Thorne, knowing the Indians well, could not imagine that anything but sheer luck had led to the capture. And it was his own curiosity, he told himself, that now made him stray from his return route and toward Fort Reno. Only curiosity, not the need to see the woman he could not forget.

By the time he rode through the gate, Thorne had decided that if Lorena Mackenzie were still visiting her friend here, he would see her and pay his respects. Maybe it was some perversity in his nature that made him so anxious to rub salt in his open wounds, but then, it could not possibly leave him more miserable than he'd been these last weeks.

He found no one at post headquarters, and so he crossed the deserted parade ground to the guardhouse and struck up a conversation with the soldier there.

"Is that the great Cheyenne chief, Spotted Wolf, you've got in there?" he asked, inclining his head toward the bolted door.

"Yes, sir," replied the corporal on duty, who seemed to be no more than a boy. "And one of his braves too. Have a look for yourself, if you like. They won't be goin' anywhere. The major's got 'em trussed up like Christmas turkeys."

"Does he, now?" Thorne replied, pulling at his chin. "I hear tell that that major of yours is one crazy son of a bitch, damn near killed half the men in his company going after these two."

Every word was true, and Ben was not ashamed of the pleasure he derived from vilifying the man. He had no respect for a man who treated Indians as little more than animals.

The guard looked askance and pulled on the brim of his kepi. "Well, sir . . . don't rightly know myself, but some of the boys

that was there been sayin' as how they'd
sooner ride into hell with the devil himself
the next time, leastwise they'd know where
they stood. Seems like Major Ackerman, he
just gets hold of a thing and he can't let go.''

"The Madman of the Shenandoah," Thorne
muttered under his breath.

"What's that you say, sir?"

"Nothing, Corporal. Do you know where I
might find Miss Mackenzie?"

"Colonel Palmer's quarters, I'd expect . . .
there's a fancy dress party in the mess hall this
evening. Is that what's brought you here, sir?"

"What? Oh . . . yes," Ben replied absently,
"thank you, Corporal."

So she was here. He could see her if he
chose to, if somehow he could overcome
that part of himself that believed she'd be
better off without him. As he wrestled with
his conscience, Thorne walked around behind the guardhouse and leaned against the
rough timber exterior of the structure. He
drew out a long cheroot and struck a match
to it.

"Good evening, sir," he heard the young
corporal inside say. "I wasn't expecting to see
you here this evening."

"I only wanted to see if our wolves have
taken to their cage," came the reply.

Ben heard the rattle of a key in the lock, and
in the twilight, peering through the barred
window at the rear of the guardhouse, he

could see a young officer standing by the door. He was resplendent in his dress uniform, and Ben guessed his identity at once.

In the shadows of the dank cell were the two braves, sitting on their haunches, their hands bound with ties of rawhide. Ben determined the younger of the two to be Spotted Wolf, since his leggings were fringed with human hair locks, a privilege reserved for only the bravest of the Cheyenne Dog Soldiers.

"Just look at them, Corporal—the flower of the Cheyenne nation. They don't look so fierce now, do they? No more than a rough, red bundle of bone and sinew and a hank of greasy hair, all wrapped up in hides. They think like animals; they hunt like animals, possessed of neither reason nor compassion, and yet they have the audacity to lay down their challenge to the Army of the United States, the greatest fighting force ever mustered."

Ben listened in fascinated disgust, but he did not miss the cunning slant in Spotted Wolf's eyes. The Indian clearly understood every word of the major's pronouncement, and turning to his companion, said in his own tongue, "I shall have the scalp of this Long Knife to wear upon my belt." At that he began to chant, in monosyllables, his song of war.

The guard let out a nervous laugh. "Well, sir, when you put it that way . . . I suppose it does sound like powerful poor judgment on their part."

"Mark my words," the young major continued, "ere long the murderous deeds of these savages will bring the military might of our great nation down upon them, and I, for one, intend to be in its vanguard."

Ben concentrated on the curl of smoke that rose from the cheroot in the crook of his finger and shook his head. This was the celebrated hero of the Shenandoah campaigns? This wild-eyed boy? Ben had seen his like on more than one occasion over these past few years: mild-tempered young gentlemen who'd been so hardened by the horrors of war that they were never again the same; men who went about spoiling for a fight, ever in search of another to call enemy. Quite obviously Charles Ackerman had chosen the Indians.

And Ben had all but delivered Lorena into his hands. His decision made for him, he took one last draw on the cheroot and dropped it, grinding it into the dust at his feet.

Sarah knocked on the door of the Palmers' quarters and when Lorena called out for her to enter, she swept inside with a rustle of lavender taffeta. Lorena was alone and flitting about the cottage like a nervous butterfly. "I can't find my other glove," she explained.

"Over there on the cot," Sarah told her and handed her a bouquet of sweet clover, sorrel, and blue gentian, all tied up with a ribbon. "It's from the officers. They made up one for each of the ladies. It must have been a sight, all of them supervising their companies of men as they scoured the prairie, picking wildflowers."

"It's lovely. How thoughtful they are," Lorena murmured in reply.

She set down the bouquet and went to stand before the looking glass that hung over Mrs. Palmer's bureau to study her reflection.

"You see," Sarah said as she came up behind her, "I told you you'd look splendid in that gown."

Lorena turned to embrace her friend as emotion welled in her. "Have I thanked you yet, Sarah, for all that you've done for me?"

"Lorena, stop that!" Sarah chided her. "You sound as though you're saying good-bye. You've another few days with us yet before the next wagon train heads out. Let's promise to enjoy the evening, and not have a care about tomorrow, shall we?"

Lorena agreed, and Sarah reached out to smooth the folds in her friend's exquisite white gown. She marveled at the feel of the rich fabric and the gauze that floated over the wide skirt like clouds of vapor. With her delicate beauty and this shimmering white dress, Lorena looked like an angel. Surely she would capture the attention of every young officer at the dance tonight, Sarah thought. In fact Sarah was counting on it.

"Well, Jed is waiting for me," she said, "so I'd best be on my way. Are you coming?"

"Not just yet. You go on ahead. I'll be along presently."

When Sarah had left her, Lorena went back to studying herself in the glass. Her features were softened by the warm, yellow light of the oil lamp on the bureau, yet she was not pleased, for she could see the emptiness she'd begun to feel. It was written there, plain upon her face, a stark contrast to the vibrant countenance of her friend, Sarah Rawlins.

Lorena was thankful that Mrs. Palmer's maid had offered to help her to dress for the evening, for she was not at all certain she'd have been able to manage the intricate fastenings of the evening dress on her own. Using a hot iron, the girl had made a neat row of ringlets out of Lorena's unruly mass of golden hair, and as Lorena reached to pin a cluster of pink rosebuds over one ear now, she noticed that her hands were trembling.

It was concern for Charles, she decided, that was affecting her. There had been a change in him, after all. She'd learned in these past few days that he was no longer the carefree young man he once had been. There was a dark side to him that had never been there before—a rage that at times threatened to consume him. Its vehemence frightened her, but then as quickly as it had come over him, the mood would vanish and he would be his old self once more.

Lorena had seen this type of behavior before. During the war she had worked for the Sanitary Commission. Though she'd told her uncle she was only rolling bandages, she'd proved to be an able nurse and, in fact, spent most of her hours at the veterans' hospital tending wounded soldiers.

And it was her work there that now told her that Charles was still nursing war wounds, and though they were not wounds one could see, they were there just the same.

Since she'd realized this about her old companion, Lorena had asked herself over and over if there were something she might do to help him. Perhaps deep within herself she believed that there was, for each time she thought of leaving, she would hesitate—as if a string around her heart tugged painfully when she contemplated starting her new life. Was it concern for Charles, though, or something else entirely?

Hot tears pooled in her eyes all at once, threatening to spill over, and through the haze of lamplight and tears she saw a reflection over her shoulder in the glass. It was Ben Thorne.

This vision was so real it startled her. It was a perfect likeness, from the wry twist of the mouth to the vivid green of the eyes. But why would her mind conjure such an apparition when she had been thinking of Charles?

"Hello, Lorena."

With a sharp intake of breath she whirled around to realize that it was him . . . truly standing there.

"How did you get in here?" she asked, astounded.

"Mrs. Rawlins told me you were here. I knocked but you must not have heard—"

"What are you doing here?"

"I had to come," he told her, following as she moved nervously from the Palmer's bedroom into the darkened parlor, where she began to pace, her skirts rustling softly in her wake. "Ackerman's not the same man, surely you've seen that now."

Lorena stopped to face him directly, angry. "And what difference could it possibly make to you, Mr. Thorne?"

Ben Thorne remained silent. His eyes dropped before her and he scuffed the toe of his moccasin on the wood-plank floor like an errant schoolboy.

Lorena went cold with fear. It was Thorne, she realized now, who was to blame for all of the turmoil within her. This man was a threat to her newly won independence. If he should declare himself, if he should say the right words, she was not at all certain she could hold firm against him. Even now, with him halfway across the room, her body betrayed her: her heart beating a frenzied rhythm against her breast, her heightened senses craving his touch.

He was a long time in replying, as if carefully weighing his thoughts. "I've promised that I would see you safely back East," he said at last, "if you've changed your mind."

Lorena ought to have known that a man of his like would never have come back for her, that what he wanted from her and what she needed of him were not the same. As her strength waned, the dam burst and tears streamed unchecked down her face. She was thankful for the darkness, which hid them from his view, and still hurting, she sought for a way to make him go. Thorne had come here to defame Charles. Did he believe that it was Charles for whom she had traveled all this way? That she was in love with him?

She turned on him, furious, her eyes flashing as the lamplight reflected in her tears. "What would you have me do, Mr. Thorne? Go back to New York? Abandon Charles because he's not as I remember him? He needs me now, and I believe I have the capacity to help him."

Lorena saw immediately, by the look in his eye, that Thorne did, indeed, imagine that she was in love with Charles Ackerman and that her words confirmed his suspicions.

"Noble sentiment, I'll admit, but not the

basis for a lifetime together," he said plainly. "You'll come to resent him, Lorena, as he will you."

"I don't believe that," she shot back, a note of regret creeping into her voice as she realized she was driving Thorne away, leading him to believe something that was not true. "I can't believe that. Charles's wounds are deep and festering. You cannot begin to understand what he suffers."

Thorne turned to stare out of the window. "Perhaps I can understand what Ackerman is going through, Lorena, better than you might imagine."

The belligerence was gone now from his manner. His words were quiet and restrained. "We all suffered, all of us who fought that war. Charles Ackerman is a fortunate man, indeed, to have someone like you—someone willing to try to help him become the man he once was. I apologize if I've misread your intentions. You've more strength and determination than I've been willing to give you credit for, and I don't doubt that you'll succeed."

By the tone of his voice, Lorena knew he was bidding her farewell.

He went to her then, gently brushing the tears from her face. Lorena caught her breath as his hands slid around her slim waist, and she tried to read something of his thoughts in the depths of his eyes, but could not. "Good-bye, Lorena," he whispered, and pressed a warm kiss against her lips.

As he stepped away, she tried to reply, but the words stuck in her throat.

She watched from the window until he had crossed the whole of the yard, mounted his Indian pony, and disappeared through the gate. Then she sat down and put her head in her hands, her eyes curiously dry.

She had made the right decision, Lorena told herself when she'd finally gathered the strength to rise again. Retrieving the wild-flower bouquet that Sarah had brought to her, she briefly touched a hand to her lips, still warm from Thorne's kiss. With only a sigh to mourn what might have been, she quit the room and went out into the darkness of a moonless night, the autumn wind whipping her skirts as she crossed the parade ground, heading for the gay sound of fiddle music coming from the mess hall.

Carried on that wind, there was, what sounded to Lorena, to be the plaintive cry of a wild bird, and it was followed in rapid succession by another, similar call. Almost instantly a commotion arose in the vicinity of the guard-house, and nearby, the stable doors burst open and the horses sheltered there broke free, racing across the yard as if the devil himself were at their heels.

Lorena stood paralyzed in the center of the parade ground, unable to comprehend what was happening. Shots were fired from the soldier standing guard over the prisoners and from those within the blockhouse near the gate as well, and then Lorena spied the intruders. A lone brave on horseback rode out of the stables at a gallop while his comrades in the guardhouse felled the soldier on guard. But the alarm had been sounded by now, and before the Cheyenne chief imprisoned within the guardhouse could be freed, the yard was filled with soldiers.

The mounted warrior veered off the course he'd made for the guardhouse as shots rang out, and instead crossed the parade ground. The earth beneath Lorena's feet shuddered at the horse's approach, and she turned and began to run toward the safety of the officer's quarters. In one swift move, though, the brave had lifted her off her feet, his arm about her waist like a steel band. She could not breathe, could not think. It was instinct alone that made her strike out at him, hoping he would loose his hold on her. But he was not fazed in the least by the blows she rained upon him.

Using her as a shield against the soldier's fire, the warrior directed his horse through the tangle of unbridled cavalry mounts rearing and stamping in confusion, and galloped through the open gate. He did not release Lorena even then, and it finally struck her that he intended to carry her off.

A few of the soldiers had collected their mounts now and were in pursuit. Though Lorena couldn't see, she imagined Charles would be at their head, driving his big bay at a breakneck pace. Perhaps she would be rescued after all, she thought, but then one of the Indians in the war party drew his rifle, turned, and fired. The lead rider was struck and his bay horse wheeled and reared up as he lost his seat.

Thinking the Indian had killed him, Lorena let out a wild scream. The evil savage, who held her in an iron grip, struck her a blow that stunned her, and she fell across the horse as he headed his mount westward toward the mountains, his confederates close behind.

Chapter Seven

✦ ✦ ✦ ✦

THE BUGLER SOUNDED the call to arms and there was a cry of "Indians!" from the blockhouse. By now all of those who were gathered for the party had spilled out onto the parade ground, where the nervous cavalry horses were still creating chaos. Through the cloud of dust they'd kicked up, the figure of the fallen corporal at the guardhouse was barely visible. Another soldier had gone to his aid, and peered through the barred window now and waved a hand across the yard, calling to Colonel Palmer. "Prisoners secure, sir!"

It was fortunate, Colonel Palmer thought to himself, that the men on guard had been able to sound the alarm before the Indians could rescue their chief, or else he'd have lost his prized captive. What a brassy lot they were, thinking they could just ride into the compound to free their leader!

The men who'd gone after the Indians rode back into the compound. "Lost them in the hills, sir," one of them called out.

At length, two of the soldiers made their way across the parade ground, supporting Major Ackerman, who'd been wounded in the melee. His head sagged and he had an arm flung over each of their shoulders.

The soldiers slowly made their way around the cavalrymen, still trying to capture their errant mounts, and approached Colonel Palmer, who had begun to shout orders to those around him. The major was dazed and blood was flowing freely down the side of his face and staining the white linen collar of his dress uniform.

When the toe of his boot struck something lying in the dirt, the major bent to pick it up, despite his injuries. Colonel Palmer could see that it was a bouquet of wildflowers, now crushed and broken, that had been tied up with a satin ribbon. Examining them, Charles's face contorted.

"Lorena!" he shouted, "Lorena, where are you?"

The colonel rushed to his side and grasped him firmly by the shoulders. "Charles, you've been injured. You must calm yourself. Do you understand? You won't be able to do anyone any good if you panic. She's been taken by the Indians. The men on duty saw one of them sweep her onto his horse and ride off."

Charles's glazed eyes were wild, and he wrung the wilted bouquet between his hands, distraught. His head was spinning like a child's top and he was overwhelmed by guilt; all of this was his fault. He'd promised that he'd protect her from the savages.

"I'm certain they won't harm her," Colonel Palmer assured him. "They'll want to trade her for this chief of theirs that you've captured. You can be thankful for that much, at least."

"Trade? For Spotted Wolf? I'll see him in Hell first!" Charles shouted, his face mottled with rage and the line of his scar whitening. "We must mount a search party at once. Find out where these devils have their camp and rescue Lorena on our own."

"Calm yourself, soldier! We shall do nothing of the kind!" the colonel snapped. "Any hostile actions on our part will only serve to bring down the Indians' wrath on Miss Mackenzie. We shall wait to hear from the Cheyenne camp. They will no doubt send a messenger with their demands before very long. We shall wait, Brevet Major Ackerman, and you shall report to the infirmary at once. Is that understood?"

Charles could feel his strength waning, but he tried to compose himself. "Yes, that is understood, sir," he replied in an uneven voice, and then fainted dead away.

The Cheyenne encampment lay in a valley nestled in the foothills of the Bighorn Mountains. There were perhaps three-dozen tepees scattered over the grassy clearing beside the creek. Lorena had regained consciousness some time ago, but thought it might prove to her advantage to pretend otherwise. So, full of dread, she hung limp across the horse's withers, allowing herself to be jostled about, biding her time.

When the horsemen drew near, some of the inhabitants of the camp let out a wild whoop, drawing still more from the tepees. Soon a crowd had gathered, and it was difficult for Lorena to remain still while dozens of hands reached out to her, touching the smooth fabric of her gown, poking and prodding as if she were some new species of animal. Just when she felt that she could take no more and would scream, the warrior who'd abducted her sent out what sounded to be a stern warning in his guttural tongue and effectively scattered the curious lot.

Lorena felt him dismount and found herself

tossed unceremoniously over his shoulder,
borne through a small opening into one of the
lodges. Without warning she was dropped
onto a bed of buffalo robes, redolent of sage
and sweet grass. Through the gauze that had
torn free of her dress and now covered her
like a veil, she looked up to see the expectant
faces of half a dozen braves, shouldering for a
space at the tepee opening. She did not have
to guess what they intended; she'd heard stories aplenty of the fate of unfortunate white
women who'd been captured by savages.
Though inexperience left her somewhat igno-
rant of the details, she felt the terror rise in
her.

Another sharp retort from the brave within
the lodge served to disperse his fellow tribes-
men, and muttering to himself, he secured the
tent flap.

Lorena's mind raced now. How could she
save herself? There could be no reasoning
with these savages, they'd murdered Charles
in cold blood. A sob caught in her throat at the
realization that he was dead. As the Indian
padded back across the dirt floor, Lorena
knew she had to keep her wits about her. She
raised herself up and edged back against one
of the lodgepoles, her eyes darting from side
to side as she sought out some weapon to use
against him.

Her captor saw that she had recovered from
the blow he'd given her earlier. He settled
himself on the buffalo robes and in one swift

move his brown arm reached out, pulling her to him. Trapped in his embrace, Lorena bit down hard on her tongue, vowing to herself that she would not cry out, no matter what happened next.

He roughly tore away the gauze that protected her face, snapping her head backward so far that she could see the blue of the morning sky out of the opened smoke flaps in the center of the lodge. The light blinded her for a moment, and when next his hand captured her chin, pulling her face close so he might examine it, she had to blink to readjust to the shadows within.

Lorena's heart drummed with such fury that she felt sure it would burst. That would be a merciful end, at least. She met his black eyes with her own fierce glare, determined to show no fear. And then, quite suddenly, he let her go, a stunned expression overtaking him.

She did not know what it was that made him hesitate at the last, but she seized the opportunity to grab for the knife that was sheathed in his belt. She snatched the weapon and lunged for him, and he reacted instantly, capturing her arm before the wicked point of the blade could reach him. Lorena's breath came in short gasps as she wrestled for control, concentrating all of her strength into the arm wielding the knife. But it was a hopeless effort. As her energies waned, she made a decision and turned the blade back toward herself, intending to plunge it into her own breast.

"No!" the Indian cried out, twisting her wrist until she was forced to release the blade.

He picked it up and returned it to its sheath. Lorena could see that he'd been alarmed by her intentions, and this puzzled her. Why should her life matter to him, when his kinsmen had murdered Charles without a second thought? He spoke a few words in his own tongue, and Lorena scrambled again back against the lodgepole, clutching the torn bodice against her breast and rubbing her bruised wrist. What had caused this change in him?

"Silver Eyes," the Indian said, in English now, almost as if he were replying to the question in her mind. "I have passed many winters awaiting the coming of the white bird with silver eyes. I am shamed to say that I doubted the truth, but now at last what was revealed to me in the vision has come to pass."

Lorena could make no sense of his words. She eyed him cautiously, not daring to move, as he pointed to a shield made of buffalo hide that hung from one of the lodgepoles. Upon this shield was painted the form of a graceful, white bird in flight. The artist had tried to depict, with a series of lines like the rays of a sunbeam, the radiant eyes of this fantastical bird. Lorena looked down at her white dress, now soiled and torn. Could it be that this Indian associated her somehow with his mythical creature?

Her captor reached for one of the decorated hide bags that lay near by him and took several items from it. While Lorena watched, he began to chant, and upon a flat stone set on the floor near the center of the lodge, he built a small fire into which he sprinkled incense he'd drawn from a small leather pouch. Fragrant smoke wreathed the air, and after taking deep breaths of it, she was quite giddy. Still his song droned on, in unintelligible monotones. All of this had the feel of a religious ceremony, but perhaps it was only meant to numb her senses, that he might not have such a fight on his hands the next time. If, indeed, that was his intent, then he was succeeding. Lorena found herself almost hypnotized and had to fight to keep her wits about her. Determined not to give way, she tried to shake the fog out of her brain.

"Why have you brought me here?" she shouted at him. "It will only serve to bring the wrath of the soldiers upon your people."

In the long silence that ensued, Lorena sized up her adversary, sitting cross-legged upon the ground, intent upon his strange ceremony. He must have been five and thirty years at least, she guessed, and had doubtless achieved some degree of status within his tribe, for as she herself had witnessed, the people listened and obeyed his words without hesitation.

His angular features gave him a harsh profile, with deep-set eyes that glittered like two beads of black jet. A foxtail and a pair of eagle feathers were tied in his black hair, which streamed long and loose to his shoulders. About his neck he wore a wide choker quilled in an elaborate design, and a rawhide thong from which hung a whistle made of bone.

Lorena had already discovered him to be as agile as a mountain cat. She must not underestimate him again, but her patience was wearing thin. "I know you can understand me," she said. "You must realize that it would not be wise to keep me here."

"You are Long Knife's woman—" he began.

Lorena started to protest, then remembered that she had been told that the Indians called the U.S. cavalrymen "long knives" because of the sabers they carried, and so she nodded, keeping a keen eye on him.

His voice was calm. "I am Blue Elk, brother of Spotted Wolf."

Now she understood. Blue Elk had intended, with his daring raid on the fort, to rescue his brother. But when his plan failed, he had taken her as a hostage, hoping that she could be traded for the Indians whom Charles had captured. So of course she'd have been no good to Blue Elk dead, that was what had disturbed him—but then what was all of that nonsense about white birds and visions?

Realizing that she was no longer in imminent danger, Lorena's fear abated. "I am to be your prisoner, then, until a trade can be arranged."

Blue Elk rose, still wearing a most obscure expression, "You will be well cared for. I will see to it."

Amidst the chaos of the sutler's store sat Ben Thorne, one hand wrapped round the neck of a whiskey bottle, the other tapping out a lazy rhythm on the tabletop. From his cramped corner of the room he watched bleary-eyed as Indians, soldiers, and emigrants alike conducted their business in a babel of tongues. Goods passed over the counter at an amazing rate: rice and coffee, calico, peppermint candy, glass beads, brass nails, ribbons, and tobacco. If Mr. Bullock had not been otherwise occupied, Ben was certain that, friend or no, he'd have thrown him out on his ear, and he couldn't say he'd have blamed him.

Ben sought out Bullock's familiar form behind the counter and saw him deep in conversation with an Indian. Ben could not recognize the Indian at this distance, since he was having difficulty focusing his eyes. He was quite sure, though, that they were discussing him, especially after the sutler's long arm stretched across the counter, pointing in Ben's direction.

Perhaps, he thought to himself, another

draw on the bottle would uncloud his vision. It did not, but by then the Indian had come close enough to make his identity clear.

"I look at you, but I see your father," he said.

Why must he always be so damned smug? "Don't give me any of your 'holier than thou' attitudes, friend. I'm past the point where I can be made to feel guilty by only a few well-chosen words from you."

Broken Hand's dark brow creased into a thoughtful frown. "All of your friends tell me that you have changed, Thorne, yet no one can say the reason why."

The Indian reached for the bottle, but Ben drew it away. "Ah, that's right. You wouldn't have heard any of it. You've been off hunting in the Black Hills with your kinsmen these past months. Well, come along with me, old friend, and I shall relate to you the whole sorry tale."

Thorne got to his feet unsteadily, but refused Broken Hand's assistance all the same, still clinging to the whiskey bottle. Together they quit the crowded sutler's store and walked out past the barracks building, where Ben propped himself against a hitching post.

"After you'd gone," he began, "I kept myself busy carrying dispatches between the forts on the Bozeman. One day I found myself at Fort Reno, and I went to see the woman."

Broken Hand regarded him disapprovingly. "The yellow-haired woman?"

"Her name was Lorena," Ben said, ignoring what he read in the Indian's eyes, "Lorena Mackenzie. I found out that that officer friend of hers was a crazy fool. He'd managed somehow to capture Spotted Wolf, the Cheyenne chief, and he was keeping him locked up like some animal in the guardhouse. Now if that isn't tempting the fates . . ."

The silence that followed was damning. Ben could hardly expect Broken Hand to understand the reasons why he was drawn to this woman, when he could scarcely understand it himself. "She and I talked," he went on, "and you'll be happy to know I did the right thing. I left her to find happiness with her officer and I went my own way, hoping I'd think no more about it. It wasn't long after that I heard she'd been kidnapped by the Cheyenne, following a thwarted attempt to rescue Spotted Wolf. I suppose they figured they could trade one for the other."

Ben stopped in his discourse and shut his eyes tightly, then downed another swig of whiskey. "It should have been a simple enough deal, but then . . . late in December, Red Cloud made good on his promise to kill any white man who ventured north of Crazy Woman's Fork. He and his band murdered eighty men out of Fort Phil Kearny, under the command of Captain Fetterman. Needless to say, after that every soldier along the trail was looking for vengeance.

"I suppose it was bound to happen. One

Indian is as good as another in the eyes of some. The guardhouse at Fort Reno was overrun, and Spotted Wolf was strung up."

"He is dead?" Broken Hand ventured.

"He was still kicking when Colonel Palmer discovered the deed, and so he was kept under close guard in the surgeon's quarters while he healed."

"And?" the Indian prompted.

"And he murdered his guard and escaped nearly two weeks ago."

"So there can be no trade, and the woman is—"

"Dead, no doubt," Ben said, his voice ice-cold. "Isn't that what you'd guess? The Cheyenne no longer have need of her."

Again he turned to the bottle, but his hand began to shake and he hurled it to the ground. Shards flew across the grassy clearing, and a sob caught in his throat.

"I warned her from the first. I told her that a gentle-bred woman had no place out here; it's too dangerous. But she was full of fire, told me I knew nothing of her life. She was right . . . and now I'll never know."

"You cannot be certain what has become of her," Broken Hand said, offering him some hope, "and you shall have no peace until you know the truth." It seemed at last that the Indian had decided to accept his friend's obsession with the Mackenzie woman. "We will ride for Reno in the morning."

Chapter Eight

◆ ◆ ◆ ◆ ◆

STANDING AT THE door of the post headquarters at Fort Reno, Ben felt the color drain suddenly from his face, and his head began to throb and spin alternately. He had not recovered entirely from his bout with the bottle, and the rigors of three days' hard ride up from Laramie had taken its toll. He was determined, though, and so he planted his feet firmly and knocked on the door.

He entered when he was told to do so and shot a glance back at Broken Hand, who was resting against the porch rail. The Indian, it seemed, had decided to let him handle this on his own.

"Come in, Captain," Colonel Palmer called to him.

Ben did so, easing himself carefully into the chair across from the colonel's desk. "Good to see you again, sir."

"I suppose you've heard of our troubles, Captain. Miss Mackenzie—snatched up by the savages as she crossed the parade ground . . . that Cheyenne chief cutting the throat of his guard and stealing off into the night like some jackal, and now the tribes seem bound and determined to push the whole of the United States Army back down the Bozeman Trail to Fort Laramie."

Ben nodded. "That's what's brought us here. Broken Hand and I know the land hereabouts as well as anyone. We thought we might be of help."

Colonel Palmer pulled on his neatly-trimmed white beard. "We could use the expertise, no doubt about that."

"I'd like to talk to Brevet Major Ackerman, if I could, sir. I understand that he's been scouting around the foothills."

"You're welcome to try, of course," the colonel replied, "but I don't think you'll learn much. Ackerman has recovered from the wounds he suffered when Miss Mackenzie was taken, but this whole affair has him unhinged. At any other time I'd have relieved him of his duties, but I need every one of my officers now. Considering the bloodletting the Indians are engaging in, I've let Ackerman have his head. Thus far he's managed to kill every stray hostile unfortunate enough to cross his path. I don't know how much longer he can hold up, though. He's obsessed by his guilt. The poor girl was here to visit him, and he holds himself accountable for her fate."

As well he ought to, Ben thought to himself. His capture of the war chief had directly led to Lorena's kidnapping. "Do you believe Miss Mackenzie could still be alive, sir?"

Palmer shook his head doubtfully. "It's not likely, but she is a pretty thing, and if she's caught the eye of some brave, who knows?"

Ben's fingers curled into a tight fist—the

only indication that the thought of such a possibility affected him. It might, however, be the only thing keeping her alive.

"I'm sorry to say," the colonel went on, "that with all things taken into consideration, she might be better off dead."

Ben's head spun crazily; he could stand no more of this, and so he pulled himself out of the chair. "Broken Hand and I will do all that we can, sir," he replied in a strangled voice. "If Lorena Mackenzie is alive, we will find her."

He had already reached the door when Palmer called after him. "Tell your friend to watch his back, Thorne," he warned. "After what happened at Fort Phil Kearny, people around here won't be too particular as to which Indian they put a hole in."

Thorne wasn't at all ready for an encounter with Charles Ackerman, but there didn't seem to be any other way to get the information he needed, so he collared an orderly to ask directions and crossed the compound to the officers' quarters.

As he approached, Ben could hear the measured step of Ackerman pacing in his room. He rapped on the door, and it opened at once, revealing a bleary-eyed young man.

"You're Thorne, aren't you?" Ackerman said as he waved him into the room.

"Well, yes, I am," Ben replied, perplexed at how the major could have known this.

Once he was inside, Ben's eyes widened as

he surveyed the room. Ackerman's quarters were a shambles, as if the man had chosen to vent his feelings of helplessness upon all of his belongings. This kind of rage was something Thorne could well understand, and he found himself beginning to reevaluate Ackerman. All along he'd imagined somehow that the self-righteous young officer would not be unduly affected by Lorena's disappearance, but he saw now that this was only what he'd wanted to believe.

Charles Ackerman was not faring well at all. He sported several days' growth of beard and his tunic was half unbuttoned, revealing a stained and badly-creased linen shirt beneath.

He cleared off a campstool for Ben to sit on. "Lorena spoke of you," he explained, then perched himself on a stack of crates in the corner opposite. "She has a gift for painting vivid portraits with only a few words. I suppose I ought to thank you for watching over her on her travels."

His tone made it quite clear that while he thought he ought to have thanked Ben, he did not intend to. Ben began to sense the other man's animosity. How much had Lorena told him?

Ben cleared his throat, ignoring the innuendo. "I've just spoken to Colonel Palmer. My friend and I have offered to help locate Spotted Wolf's camp, and I thought you might tell me what areas you'd been concentrating on, so that we'll not be going over ground you and your men have already covered."

"This is my fight," Ackerman said plainly. "Besides, what sort of help can I expect from an Army officer who resigned his commission because of his sympathies for the red man?"

"I have lived and scouted in this country for more than fifteen years," Ben said, trying to maintain his composure, "and my friend was born on this land. The two of us can cover more ground in less time than an entire company of your men, and time is of the essence, Major, if we hope to find Miss Mackenzie alive."

"If? If!" Ackerman was becoming agitated now. "Of course Lorena is still alive, and I don't need the likes of you nor your Indian friend to aid in the rescue. Mark my words, Thorne, I shall find the savages who have captured her myself and make them pay, the lot of them!"

Ben was tired and vexed. He had managed to control his temper till now, but with Ackerman's outburst, he struck out. "Haven't you done enough already? She'd never have come out here at all if she weren't in love with you. It was purely selfish of you to allow her to stay, knowing the dangers. You're the one who captured Spotted Wolf and angered his tribe, and you alone are to blame for Lorena's fate."

Clearly Thorne had struck home. Ackerman paled, but regrouped and lashed back. "You don't know what you're talking about! Lorena Mackenzie isn't in love with me. She's come out here to be a schoolmarm. I told her this wasn't a safe place for a woman on her own, but I thought that, while she was here at least, I could keep watch over her."

"Fine job you've done of that," Ben shot back. The retort was unfair, and he knew it, but he couldn't help himself.

"You don't know Lorena," Ackerman told him, shaking his head. "You don't know her at all. I watched her grow from a little girl. Year after year I followed her on her wild escapades, doing my best to keep her out of harm's way. From the time she was old enough to get about on her own, she was a hell raiser, in spite of her upbringing. I've never met a woman of her like, and I never shall again. She's forceful and determined and probably damned near as strong as you and I put together. So don't tell me what I've done, Thorne. She'd have found her way out here, with or without me."

It was almost as though Ackerman were trying to convince himself with his words. Ben knew, though, that all of what he'd said was probably true, and once again he realized that his own feelings for Lorena had caused him to

misjudge Charles Ackerman. The man may
have been battle scarred, and his hatred of the
Indian people had grown to near obsession,
but his concern for Lorena Mackenzie was
genuine.

Ben noticed then that Ackerman had gone
to his makeshift desk to take up a crumbled page. He read it more than once, as if
the written words might somehow change.
Finally, though, he let the paper slip to
the floor and cradled his head in his
hands.

Ben got up to a retrieve the page, and could
not help but glance at the words penned upon
it, which had so affected Ackerman.

> *My dear friend,*
>
> *I hope this letter finds you well. I am well
> enough myself—*
>
> *No, that isn't so at all. Life here has become
> a misery, for my uncle insists that I marry a man
> whom I despise, and he will not be dissuaded. I
> have no choice therefore but to leave his house at
> once.*
>
> *You mustn't worry for me, though,
> Charles, as my future is not so bleak as it might
> seem. I have secured a position for myself, as a
> schoolmistress in Virginia City in the Montana
> Territory. This town is, I have discovered, not so
> far from your Fort Reno, and so I shall be stopping by to visit you on my way. If there is yet*

some small space in your heart for your child-hood friend, do write at once to tell me what you think of my plans and that you are pleased at the prospect of my visit.

> *With warmest regards,*
> *Lorena*

"So you see," Ackerman said, as though he'd expected all along that Ben should read the letter, "she didn't come here on my account. She only wanted to escape an arranged marriage.

"The damnedest thing of all," he continued, his voice hoarse with emotion, "is that this letter only arrived last week. What must she have thought as she waited for my reply, week after week, and none came?"

There was a long silence.

"And then to have come all this way on her own, not sure if I'd received the letter, or if I even cared."

He hit his fist on the plank desk and sent papers flying. "Lorena trusted me, Thorne, and I'll not let her down. I swear I'll find her or die trying."

Ben could not reply. Certainly Charles Ackerman had suffered as much as anyone in all of this.

"I'll get my maps and show you those areas where we've concentrated our search," Ackerman told him.

"I'm truly sorry about all of this," Ben said at last.

Ackerman managed a weak smile. "Lorena will be fine, you know. She's a survivor."

She clambered up the bank of the shallow creek with all of the excitement of a child. The bells tied into the long fringe of her white doeskin dress tinkled gently as she ran, and watching her, Blue Elk smiled. It had been autumn when he'd brought her here, and now it was spring. Not such a long time, he thought, and yet she'd taken to the ways of his people as he'd never expected her to. If not for her fair skin and the long braids of yellow hair, she'd have been no different from any other young Indian maiden. But there was one difference: Blue Elk had never seen a woman so beautiful nor so quick-witted as the one he called Silver Eyes.

She came to him breathless, clutching plants in both her hands, and knelt down beside him.

"Bindweed," she said, setting one of her treasures down on the rawhide mat spread before him, "we shall powder the root and make a tonic to cure an upset stomach. Cohosh," she said upon laying down another. "A tea made from its root will ease the pains of childbirth."

Blue Elk held up a thick, knobby brown root. "And this?" he inquired.

She took it from him, broke it into sections

and held it under her nose, taking a whiff. "Crowfoot," she concluded, "to stop bleeding."

"You have done well," he told her.

"Not so well as my teacher," she replied, sorting through the collection of roots, stems, and leaves on the mat. "Look, here are snakeroot and gumweed and mare's tail. All powerful medicine."

"You are pleased, then, that I have brought you here?"

Her full lips curved into a smile as she looked upon him. "The medicine spring is indeed a wondrous place, just as you told me. I have learned much."

But teaching her the secrets of his medicine was not the only reason Blue Elk had taken her away from the main camp. Word had reached him that since the great Sioux victory in the north, the soldiers were not so eager to trade away the war chief they'd captured. Some said that to free Spotted Wolf was to condemn hundreds more of the whites to death.

Blue Elk could not deny the truth of this. Since their parents and two sisters had been so viciously murdered by the white soldiers at Sand Creek, Spotted Wolf had carried a strong hatred within him. If he were freed, Blue Elk had no doubt that many more whites would die.

Though his love for his younger brother was great, Blue Elk knew that he had been entrusted, as well, by his sacred vision to care for the one with silver eyes. He was not certain that the power he had over his people would prove enough to save her if the soldiers should harm Spotted Wolf. And as he had foreseen, if the white bird should die, then Blue Elk and the last hope of his people would die as well.

Lorena sensed that her companion was more thoughtful than usual. When Blue Elk had first swept her off the parade ground at Fort Reno, she'd thought of him as little more than a savage. But the months she'd spent with him had made her see otherwise. He was called *nama-eyoni* by those of his tribe. This meant holy man—a man with special gifts. He was much respected by his people, and Lorena had come to respect him as well. Even lacking the benefit of the white man's education, he was very wise, and he'd taught her many things.

From the time Blue Elk had brought her into the camp, he had shared his lodge with her. He had no wife of his own, though he was still young and virile, and Lorena came to see that many young women of the tribe envied her her place. They did not know the truth, however. After their first confrontation, Blue Elk never touched her as a man does a woman. He treated her rather as a cherished sister. She was thankful for this at first, but wondered still, and came to believe finally, that the change in him had some religious significance, like the mystical white bird that was his special symbol.

"You have taken to our ways quickly and with none of the white man's scorn," he said to her at last. "This pleases me."

"My heart has found peace among your people," Lorena admitted as she took up his rough hand, for indeed it was true, "I am free as I never thought I could be."

"You can forgive me when my people killed your friend?" he wondered aloud. "When I carried you away from the old life and took you as my prisoner?"

Lorena pondered his words. She hadn't thought about her life as it had been in a very long while. It was easier not to think on it. Charles was gone; her hatred of the Cheyenne would not bring him back. And perhaps Charles had been right when he'd said that Lorena hadn't the patience for teaching. These months with Blue Elk's tribe had afforded her many quiet hours to consider. What was there for her to go back to now?

Memories of Ben Thorne crept up on her unexpectedly, as they had often lately in her unguarded moments, but she shut them out. She'd been afraid of him from the first, afraid of the way he'd been able to control her senses and obscure her reason. Even now at the thought of him she trembled. But he was not the sort of man to speak his mind nor settle in one place—with only one woman, as Lorena had learned well enough. Thorne had gone out of her life, and good riddance to him.

Blue Elk, by contrast, was patient and kind. He'd insisted that Lorena be treated by the tribe with all of the respect that was due his woman. He cared for her and provided her with all that she needed, asking no more than her friendship in return. Lately, though—and Lorena was ashamed to admit it even to herself—she had begun to wish that he'd ask for more.

"I would stay with you now willingly, Blue Elk," she told him, increasing the pressure of her hand on his as she repeated the word once more, "Willingly."

The Indian seemed fretful, and disentangling himself quickly, got to his feet. "I have brought a gift for you," he said, "come and see."

He led Lorena by the hand around behind the lodge, and there, nibbling on the tender, green shoots of a low bush, was a white stallion.

"This is far too costly a gift," she told him.

Blue Elk captured her gaze, and there was a meaningful look in his eyes which Lorena could not fathom. "He is for you to ride, Silver Eyes, that you may be truly free."

"Thank you, my friend," she said, embracing him.

Lorena stood on tiptoe and brushed her lips

gently over his. She felt him stiffen, and he drew away from her suddenly, as if he'd been burned.

They'd grown so close in these past months that Lorena thought she knew him. All of Blue Elk's actions had led her to believe that he cared for her as much as she'd come to care for him. Why, then, had he pulled away?

Struggling to control her disappointment, Lorena turned her attention on the white horse. Approaching him slowly, she patted him with a gentle hand until he decided there was nothing to fear and allowed her to whisper in his ear and stroke his muzzle. Blue Elk watched them from a safe distance, no trace of emotion marring his dark features. Had Lorena only imagined his affection?

Even without the creature comforts she'd learned to take for granted, Lorena had discovered early on that life among the Cheyenne appealed to her. There was none of the hypocrisy of polite society; she could do exactly as she pleased. She found an indescribable satisfaction in this simple life, traveling light and trusting in nature to provide the necessities.

It might have been the perfect existence, but for the loneliness. Try as she might, Lorena had not been able in her time with the Cheyenne band to bridge the gap, in culture as well as language, that separated her from the rest of the tribe. They accepted her presence among them as Blue Elk's woman, but had not the patience to wait while she struggled with their difficult tongue. Blue Elk alone had come to be her mentor, her translator, her friend, and it pained her to think he was abandoning her.

The white horse nudged her arm, and she scratched his withers in reply. She noticed then the blanket roll and parfleche on his back, and was struck all at once by what this gift of Blue Elk's really meant. She had come to the Cheyenne as his prisoner, and now he was setting her free.

His actions made sense now. He'd told her all along that before much more time had passed, he would take on a great responsibility within his tribe's council of forty-four. That time must be upon them now, she realized, and he could scarcely be expected to go on nursemaiding a lonely white woman. Without a word Lorena mounted the stallion and, not daring to look back at Blue Elk, gave the horse his head.

Blue Elk watched until the pair had disappeared over a distant hill, and then turned away, determined to ignore the emptiness he'd already begun to feel inside. The white bird had taken flight; all was as it should be.

The thunder of hoofbeats rumbling across the meadow made him look back in time to see her return, tears streaming down her pale face. She drew up beside him and slid down from her horse, throwing her arms about his neck.

She was still so young, Blue Elk reminded himself. She did not realize what a trial it was for a man such as he to be this near to her. Her skin was scented with sweet blossoms, her golden hair soft as down. Against his will, Blue Elk's arms reached out to enfold her, then his hands slipped down from her shoulders to caress the small of her back and press her closer to him. Silver Eyes turned her tear-stained face up to his and her full lips parted as if awaiting his kiss. He could fight no longer.

When Blue Elk's mouth closed over hers, Lorena's heart gave a leap. For months now she'd lived at close quarters to this man and come to crave his tenderness, hoping that one day he might respond to her as a man instead of just a friend.

Lorena did not realize until this moment how deeply she'd longed to feel again the thrill of passion that Ben Thorne had only just awakened in her. Caught in Blue Elk's embrace, her hands eagerly explored the breadth of him, from the taut cords that stood out on his long neck, to the slick, copper skin of his heaving chest and sinewed arms.

Lorena found to her dismay, though, that her mind was playing tricks with her. For each sensation wrought by Blue Elk's hand, she experienced a flash of memory: the drumming of thunder and the patter of rain, the smell of weathered buckskins and rain-dampened earth, the peculiar taste of salty kisses mingled with raindrops. . . . Held fast in one man's arms, Lorena Mackenzie could think only of another.

When Blue Elk's dark eyes met hers, Lorena could see the puzzlement in them. How could she explain to him what she herself did not understand? She buried her face against the warmth of his chest. Soon, she told herself, soon these memories would fade. . . .

"I cannot go back," she whispered to him. "I belong here. Do not send me away."

"We shall speak of this no more," he promised, stroking her hair.

Blue Elk allowed her to cling to him only a moment more before he drew away. It was, he saw now, as the vision had foretold. He would not take a wife. He could never know the sweetest of embraces that Silver Eyes offered to him. He must make this great sacrifice that he might be worthy of the title of Great Prophet in the Eyes of his People, Keeper of the Sacred Medicine Arrows.

As the sun slipped low on the horizon, Lorena went to fetch the plants that had been drying upon the rawhide mat. She was not proud of the way she'd run to Blue Elk, like a frightened child. It was cowardice, she had to admit. She could not think of leaving, though; there was nothing for her outside of this camp. Lorena had always borne a wild streak within her, but now she felt herself more Indian than white. She thrived in this wilderness, with these people, and knew it was something her own society would never accept.

Better by far that she should remain here with Blue Elk and make a place for herself in the tribe. She vowed then never to be a hindrance to him. Using those skills Blue Elk had taught her, she would make a comfortable life for the two of them and not stand in the way of his duty to his people. And when he came to her the next time, she would put away these memories of Ben Thorne and the foolish dreams she harbored deep within her, and she would give herself to Blue Elk . . . gladly.

On her knees before the mat, Lorena sorted through the precious herbs, placing them carefully into a parfleche bag painted with special symbols. She did not hear the intruder approach until it was too late. He grabbed her by the hair, jerking her head back sharply, and she screamed as a sinewy brown arm coiled itself around her throat, threatening to crush her windpipe.

Chapter Nine

✦ ✦ ✦ ✦ ✦

BLUE ELK RUSHED out of the lodge with his knife unsheathed, its point glittering in the red-tinged twilight.

"Brother, no!" he shouted. "Kill her and I die as well."

"This is the crazy Long Knife's woman," said the man who held Lorena in a death grip. "What can she be to you?"

Blue Elk approached his brother slowly. "She is called Silver Eyes, the one entrusted to my care by the Great Spirit, *Macha-Mahaiyu*, and she belongs to no white man."

"I will have my revenge on the Long Knives," Spotted Wolf insisted.

Stars flashed before Lorena's eyes as he tightened his hold on her. Blue Elk stuck his knife back in the sheath on his belt. He was only a few steps away now. Crossing his long arms over his chest, he faced Spotted Wolf with no more than a malevolent glare. "You do not wish to kill this one, little brother."

"Leave me be, *ma-achis*," Spotted Wolf replied, ". . . old man."

Lorena could feel a slackening in her captor's strength, and then all at once he let her go. She ran to Blue Elk, who folded his arms around her. "*Natomo-wonotziyi*," she managed to say to him in his own tongue. "He frightens me."

125

"The soldiers have let you go then?" Blue Elk asked his brother.

"Ha!" Spotted Wolf spat upon the ground. "This is what her people think of the Indian."

With one swift move he tore open the tattered remnant of a blue Army tunic he was wearing to reveal a festering bullet wound on his shoulder and an ugly weal about his neck that was badly infected as well. "The white men tried to kill me, but a Cheyenne Dog Soldier does not die so easily."

Lorena turned away from the sight of Spotted Wolf's festering wounds, trying to deny that he could have received them at the hands of the soldiers of Fort Reno, but she could not. She looked back at him in time to see him sway on his feet and then drop to his knees.

Blue Elk went to his brother, lifting him into his arms. "We must take him to the medicine spring," he told Lorena, "to cleanse his wounds. Fetch some blankets and the medicine bag."

Lorena did as he bade her, following him across the clearing, wading through a tangle of brambles and past the sheltering grove of tall pines to the secluded glade he'd told her so much of and the natural mineral baths which gave this spot its name.

Steam rose up like curls of smoke from the bubbling waters but dissipated quickly in the cool evening air. Blue Elk stripped down to his breechclout and carried Spotted Wolf into the deep pool. The light was nearly gone, but he worked quickly, bathing his brother's wounds in the healing waters of the hot spring, then daubing them with salve from the medicine bag. It was well after dark when they returned to their lodge.

Despite his hatred of her, Lorena did what she could for Spotted Wolf, examining the wound in his shoulder to find that the ball had gone clean through, then binding his arm with strips of cotton cloth. He was only barely conscious during most of their ministrations but still was able, in bits and pieces, to relate the story of his escape from Fort Reno after a mutinous band of soldiers had killed his compatriot and tried to hang him. Spotted Wolf vowed, in his delirium, that he would rise once more to drive the white man off the Indian lands, and promised death to those who would not be moved.

Lorena took in his story impassively enough, but it sent a chill through her, much the same as she'd experienced when she witnessed Charles vent his hatred of all Indians. Soldier and red man alike were poised for war; there was no point in denying it. What would become of them all? she wondered.

Lorena was amazed at how quickly Spotted Wolf healed. He spent his days of recuperation eyeing her with mistrust as she went about her work, yet still allowed her to nurse him, and though he would not speak nor even meet her eyes, she could tell that he was surprised at her skill.

When he was lucid enough to converse, Spotted Wolf began to plot a course of all-out war against the whites. Blue Elk was patient with his headstrong brother, trying to temper the young man's hatred, but without success. Spotted Wolf's thirst would only be quenched with blood.

Only two weeks went by before Spotted Wolf had recovered enough to pace the lodge like a caged cat. He was anxious to rejoin the tribe. Blue Elk ruefully agreed, and so, in late June they rode into the main Cheyenne encampment, the two brothers leading the way and Lorena, on the white horse, pulling the travois.

Tepees were spread over the lush green valley in the shadow of Cloud Peak, a magnificent snow-capped summit crowning the Bighorn Mountains to the north. There were many more tepees than Lorena remembered, and when the travelers were within shouting distance, Spotted Wolf let go a loud war whoop and galloped triumphantly into the center of the camp, where he was met by a great throng of young warriors, all trilling a joyous welcome.

Lorena watched him as he sowed the seeds of hatred among his people, exhibiting his scars for all to see, relating the harrowing tale of his escape from the Long Knives and his journey to the sacred medicine spring. It was an effective display, indeed.

That night there was a gathering of all the warrior societies of the tribe in their full regalia: Red Shields with their buffalo horn headdresses and long-fringed belts, Elk Soldiers carrying their magic buckskin rattles which could charm whole herds of buffalo, Coyotes painted yellow and black—two eagle feathers in their scalp locks—and the fierce Dog Soldiers, daubed in red paint and sporting their elaborate plumed headdresses of raven and golden eagle feathers.

With growing foreboding Lorena observed the proceedings from behind the hide door flap of the lodge she shared with Blue Elk. The light of the campfires cast an eerie red glow over the dancers in their garish costumes, and ere long the war chants had reached a fevered pitch. Yet within the tepee, Blue Elk sat impassively over his offering fire of sweet grass and sage, concentrating on the prayers he was sending heavenward along with the spiraling smoke.

Spotted Wolf approached the center of the camp circle then and was illuminated by the firelight. He was dressed in the same manner as the others of his society, but his costume seemed more ornate. "Why does your brother wear such an unusual sash?" Lorena asked.

"It is his dog string," Blue Elk explained. "Only the bravest of the Dog Soldiers wear them. When in battle, the warrior drives a stake fastened to its end into the earth and fights where he stands. He may not retreat unless one of his comrades orders him to do so.''

Not an enviable position, Lorena thought to herself, but Spotted Wolf wore this dog string with pride. As she thought on it, she decided that this would account for the relative ease with which Charles had been able to capture the Indian. Without a friend to order his retreat, Spotted Wolf would have been easy prey for the soldiers.

''Why are you not taking part in these rites?'' she asked Blue Elk as she turned back into the lodge with a shudder that was not caused by the evening's chill.

He opened his eyes and regarded her with an inscrutable expression. ''My time has not yet come.''

She let the door flap slip down to shut them in and went to sit beside him. ''Can't you do anything to stop them? Your brother does not understand what he's begun here tonight. There is more to this than he can see. The Army is like a nest of hornets—disturb a few and the rest will come after you by the thousands, until your people are destroyed.''

''They would destroy us regardless. Can you not see that, little sister? The white man would make us farmers—to tie us to a single plot of land. But we are a proud people, and without the freedom to roam the prairies and shelter in the bosom of the sacred mountains as we wish, the spirit of our people would die. Better that these young warriors should find an honorable death on the field of battle."

Lorena dropped her head; it was difficult to argue with his logic. The sincerity of his words touched her heart; she could well understand the need for freedom. "Is there not one man who will speak for peace?" she wondered, though.

"My father was such a man," Blue Elk replied. "He knew that the whites had come to stay, and convinced some of our people to settle with our brothers in the south. They camped under the protection of the white soldier's flag . . . at a place the white men call Sand Creek."

Lorena caught her breath. She had heard of this place. It had been mentioned in the newspapers time and again. Only three years ago a band of five hundred Cheyenne, most of them women and children, had been slaughtered at Sand Creek in the Colorado Territory by a detachment of U.S. Army volunteers. "Your people?" she asked, her voice barely a whisper.

Light from the fire flickered over his solemn features. He nodded once. "Father, mother, sisters . . . Spotted Wolf and I had gone off to hunt," he explained. "When we returned, all of them were dead . . . helpless elders, innocent children. . . ."

Lorena got to her feet and turned away,

filled with shame to think she had ever considered this man a mindless savage. She pushed the door flap aside once more and stared out at the warriors. "I don't wonder that your brother hates us so."

"I was once as he is now," Blue Elk said to her. "My hands, too, were stained with white man's blood."

"And yet you've spared my life—"

He drew up behind her before she'd realized it, and when she turned back, he was very close. His chest vibrated with a long, uneven breath as he reached out to touch her arm. "You are like no other, Silver Eyes."

There was so much in his eyes that Lorena could not fathom yet dared not question. Every muscle in his frame seemed taut as a bowstring. Lorena wished that she could understand this enigmatic man. Was this friendship? She sensed that even he could not decide, but without some clear indication of what he wanted of her, she would not even begin to examine her own feelings. She feared she'd be hurt in the end. "Tell me about the white bird," she asked him.

"One day, little sister," he whispered, "but now the time is not right."

Lorena sighed, confused. Never would she have guessed that such a man as he could be so complex, and yet it was so. "Perhaps you are meant to be the one man who will stand for reason, my brother," she ventured.

With these words the spell was broken. Blue

Elk stepped back and shook his head, a move designed to restore his senses, then retreated to the far side of the lodge and dropped cross-legged on the floor. "The peacemakers are dead," he snapped. It was clearly a warning. If such a decision must be made, there was no doubt which side he would take.

"Then many will die before there's an end to this," Lorena said.

He only nodded.

Broken Hand stretched his arm toward the horizon, pointing to a billowing column of black smoke far across the open plain. "Look, there to the north," he called out.

Ben rode up beside him and studied the dark plume standing out against the clear, azure sky. "There's more burning there than a campfire, I'd say."

The two spurred their horses and made for the site, and Ben could feel the apprehension crawling up his spine. It had been a bloody summer, with one incident following upon another. The Cheyenne and Sioux were reported to have massed thousands of their warriors along the Tongue River, and it seemed to be so, for wave upon wave of them had spread southward across the Bozeman in the past few months. At first they'd only stolen horses and harassed the soldiers of the northernmost Army posts, but more recently they'd stepped up their hostilities, and now the fate of any soldier, freighter, or emigrant they might happen upon was certain to be death.

More than once in their search for Spotted Wolf's camp, Ben and Broken Hand had stumbled across the remains of a burnt-out wagon . . . or worse, and Ben had an awful suspicion that this time it would be the latter.

He'd all but given up hope of finding Lorena alive, though he had not said as much to his friend. In the past four months, they'd served as outriders for a northbound emigrant train, scouted for the Army, and searched damn near every inch of ground from the North Platte to the Tongue River, but with no sign of Spotted Wolf's band. The Indians had either kept on the move or had hidden themselves deep in the mountains, yet still they struck out at the whites with increasing frequency, bent on forcing them to abandon the Bozeman Trail altogether.

It was a half-hour's ride to Clear Creek, where Ben and the Indian finally came upon the battleground. Half a dozen wagons were drawn up in a circle on a desolate plain dotted with sagebrush and cactus. At first glance it appeared that an emigrant train had been attacked. One of the wagons had been set afire and was now smoldering nearby. But upon closer inspection, Ben noticed the blue uniforms. Bodies of soldier and Indian alike lay strewn over the sunbaked earth. It was difficult to tell exactly who'd been the victor in this engagement.

The stillness was eerie. Only the cry of buzzards overhead and the nickering of a few, riderless Indian ponies, still loitering near the bodies of their dead masters, disturbed the absolute quiet of the scene. Ben and Broken Hand rode in, silent in the face of utter destruction.

If the Indians had been the victors, Ben reasoned to himself, they'd surely still have been about, dancing in celebration, gathering up their war trophies and going about the grisly business of mutilating the bodies of their slain enemies so that they'd not prove a threat in the spirit world. The U.S. Army must then have won this conflict.

Near the center of the wagon circle Ben dismounted. Sure enough, there was a handful of soldiers there, assembled to receive orders from their superior.

"Sergeant Reynolds!" Ben called out to him as he approached. "What happened here?"

"Is that you, Captain Thorne?" the burly man asked, squinting his eyes against the sun. "We stood 'em off, sir. Forty-five of our men against five times that many Cheyenne braves. Took 'em by surprise, we did. Six wagonloads of our best marksmen and an arsenal of ammunition, disguised to look like an emigrant train. It was all part of Major Ackerman's plan. Too bad, though. It's not likely he'll live to enjoy his victory."

"Ackerman's here?" Ben asked, surprised.

"Rode right into the thick of it, he did. We

put him in that wagon over there," Sergeant Reynolds said, pointing. "He's gutshot, sir. The surgeon's gone to tend him, but it don't look good."

Ben thanked him and headed for the wagon, but was sidetracked when Broken Hand beckoned him onto the battlefield.

"Thorne, look here!"

Broken Hand was bent over the still form of a warrior, his body riddled with bullets. Ben could see that he was a Dog Soldier; the rawhide sash that he'd worn draped across his body was still staked to the ground. The design painted on his face identified him clearly as the war party leader, but Ben would have known that in any case. The dead Indian was Spotted Wolf.

"Thorne! Are you there? Thorne, I know you're out there. Come here, damn you!"

Ackerman's voice dissolved in a fit of coughing, and Ben ran toward the sound. The Army surgeon stopped him halfway.

"How bad is he, Doctor?" Ben asked.

The man shook his head. "There's serious abdominal bleeding. This type of wound is nearly always fatal, I'm afraid. I've bandaged him up, but there's no more I can do. I've got to see to the others."

Charles Ackerman lay in the bed of the wagon, propped up on his elbow, one hand pressed against the width of cotton flannel wrapped about his midsection. Dark red blood had stained the bandage and was now oozing between his fingers. His complexion had an ominous, ashen pallor. Ben pulled himself up into the wagon and knelt beside him. "I'm here, Major. What is it?"

"I'm dying, Thorne."

Ben had seen enough dying men during the war to know it was so. The whole of this battle scene, in fact, was calling up unpleasant memories that he would just as soon have kept buried forever. The acrid smell of gunpowder that hung on the air, the tangle of blue-clad bodies spread over the site with limbs frozen by death in awkward pose, the pitiful whimpering of those yet clinging to life—all of this combined as a powerful stimulant, forcing Ben to relive the horrors of the war again in his mind.

It took a great deal of effort to quell the tremor that ran through him, and only then could he face Ackerman to reply.

"The wagons will be on the move shortly. We're only a few hours from Fort Reno. The doctor can patch you up properly there, and you'll be on the mend in no time."

"You're not a good liar by any means, Mr. Thorne," Ackerman told him, his words punctuated by a spate of coughing, "and I haven't the time for pleasant imaginings. We both know I'll be dead long before we reach the fort."

Thorne dropped his head. "What is it I can do for you then, Major?"

"It's providence, no less, that's brought you here."

Edging back to lean against a canvas tarpaulin folded in the corner of the wagon, Ackerman clutched his middle with one hand and pushed the other at Thorne. "Take this," he said, unfurling his fingers to reveal what appeared to be an Indian fetish.

Ben lifted it up carefully and examined it. It was a necklace of sorts. Strung on a rawhide thong were a pair of ermine tails, several dew claws, and a small white pouch, stuffed with powdered herbs. The importance of this find was lost on Ben until he realized that the pouch was sewn of a rich fabric, such as that used to make a lady's fancy evening dress, and Lorena had been wearing just such a dress when she'd been abducted.

"Where did you come by this?" Ben wanted to know.

"One of these warriors had it 'round his neck."

Ben's brow creased as he stared at the charm he held in his hand, and a numbness spread over him. She was dead, and here was the proof. Slowly his hand closed over the necklace, his knuckles whitening.

"No. You don't understand," Ackerman said, labored breathing a sign of the pain he was suffering. "There's talk among the Indians who've come to trade at Laramie . . . of a powerful medicine man among the Cheyenne . . . who's taken himself a white squaw. They call her Silver Eyes.''

Charles Ackerman pooled what strength was left in him and reached out to grab Ben's arm. ''Damn it, Thorne, it's Lorena! It has to be! That Indian charm proves it.''

''Or it could mean something else entirely.''

Ackerman slipped back against the canvas, squeezing his eyes shut. Perspiration beaded his pale brow and he lay very still. The rasp of his breathing filled the silence. ''You don't believe that, nor do I,'' he whispered. ''I'd have fought you for her, you know, even though she didn't love me . . . but now—''

His lids fluttered open once more, his eyes glittering fiercely. ''Find her, Thorne. Take her far away from here . . . where she'll be safe. Do you hear me, Thorne? Find her!''

Chapter Ten

◆ ◆ ◆ ◆

HENRY EDGINGTON STARED out of the tall, leaded windows, watching impassively as a whirlwind picked up a scattering of dry leaves and carried them across the neatly-trimmed lawns that stretched out to the banks of the Hudson

River. "So, Mr. Crowell, what you're telling me is that my stepfather had very little in the way of cash assets. Is that correct?"

"Mr. Gilmore's finances suffered greatly as a result of the war," the attorney replied. "I'm afraid that the bulk of the estate inherited by your mother entails this house and the surrounding properties. There is, of course, the allowance that Mr. Gilmore has provided for his niece—"

Ungrateful little wretch! Henry thought. *She ran off without so much as a good-bye, and the old man left her what was left of his money.*

"Thank you," he replied sharply, dismissing the aging attorney who was the executor of his stepfather's estate.

Crowell gathered up the papers he'd left on the desk, pushed them into his portfolio and beat a hasty retreat. Clasping his hands behind his back, Edgington began to pace before the windows. He hadn't anticipated this, not at all. He'd always thought old Gilmore had money, at least enough to cover the gambling debts that he'd incurred in the past few months, but it didn't appear to be so. Last year Edgington had been forced to sell the house his own father had left him just to keep the creditors off his back, and the people he owed now were not nearly so polite.

If only his mother had been the one to get the money, it would have been his for the asking. But instead the old man had gone soft and left it to his niece, Lorena Mackenzie.

What need did she have of it? She had all of her father's fortune just there for the taking in California when she turned twenty-one.

Edgington's pacing increased as his mind worked to figure a way out of his tangle. If he could talk his mother into selling off the property—but that was something she would never agree to, not even for him. Still, though, he had no intention of changing his style of living. He realized full well that a certain status was required to move in the elite circle to which he had grown accustomed, and this estate provided at least the semblance of prosperity. It would not be wise to give that up.

Damn Lorena Mackenzie! Damn her and her fortunes! he told himself. *But wait—*

He rushed to the desk and sat down to rifle through the stack of papers there. A triumphant gleam in his eye, he pulled out a newspaper, several days old, and there, halfway down the page, was the item he'd remembered; U.S. ARMY STRIKES BACK ONE HUNDRED HOSTILE INDIANS KILLED IN DAKOTA TERRITORY.

Yes, this was it. He scanned the article, reading only what caught his eye. "In response to the growing frustration of those soldiers manning the beseiged outposts along the Bozeman Trail . . . a brilliant stratagem devised by Brevet Major Charles Ackerman . . .unsuspecting savages . . . a stunning victory . . . resulting, however, in the unfortunate death of Ackerman."

Edgington had taken this in with a shrug

when he'd read it at first, although he knew that Ackerman had been a close friend of Lorena Mackenzie's, but now the news took on an entirely new meaning.

Charles Ackerman had been killed by rampaging Indians, so thirsty for the white man's blood that no one in that part of the country was safe from their wrath.

Edgington pulled open the center drawer of the desk and rummaged through the contents, finally coming upon Harrison Gilmore's appointment book. He was sure he'd seen the old man put that scrap of paper in here. A few weeks after Lorena Mackenzie had disappeared, one of the maids had brought it to him; she'd come upon it while she was cleaning Lorena's room. It still had to be here, it had to be . . . Edgington leafed through the book and found what he'd been searching for, nestled between the last two pages.

January 17, 1866—Madison County school authorities announced today their requirements for one dozen young women . . . willing to take up the position of schoolmistress . . . contact Mr. N. P. Langford, Virginia City, Montana Territory.

It was an advertisement from the *Montana Post*, a Western journal, which had been reprinted in a New York newspaper. When Harrison Gilmore had first shown it to him, the old man had been apoplectic. How could his niece, a mere slip of a girl, think to defy him? He'd urged Edgington to go after her and bring her back, but it had seemed far too much trouble at the time. Now, though, Lorena Mackenzie's fortune was a prize too tempting to resist.

The poor girl was all alone in a God-forsaken country. Edgington quickly decided that it was his duty, no less, to go to the aid of his dear cousin and offer her comfort in her time of need. But this time he would not play the excruciatingly polite gentleman, as he had when he'd courted her. This time he would insist that, for her own safety, she must come home where she belonged, and if he played his cards right, they could be married before the coming of the new year.

"We'll need coffee, tobacco, and a box of cartridges," Ben Thorne said to Mr. Leighton, the sutler at Fort Reno.

"Happy to oblige, Captain," the man replied.

Thorne leaned over the long counter and lowered his voice. "And if you're still hiding that flask of bourbon behind the yard goods, I'll take it as well."

Leighton laughed, shaking his head, and went off to fill the order. In the meanwhile Ben pondered his course. Charles Ackerman and his men had been buried. Those who'd managed to stay alive were boasting of their bravado, but the victory was a questionable one, and the Army had decided to maintain a defensive stance, shutting themselves up in those outposts along the Bozeman in anticipation of the hard winter ahead. Ben wondered if it mightn't be wise for him to do the same, but the promise he'd made to Ackerman as the man lay on his deathbed gnawed at him.

It had been more than a year now since Lorena Mackenzie was captured by the Cheyenne. There was little chance that she was still alive, especially given the hostility of the tribe toward whites in past months. Ben had let Ackerman go on, nevertheless, with his speculations; they were only the ramblings of a desperate man, trying to find peace. And in the end Ben had given his promise so Charles Ackerman might have that peace.

Though he didn't like to admit it, Ben was afraid. Each night he went to sleep clutching an unopened whiskey bottle, daring himself to take a drink. He'd managed thus far not to, though the temptation was great. Lorena Mackenzie haunted his dreams. He had only to close his eyes and he was assailed by memories of the scent of sweet violets, of the feel of her supple body pressed against his. He could see her standing there before him, her soft blond curls cascading over bared white shoulders, and she was staring a him with—what was it Ackerman had called them?—silver eyes. Yes, that was an apt description. Ben had never before seen such unusual eyes. A chill ran through him to realize that Ackerman could have been right about the white squaw of the Cheyenne. Though Ben feared he might have to come to accept the fact of Lorena's death, he realized that there was yet a greater fear in him. What horrors might she have had to endure at the hands of Spotted Wolf's brutal band, and how might she have suffered on account of it?

"Mr. Thorne? Mr. Thorne?"

Ben dragged himself from his thoughts to look upon the fresh-faced young woman who stood before him, a bundled babe in her arms. "Sorry, ma'am," he said, shaking off the reverie. "What can I do for you?"

"My name is Sarah Rawlins," she began. "You might not recall, but I was—that is to say, I am a friend of Lorena Mackenzie." She paused to wipe from her brow a stray lock of chestnut hair that had escaped her bonnet. "It would seem," she continued, "that since Major Ackerman's death the Army has given off searching for her. Everyone I've talked to seems to think it's a lost cause. My husband tells me that you would know these Indians as well as anyone, so I've come to ask you . . . Do you think there is any hope that Lorena is still alive?"

Ben stood there, pulling at his stubbled chin

as he struggled to conceal the turmoil within him. "Well, Mrs. Rawlins," he began, "there's no saying for certain, but there is talk of a white woman living with the Cheyenne."

Ben reached beneath his buckskin shirt and pulled out the Indian fetish that he'd worn around his neck since Ackerman had entrusted it to him. He showed it to her. "Before he died, Major Ackerman gave this to me."

Cautiously, she reached out a hand to touch the white pouch. "This is fabric from Lorena's dress," she said, her voice unsteady. "Do you see the pattern in the weave? It's very distinctive. I'd know it anywhere, Mr. Thorne. I helped her to mend it, so I would remember."

The child in her arms began to fuss, and Sarah rocked him absently. "What are we to think?" she asked.

"Charles Ackerman believed that Lorena was alive and still living with the Cheyenne," Ben told her. "He could well be right."

"Then someone ought to try and bring her back. Surely there are men enough here for the job. I cannot bear to imagine what cruelties poor Lorena might have been made to suffer at the hands of those savages, forced to live like an animal. I shall speak to Colonel Palmer at once."

"He's a soldier, ma'am," Ben tried to explain, "and same as any other, he must obey his orders. He'd never be allowed to appropriate the whole of his command in the search for one white woman held by the Indians.

Why, it's a wonder he allowed Ackerman to go on for as long as he did.''

She fixed her wide brown eyes on him, and the accusing look she sent stabbed at him no less than his own conscience. He turned away so that she could not see the anguish that was surely written on his face. Did she think he didn't care? He, who'd lain awake at night, tortured by imaginings of Lorena in the hands of the Cheyenne? The fault was that he cared too much!

Ben had come to accept that he was in love with Lorena Mackenzie, inextricably, and in giving up his heart, his peace of mind was forfeit as well.

He wondered if perhaps Colonel Palmer hadn't been right to suggest that she'd be better off dead. Even Broken Hand could not deny that if she were still alive, she'd not be the same woman Ben had come to love; not at all. It was this fact, then, that had made a part of him relieved that they'd not yet found her, for he feared to think what the spirited, willful beauty might have become.

"I made a promise to Ackerman," Ben said to her at last, "before he died. I swore I'd find Lorena Mackenzie and send her home where she belongs. Rest assured, I intend to keep that promise, ma'am."

Touching the brim of his hat in deference to her, he picked up his parcel from the sutler's counter and went out, hoping that the brisk November chill would revive him. He'd gone only a short distance, though, before a stranger stepped into his path, a gaunt-faced gentleman, too well-dressed to be an emigrant or a miner en route to the goldfields. Ben did not miss, either, the pair of men, of rougher caste, who loitered nearby.

"Excuse me, sir. Might you be Ben Thorne?" asked the man.

"I am," Ben replied warily.

The stranger pulled one hand from the pocket of his expensive overcoat and held it out toward Ben. "My name is Henry Edgington. I have been told that if one needs to find something in this part of the country, you are the man to see."

"And what is it, exactly, that you wish to find, Mr. Edgington?"

"Not what, but whom," the man replied, and shivered against the cold. "Is there someplace we might talk?"

Ben's suspicions were aroused, but then so was his curiosity, and so he led Edgington to the small outbuilding the Army was allowing him to use as his quarters while in their employ. Broken Hand had gotten there before him and was nursing a fire he'd started in the ramshackle stove. Ben walked through the door with Edgington following close behind and his retainers still keeping a discreet distance. When he spotted the Indian, Edgington stepped back, alarmed.

"Rest easy," Ben told him, "that's my partner, Broken Hand. I can guarantee, sir, he's not after your scalp."

Ben tossed the parcel he'd been carrying to Broken Hand and motioned Henry Edgington toward one of the campstools as he himself leaned back against the wall. He could feel the cold seeping through the spaces between the planked boards, and crossed his arms across his chest against the chill as he studied the man who sat before him. Edgington had removed his fur cap and set it on his knee and was now smoothing the sparse strands of black hair that had been plastered against his forehead.

Once he had the hearth fire blazing, Broken Hand took a battered tin coffeepot and went outside to fill it from the water barrel. When he returned, he captured Ben's eye, inclining his head to indicate the rough pair lingering just outside the door.

"Those two outside belong to you?" Ben asked Edgington.

Edgington looked a trifle too nervous. "Yes. They are 'associates' of mine. One cannot be too careful in this unfriendly territory."

"Now tell me about this person you wish me to find," Ben prompted.

Across the room a hammering distracted them. Broken Hand was using the handle of his knife to pulverize the coffee beans he'd put into a small sack. Edgington shot him an anxious glance, then addressed Ben. "You must excuse me, Mr. Thorne. I'm a New York City attorney and quite out of my element here. I've come here only because I must. You see, I'm searching for my dear cousin, Lorena."

If Ben had been disinterested before, he was not so now. His attention was fully focused on the overdressed, overmannered gentleman.

"What did you say?"

"I've come to find my cousin, Lorena Mackenzie. When we received word of the death of Charles Ackerman and of the Indian wars being waged in these parts, I came after her at once. This is not the place for a young woman alone. I was on my way to Virginia City, where Lorena was to have taken up a position teaching school. The post commander here, however, has informed me that she never reached there, that she has been abducted by Indians. I will pay any price, anything you ask, Mr. Thorne, only rescue my dear cousin that I might return her to the bosom of her family."

Edgington weaved his fingers together in his lap and stared down on them. The concern was plain upon his face, but still Ben was cautious, determined not to reveal anything of himself with his words. "I am acquainted with Miss Mackenzie," he told Edgington, "and I knew Major Ackerman as well. I can tell you, sir, that this is not a question of money. Miss Mackenzie has been captured by a hostile tribe. There is no telling at this point whether or not she is even still alive. And if by some chance her life has been spared, she has likely been subjected to evils which a lady of her delicate sensibilities could scarce imagine. If she lives, Mr. Edgington, she will not be the same woman you remember."

There was a crease in Henry Edgington's heavy brow. He tried to rub it out with his hand and squeezed his eyes shut. "My mother, Lorena's aunt, has been distraught with worry since the girl ran off to this wilderness, and I see now that her fears were not unfounded. How can I face her with such news?"

But Ben was consumed by visions of his own, as evidenced by the whitened knuckles of his clenched fists. "I cannot promise anything. . . ."

Edgington rose, twisting his cap in his hand. "Just find her, Mr. Thorne . . . if she is alive. We will care for her, my mother and I, regardless of her state."

He tossed a heavy sack of coins on the crate that served as a table, walked to the door, then turned before going out. "That's for expenses. I will be staying at Fort Laramie, where more pleasant accommodations can be found. You may contact me there when you have news."

Ben said that he would and saw the man out. When he returned, he tossed his saddle-bags up on the iron bedstead in the corner and began at once to gather up his things. Broken Hand came to him and pushed a tin cup of coffee into his hand. "Sit," he commanded, "and we will talk about this, you and I."

"My mind is made up," Ben told him. "I'm going after her, and this time I'm not coming back until I know for certain. You can come along or stay, as you like."

He swigged the coffee, scalding the roof of his mouth.

"Something about that one is not right," Broken Hand said, tossing his head in the direction of the door that Edgington had gone out of not long before.

"He's a high-class, city-bred lawyer and not the type you'd likely have run across before; that's what's got your hackles up."

The Indian paused to consider, then shook his head as he began to roll up his blanket. "He has the eyes of a wolf. I do not trust him."

Ben laughed despite himself. The image of the pale, spindle-legged gentleman in wolf's guise was amusing. "I'm sure he feels the same about you. Now are you coming with me or not?"

"I will come, Thorne," the Indian replied, as he tied up the blanket roll and reached for his parfleche. "We have been as brothers for many winters, and you will need me to ride with you now. But I ask you this: If you find this woman, what will you do then?"

Ben's smile quickly disappeared as he stood there, meeting his friend's dark eyes. No matter what his heart was telling him, he could not utter a word.

Chapter Eleven
◆ ◆ ◆ ◆

JANUARY 1868

THE UNITED STATES ARMY was not, by and large, an experienced Indian-fighting force, and had not yet learned what Ben Thorne knew already. The Indian was at his most vulnerable in the winter. Game was scarce, and when there was no fresh meat, the tribe had to make do with what could be stored. The normally hardy Indian ponies were weakened from lack of grass to graze upon, and mobility was cut to a minimum. The Indians broke into smaller bands; the winter-scarred land could not provide the resources to sustain large numbers all in one camp.

And thus was the situation as Ben and Broken Hand meandered through the snow-laden valleys at the base of the Bighorn Mountains. They came upon more than one of these small camps in their travels. There were small bands of Cheyenne, Sioux, and Arapaho, and while wary at first, most proved friendly enough. Ben made cautious inquiries among them about the white squaw of the Cheyenne, the one called Silver Eyes. He found, to his surprise, that many had, indeed, heard the name. When he'd put all the information he'd gathered together, it made a fascinating tale. . . .

It began as a story of two brothers of the Cheyenne tribe: Spotted Wolf and his elder brother Blue Elk. The pair were brave young men who belonged to the warrior society known as the Dog Soldiers. They had distinguished themselves in raids on their enemies and were destined to bring great honor to their people. When the members of their family were slain by the white soldiers, the pair unleashed their hatred upon all whites in a rage that could only be sated with blood.

Then there came a day when the eldest brother realized that there was a sickness in his heart. To purge it, he went into the mountains, blood still thick upon his hands, to seek a vision. When Blue Elk returned to his people, he turned from the life he had led and became a holy man. He healed many and his advice was sought often. He took his place on the council of forty-four, and his brother, Spotted Wolf, continued his fight against the white man alone.

Spotted Wolf was taken prisoner not long after, and his brother set out to free him, returning instead with a white squaw. The people were angry, but Blue Elk told them that through this woman, whom he called Silver Eyes, he would make powerful medicine. He forbade the people to treat her ill and took her as his woman. When the spring came, Blue Elk and the white squaw set off alone for the sacred medicine spring and, lo, when they had returned, they had with them Spotted Wolf, the beloved warrior chief of the people. Blue Elk and his woman had indeed made powerful medicine.

Ben ought to have been relieved. It certainly appeared as though Lorena Mackenzie were still alive and living with the Cheyenne, but there was something in the tales that disturbed him. Perhaps it was in the nuance of the translation or just his own interpretation of what was said, but in each of the tellings, it did not seem to him that the woman called Silver Eyes was a victim. She followed the medicine man, Blue Elk, willingly through their adventure . . . as a loving wife might follow her husband.

Ben Thorne and Broken Hand had set up their base camp in an old abandoned cabin that had once belonged to a mountain man. A part of the structure was dug out of a low hillside, with the earth itself forming the rear walls, and the rest was finished with hewn logs. Having been so long neglected, its interior was laced with cobwebs and had become home to a host of woodland creatures, but it proved a snug shelter from which to conduct their winter search nonetheless.

Broken Hand left with the dawn to investigate claims made by a pair of Sioux hunters they'd run across several days before of a Cheyenne encampment that lay only a few miles north. Ben elected to stay behind as his friend checked out this latest information. He bagged a brace of hare for supper and then returned to pace the breadth of the cabin, but after only a short while he'd decided that waiting was not to his liking and so decided to follow the same path Broken Hand had taken.

A wet, heavy snow had fallen early in the afternoon, blanketing the landscape and making it hard for him to track the Indian. But by heading due north he did, indeed, come upon a cluster of half a dozen tepees just as the sun began to disappear behind the mountains. Ben picketed his horse some distance away and sheltered himself in an evergreen copse to get a better look at things.

He spotted Broken Hand's piebald pony near the camp circle with the other Indian mounts, but there was very little activity to observe. In the twilight the tepees glowed red from the fires within, and white clouds of smoke rose up into the night sky from the opened flaps atop each.

Ben hesitated, deciding not to enter the camp. Many times these Indians were freer with their information if no white man was on hand. Broken Hand alone could learn much more of what they needed to know. And so Ben settled himself beneath the low-hanging branches of an evergreen, on a bed of fragrant pine needles, with only his bedroll for warmth, and drifted into a fitful sleep.

He was awakened just before dawn by the chatter of a gray whiskeyjack in the branches above him. The morning air was frigid and still, and he stifled a yawn as he stretched his stiff limbs. The only movement from the camp was the emergence of a lone squaw from one of the lodges. She pulled up the picket pin that secured a white stallion which had been stamping at the snowpacked ground as if anticipating the arrival of his mistress. The woman whispered a few gentle words into his ear, and he allowed her to slip on a bridle made of buffalo hair.

Ben threw off his bedroll and crept closer to the camp, still hidden by the evergreen thicket. Wanting a better view, he got to his feet and pressed himself against the wide trunk of a lodgepole pine. Yes, he could see quite clearly from this vantage point, and his mouth dropped open in disbelief.

But for the dark blond hair that hung in two long plaits, tied with rawhide thongs, he'd not have guessed that this Indian was Lorena. He watched, mesmerized, as she pulled off her buffalo robe and tossed it over her horse's back. Beneath, she wore a white doeskin dress edged in long fringes, leggings, and a wide belt and moccasins that had been decorated with various hues of blue beads, all arranged in geometric design. Nothing at all remained of the fashionable Eastern lady he remembered so well but the delicate heart-shaped face and those amazingly brilliant eyes.

Wrapping a hand in the horse's mane, she pulled herself up, easily throwing one long leg over his back, and then nudged him with her heels. The pair of them bolted off across the open ground, heading for the shallow stream opposite the camp. She let him have his head, and the great white horse galloped over the frozen streambed, breaking the ice that had formed there, his hooves beating a rhythmic cadence in the snow as he carried her farther still, until both disappeared over a distant hillside.

As Ben stood there looking after her, he imagined that she might have made her own escape. But before very much time had passed, horse and rider reappeared, approaching the camp at breakneck pace. This could not be Lorena, he told himself. No young lady of breeding would have been taught to ride like this, molded to her mount as if they were one. Ben stepped back for cover as she drew up near the place where he stood and dismounted in one easy movement.

The sound of her breathless laughter was carried to him on the wind; it was a pleasant sound. She slid the buffalo robe off the horse's back and stroked the great white beast as if he were a docile pet. He stamped and tossed his head, flared nostrils sending clouds of steam into the chill air, but she cajoled him into quiet obedience with her soft words. Oh yes, Ben decided as he watched her, it was indeed Lorena.

A quick survey of the camp told him that no one else was stirring yet, and so he crept up behind her and slipped one hand around her waist and the other over her mouth lest she cry out. Lorena stiffened at his touch and began to struggle, but he pulled her back against him so that she could see she had nothing to fear.

As he'd expected, her eyes went wide at the sight of him and she ceased her thrashing. But when he loosed his hold on her, she bolted back toward the circle of tepees. Despair pierced him like a sharp blade. The look she'd worn had not been one of relief, not one of a woman eager for rescue. He sprinted after her and caught her, wrestling her to the snow-covered ground and throwing his body over hers, pinning her arms at the wrists.

She did not cry out. She did not utter a single word, though her breath was drawn in ragged gasps. Ben stared full into her eyes, looking for some trace of the woman he'd become obsessed by, for some sign that she was glad of his presence, but could find none. All of the fears he'd had about her these past few months came to the fore. That Indian medicine man had weaved a spell of some sort over her. Damn him! Damn him! Ben could not see in those precious eyes one iota of the emotion that had been there the last time he'd held her in his arms.

Determined to bring it back, he lowered his mouth on hers, stilling her breath. He was not gentle; he could not afford to be. Desperation fueled his actions. His kiss was deep and intimate, and his body moved on hers in a way designed to rouse her senses, to stir the memories of that night so very long ago when she'd wanted him.

But Ben could not play this game and remain aloof himself. His head had begun to swim. His hungry mouth followed a course along her jawline and lingered over the silken softness at the nape of her neck. Blood surged against his temples when at last he felt her relax and he saw victory before him. He freed her hands, using his own to explore the supple body pinned beneath him.

Lorena had sworn that she would not allow this to happen. Now, when she'd settled into some semblance of a peaceful existence at last, here came Ben Thorne to dredge up all the old hurts, to play upon her emotions, as he seemed so fond of doing.

She could not forget how he'd toyed with her that night in the rain, then left her with every nerve raw. And then later he'd reappeared in her life, only to try once more to persuade her to go back east. Not once had he spoken for himself nor explained why he sought her out. What was his game now? she wondered.

Of one thing Lorena was certain. Thorne used his hard body as a weapon, preying on her weakness and summoning up emotions that she sought to deny. The bold explorations of his rough hands were rekindling a fire deep within her that threatened to melt the snows upon which she lay. She must fight him!

There was a slackening of strength that came as his desire was aroused, and at this Lorena made her move. With one great shove, she pushed him off and scrambled to her feet. Her head reeling, she ran haphazardly over the snow, sinking again and again as the light crust gave way beneath her feet, pulling her down. Her lungs ached then burned as a gasp for breath filled them with frigid air. She fled without direction, knowing he was at her heels, knowing that if he caught her, he would win. . . .

"Lorena, come back!"

Ben swore beneath his breath and bolted after her. She had come around in a circle, leading him again within sight of the Indians' camp. He followed her into the clearing just as Broken Hand and Blue Elk emerged from one of the tepees, but he only stopped short when he saw Lorena run straight into the arms of the Indian medicine man, burying her head against his chest.

Rage welled in him as he watched Blue Elk stroke her hair, but it pained him more to see that Lorena took comfort in the gesture. He'd expected a change in her, yes, but not this. More of the Indians had awakened now and were peering out of their lodges, perplexed at the scene that unfolded before them. Ben paid them no mind, however. All he could see was the woman he loved seeking shelter in the arms of another. Boldly, he stepped toward her, hesitating only when Blue Elk made a move to shield Lorena and put a hand on the hilt of the knife sheathed on his belt.

"You know this man?" the Indian asked Lorena.

She nodded, stepping out from behind him to put herself between the two. At the same time Broken Hand crossed to Ben's side. "Take care, my friend," he cautioned, "this is no way to die."

But Ben would not listen. "You run from me as if I were the devil himself," he said, "yet you seek comfort from this man, whose people are responsible for the death of your friend."

Lorena looked up, her eyes wide. "Charles was killed when I was taken captive. I've had a long time to accept that."

Snow crunched beneath Ben's moccasined feet as he edged closer, shaking his head. "That wound wasn't fatal. Charles Ackerman has spent the past year searching for you, trying to exact retribution from this tribe for what he believed they'd done to you. He was killed," Thorne went on to explain, "leading his men in a charge against the Cheyenne at Clear Creek. Surely you've heard of that engagement. It also claimed the life of Spotted Wolf."

"I'd heard of this fight with the Army," Lorena admitted, "but I did not know that Charles had been—that he—"

Her voice broke off and she buried her face in her hands.

Ben went to her and wrapped his arms around her. "Come with me, Lorena," he pleaded, "back where you belong."

She looked up, eyes brimming with tears. "I belong here. I am not a prisoner."

There was nothing she could have said that would have hurt more. Ben's frustrations spilled over in a torrent of angry words, and he caught her arms in a cruel grip, meaning to hurt her as much as he was being hurt. "Charles Ackerman was not the first to die in this war," he shouted, "nor will he be the last. The United States Army is bent on the destruction of these people you've allied yourself with, and that puts you in a damned precarious spot!"

He released her with a shove, and she fell, bottom first, into a snowbank. With the last of his strength, he turned on her. "And don't think your Indian lover will be able to protect you when the time comes," he warned. "All the honor and traditions of his warrior society amount to less than nothing in the face of a superior army determined to claim every inch of this land you and I are standing on. These people are a doomed race, and the wise among them already know it."

Lorena struggled to her feet as Blue Elk swept past her. The narrowing of his dark eyes told her that he could no longer restrain his anger at Ben's mistreatment of her. Before Ben could anticipate his move, Blue Elk had struck him a hard blow, knocking him off his feet. Ben retaliated by dragging his foe down as well, and the pair wrestled over the frozen ground to the taunts and cheers of the Indian onlookers.

Lorena was stunned; Ben Thorne's bitter words were still ringing in her ears. He believed that she and Blue Elk were lovers, and clearly it upset him. She had only to look upon his face as he struggled with Blue Elk to know that there was more, much more than anger there. For the first time Lorena asked herself why he had come after her, and the answer led to a painful examination of her own heart. She had run from him like a frightened child, so she need not admit the truth to herself. She was in love with Ben Thorne. Could it be that he loved her as well?

The two men pummeling one another were evenly matched, and so none of those who watched them sought to put a stop to the spectacle, not even Broken Hand. As she looked on their bloodied faces, Lorena's heart was torn by concern for them both, but neither listened as she cried out for them to stop. Again and again they clashed then drew themselves apart, only to face off once more. They'd gone on this way for some time before Blue Elk gained the advantage. After delivering a stunning blow, he wrestled his dazed adversary to the ground. Instinct made him draw his knife, and silence fell over all. The sound of the two men's harsh breathing filled the quiet clearing.

"No!" Lorena screamed, the panic in her voice finally bringing Blue Elk to his senses. The Indian stared hard at the knife in his hand, then plunged it into the snowbank beside him and rolled off of Ben.

Lorena went at once to the place where Ben lay and dropped to her knees beside him. With a gentle hand she caressed his bruised face. "Forgive me, Ben. You've come all this way for me, and I— Forgive me."

Ben raised himself up, using the back of his hand to wipe away the blood that oozed from a cut on his lip. "You have a choice to make," he told her, a chill in his voice. Lorena winced to feel the hatred in those cold, green eyes.

Getting to his feet, he went to join Broken Hand across the clearing.

*　　*　　*

Lorena rose, and Blue Elk came to her side. Before she could speak, he took up both her hands and made her look at him. "You must go with him," he said, "the time has come for the white bird to take flight."

"What does that mean, my brother?" she asked of him, unable to check the stinging tears that flooded over now.

"I will tell you the tale of the white bird, my *tsiso*," he began, "so that you may understand.

"I lived the warrior's life for many years, but one day my heart grew sick of the hatred and the killing and I went into the mountains on a vision quest. For many days I fasted and prayed to the Great Spirit, *Macha-Mahaiyu*, to show me the way, and at last I was granted my vision. A graceful white bird, with eyes that shone like stars, came down out of the sky and lit upon my shoulder, and then a voice called out to me. 'You are Blue Elk, he who shall be the great prophet of his people,' it said. 'This cannot be so,' I replied, 'I am not worthy.' 'Watch for the white bird,' the voice told me, 'for it is your sacred duty to care for her and keep her from the evils of man. This will prove you are worthy of the name, and when the white bird takes flight, you will know the time is come.'"

Lorena met his eyes, still puzzled. "And you think that I—"

"I knew it was so from the first moment that I looked upon your face. You must go now, Silver Eyes, that I may care for my people, who need me."

"But what Thorne said," Lorena put in, "about the Army, if all that is true—"

"Then my people will need me all the more."

Ben had gone for his horse and returned in time to see Lorena again in the arms of the medicine man. He pulled himself into the saddle, trying to ignore the pains of his bruised body, though it was the ache in his heart that plagued him most of all.

He forced himself to watch their embrace, and his eyes went wide when he saw her reach for Blue Elk's knife. Lorena seemed so unpredictable that there was no telling what she intended now, but then Ben saw her cut the rawhide thongs that bound her two thick braids, and he breathed a sigh of relief. She combed out the plaiting with her fingers and then cut a lock of hair, which she put into Blue Elk's hand along with his knife. Then she turned from him and walked away.

When she crossed the clearing to join him at last, Ben was surprised, but put out his hand and, without a word, pulled her up behind his saddle.

"You will ride for Wind River?" Broken Hand asked him.

"We'll stay the night at the cabin," Ben said, "and go on from there in the morning."

Broken Hand nodded. "You'll have no need of me, then. I will carry your news to the man who waits at Laramie."

If Ben had thought that there was any chance at all that Lorena could care for him, he'd not have sent his friend off to Edgington with the good news, but she'd made it quite clear where her affections lay. "Tell him we'll be there in two weeks' time," he said.

Chapter Twelve

✦✦✦✦✦

LORENA STOOD IN the shadows at the far corner of the cabin, shivering against the cold as Ben lit the hearth fire. Her soft doeskin dress and leggings were still damp from the morning's chase through the snow. But even after the fire was a blaze of golden light and the waves of warmth had drifted across the room to her, Lorena could not shake the cold within her. Ben had spoken not a word since they'd left the Cheyenne camp, and now, settled on his side of the cabin, he was all but ignoring her.

She watched as he pulled off his buckskin shirt, hanging it over a chair near the fire to dry. The firelight gleamed on the well-defined muscles of his chest and back and highlighted several jagged lines of scar tissue. Were they old war wounds, she wondered, or just more evidence of the hazards of living in the wilderness?

Lorena noticed, too, the Indian fetish he wore on a rawhide thong. It looked to her to be of Blue Elk's making, but however could Thorne have come by it? When he saw that it had caught her eye, he tore it from around his neck at once and hurled it across the room, where it struck the rough log wall and dropped to the floor.

Ben went next to the water barrel near the door and broke the crust of ice to fill the washbasin. Setting it on the crude table before the fire, he dashed the water over his face and wiped away the traces of dried blood still remaining from his encounter with Blue Elk. He winced when his hand moved over the purplish bruise on his brow. Lorena would have gone to him then to offer comfort but for the harsh look he sent her.

Instead, she turned to the other subject that had been gnawing at her throughout the silence of their morning ride. "Tell me about Charles," she asked, finding her voice at last.

"He's dead," Ben replied sharply. "What else would you have me tell you? . . . that he spent every waking moment of his last months searching for you? . . . that he died wracked with guilt that he hadn't been more concerned for your safety . . . that as he lay bleeding to death, he made me swear an oath that I'd find you and bring you back? All of that is true as well, Miss Mackenzie. How does it feel to know that while you were warming that Indian's bed, your friend was suffering?"

Each of his words struck her like a blow. She turned from him, her chin held up, and went to kneel before the fire. She would not show him how she was hurting. The vision that Ben had painted for her of Charles's last days tormented her, as well as his accusations about her life with Blue Elk. But what hurt most of all was the truth she now had to face. Ben Thorne had not come after her out of any personal concern, but only because of the promise he'd made to Charles.

Ben could not help but be touched by the sight of her, distraught and trembling, yet still trying to maintain her composure. He had wanted to hurt her, and he'd succeeded. Now, though, the guilt overwhelmed him. "I'm sorry, Lorena," he said as he went to her and knelt to lay a hand on her shoulder.

She did not respond to the words, only shivered at the warmth of his touch. Instinctively, Ben pulled her close, but she bowed her head, determined not to meet his eyes.

For months following her capture Ben had been made miserable by thoughts of what Lorena might have had to endure at the hands of the Cheyenne, and these thoughts were not

mere wild imaginings. He knew well enough
that the Indians did not feel a need for compassion where their enemies were concerned.
A woman, and a white woman at that, could
expect to be treated no better than a slave. Ben
realized, too late, that Lorena might only have
accepted Blue Elk as her protector to forego a
far worse fate.

Her clothes were damp. She was chilled to
the bone and her slim form began to shake
with renewed sobbing. Ben took her heart-
shaped face into his hands, and wanting to
ease some of the pain he'd caused her, he
breathed a warm kiss against her lips. Lorena
responded, as he'd hoped she would, her soft
mouth yielding under his.

It was a long, languorous kiss, and though
it had begun innocently enough, when his
tongue sought the velvet warmth of her
mouth, Lorena's hands began to move over
him in response, caressing the hard planes of
his bare chest and back, tracing lovingly over
each of his long-healed scars with her smooth
fingertips. Sliding upward, those fingers
hooked together behind his neck to draw him
down still closer to her.

When Ben drew back to catch his breath, a
soft sigh of regret escaped Lorena's parted
lips. The sound pleased him more than he
could have imagined. His own callused hands
smoothed the silken wisps of hair that
threaded across her brow, played lightly over
the familiar curves of her face, fingered the

unbound mane of curls that tumbled behind her back to her waist. Lorena had begun to relax, but Ben, regretful, held himself back, to stem the passions rising within him. He would not risk frightening her away again.

"You've got to get out of those clothes or you'll catch your death," he said huskily, then coughed to clear his throat. Clearing his head would not be quite so easy.

Still shaking from the assault on her senses, Lorena gathered what little strength was left to her and reached a decision. She rose, leaving him still on his knees. Her eyes, glittering now with determination, captured his as she unlaced her moccasins, drew off the long leggings, and reached to unfasten her belt. She wasn't thinking about tomorrows, only of this moment and the man who knelt before her. Her family was gone, so was Charles, and Blue Elk had set her free. There were no other needs to consider now but her own, and what she needed was for Ben Thorne to love her.

In one swift move Lorena pulled the fringed dress over her head and tossed it aside to stand naked before him, a proud tilt to her head. A muscle knotted in Ben's jaw as he strove to contain the desire that surged through him at the sight of her exquisite body, bathed in shadows and amber firelight: the perfectly-formed breasts, soft coral nipples upthrust against the chill air, the slender waist and long, well-shaped legs.

The sheen of sweat on his brow betrayed

his struggle for self-control. He had to keep
his wits about him, he thought, for Lorena
was most definitely not the predictable sort.
He got to his feet and crossed the room to
fetch a blanket from the bed for her to cover
herself with, but as he put it around her, she
purposefully let it slip from her grasp and
drop to the cabin floor. Then Ben reached out
for her and she entwined her arms about his
neck, pressing herself intimately against him.

He squeezed his eyes tightly shut. The ache
in his loins would not be denied much longer.
He had waited far too long already for this
moment, and so at last he succumbed to the
overwhelming need, covering her mouth hun-
grily with his own. He felt the sharp bite of
the cuts he'd received at the hand of Blue Elk,
and a traitorous thought fought its way to the
surface against the rising tide of his emotions,
demanding to be heard: How much of Lorena's lovemaking had been taught her by that
damnable medicine man?

Lorena felt him hesitate and assumed it was
a twinge of pain from his wounds. Gently she
put her hand to the mottled crimson bruise
over his brow, wishing she could make it disappear. She stood on tiptoe and pressed her
lips to the spot, aware now that Ben's eyes
had narrowed, glittering like shards of green
glass. His rough hands grew more insistent,
sliding off of her shoulders to knead her
breasts, slipping lower still and trailing back
along the curve of her spine to press her hips

full against his hard thighs. Lorena could feel his need, there between them, and it sent a shiver of apprehension through her.

She was treading unfamiliar ground now, but there was no turning back. What if Ben found her inexperience tiresome? Once before he'd turned away, and she felt she couldn't bear that reaction again.

His mouth found hers and was coaxing a response from her as his practiced hands continued to explore her body in a most intimate fashion. Lorena was soon lost in the sensual dream. With all coherent thought suspended, she gave over to the tingling currents of pleasure that coursed through her body.

Abruptly, he swung her into his arms and carried her across the cabin to the bed, tossing her lightly upon the blankets. He swore as he struggled to unlace his moccasins and unbutton his trousers, then shedding them on the floor, he came to stretch out beside her, teasing her with the feather-light kisses he breathed against her charged flesh.

When he could stand it no longer, Ben rolled over, pinning her beneath him, and his knee opened her thighs. He stared for a long while into the depths of those silver eyes, dark with passion, before he took her. He was trying to wipe from his memory the enraged face of the Cheyenne brave who'd fought him for possession of her, but the temptation of the soft, warm body beneath him soon drove out all save a fierce longing to possess her himself.

His first thrust was met with a small cry, silenced almost immediately by his hungry kiss. He gave over to the driving urgency of his body and concentrated on Lorena's labored breathing, which matched the rhythm of his movements, quickening, until together they were swept by a surge of pleasure that heralded fulfillment.

Ben had not missed that first moment of resistance, though, and later, when Lorena lay cradled on his arm sleeping as peacefully as a child, he pondered how she could have lived a year with the Cheyenne, in the company of a man such as Blue Elk, and still have been a virgin.

He knew then that he had grievously wronged Lorena. He could not begin to understand what sort of relationship she had shared with the Indian medicine man, but it was obvious that Blue Elk had been the one to care for her and keep her safe in the time they'd been together.

It was more than Ben could say for himself. He cared more for Lorena Mackenzie than he had ever cared for any woman, and yet he began to wonder if perhaps he weren't using that as an excuse to pursue his own selfish needs. This love of his was no noble sentiment. It had caused the fight with Blue Elk and even made him lash out at Lorena herself when he thought she cared for the Indian.

He lay there for a long while, contemplating the future. Much as he wanted to keep Lorena for himself, he wondered if he could be so selfish. He'd grown accustomed to a simple, untrammeled existence, living from day to day, and even though she had endured such a life among the Cheyenne, she deserved more. Back at Fort Laramie waited a cousin anxious to return her to the comfort of her family in New York; perhaps it would be best if he let her go.

With the sound of horses approaching, Ben got up and dressed quickly, reached for his rifle, then cautiously poked his head out of the cabin door. The late afternoon sun gleamed a brilliant red-orange. Its beams filtered through the tall pines, casting long shadows on the snow and blinding him for a moment. "Thorne!" a voice called out.

It was Broken Hand who rode up, with Lorena's white horse trailing behind. Ben came out to meet him.

"I thought you were bound for Laramie," he said.

The Indian did not dismount, but threw the reins of the white horse down to him. "I have brought this horse—a gift from Blue Elk for the one he calls Silver Eyes. You have made your peace with her?"

Ben cast a quick glance back at the cabin. "Yes," he said, "you could say that. But let's not both stand out here freezing. Come in. We'll have supper and talk."

Now it was Broken Hand's turn to glance toward the cabin. He shook his head. "I'll be on my way," he said. "What shall I tell the man at Laramie?"

Ben was very still and thought for a long time. "Nothing's changed. Tell him we'll be there in two weeks."

He watched his friend ride away, and when the Indian had disappeared at last into the landscape, Ben went back into the cabin and bolted the door. Stripping off his clothes, he went to Lorena once more and roused her from her sleep to make love for what he swore to himself must be the last time. And he hated himself for doing it.

Lorena told herself that she ought to have guessed by now that, by his very nature, Ben Thorne was a contrary sort. After that first glorious night of lovemaking in the mountain cabin, she'd expected there to be a change in him, but certainly not the one that occurred. She awoke that next morning to find herself face-to-face with a stranger. He'd shut himself off completely from her, as if there'd never been any bond between them. She was hurt but soon gathered up her pride and forced herself to admit finally what she'd feared all along. He had had what he wanted from her, and now he'd lost interest.

Though they rode side-by-side for the next two days, conversation was scarce. Lorena let her thoughts take over. She'd have to make plans for her future. For a few sweet hours

she'd allowed herself to believe that Ben
Thorne could fit into those plans, but now she
knew otherwise. Several times she'd had the
urge to break away and run back to the Cheyenne, but she'd resisted. Blue Elk had a duty
to his people now; there would be no room for
her in his life. She had to get by on her own.

She decided finally that when he delivered
her to the nearest fort, if indeed that was his
plan for her, she would secure a place for
herself on the first wagon train heading west
in the spring. She'd go to California to see
firsthand all of the wonders about which her
father had written, and to at last meet Tyler
Sanderson, the man who'd been her father's
partner and with whom his fortune was now
entrusted. Thus decided, she was able to relax
and let Ben lead the way.

It was late afternoon when they reached
their destination. Near the frozen track of a
meandering river, in a stark, windswept valley overshadowed by a rugged gray mountain
range, lay a single log house with a curl of
smoke beckoning from its chimney. The structure was dwarfed by the imposing landscape,
but as they rode in, Lorena could see that it
was a snugly-built ranch house with a barn
nearby and a pasture hemmed in by a snake
fence of split rails.

Her fingers and toes were numb from the
cold, and the thought of a blazing fire was

enough to send waves of imagined warmth coursing through her body. She would not have Ben Thorne know of her discomfort, though, and so she nudged her mount to keep pace with his piebald pony until they had both drawn up before the ranch house.

Lorena dismounted and stepped up onto the veranda with its rough-sawn log pillars, stopping to admire the pair of multipaned glass windows on either side of the central door.

"Imagine all of this out here in the middle of nowhere," she said, musing aloud.

"It's improved a great deal since I was here last," Ben noted.

There was a hint of emotion in his voice now. This was the most information he'd volunteered all day. "Where are we now, exactly?" Lorena asked, taking advantage of his change in attitude.

Ben pointed to the snowcapped peaks in the distance as he, too, dismounted, tossing both of their horses' reins over the porch rail. "You see those mountains to the west? That's the Wind River Range. There's not another white man living within a hundred miles of this place."

"Someone chooses to live here, unprotected, in the face of all the Indian trouble?"

"You've not seen it here when the valley is green," Ben replied wistfully, "and the water rushes down from the mountains, cold and clear as glass. Besides which," he said, shaking off his reverie as he reached for his saddlebags and tossed them over one shoulder, "the man who lives here has nothing to fear from the Indians. They're a superstitious lot, and they think he's crazy. Can't say as how I'd argue with them, either."

Lorena, who had been hovering very near the door, stepped back suddenly. Ben laughed and pushed his way through without even knocking. Lorena followed close behind him, and once inside, glanced quickly around the large room, expecting to be met by a grizzled, old mountain man sporting a wild look in his eyes. But there was no one there.

What she did see within surprised her. This was no rustic cabin. It was a comfortable home, with a pegged wood floor covered by a large Turkish carpet, a clock on the mantel, and even a rocking chair beside the fire. The kitchen was a room by itself at the rear of the house, and Lorena could see at least two other rooms through the open doorway.

After recovering from her surprise, she joined Ben before the hearth, and tossing off the buffalo robes and blankets that had kept her from freezing during the long ride, she put her hands out toward the blazing fire and let its warmth caress her face.

"Well, I must say I never expected such luxury," she said.

"As I said before, there's been quite an improvement in the place since my last visit."

He went to explore the rest of the house and

had barely returned when the front door swung open. Lorena looked up, startled, and her eyes came to rest on a tall, lank man, bundled in a heavy woolen coat. He raised a brow when he saw her, in her Indian garb, sitting before the fire, but then promptly turned his attention to Ben.

The two shared a long look, and Lorena could not miss the undercurrent of strong emotions that threaded through the silence. Focusing on Ben, she awaited an introduction.

"Lorena Mackenzie," he said at last, and she could not help but notice the disdain with which Ben regarded the man, "this is Martin Thorne."

With that he turned away, and the older man, looking saddened, pulled off his felt hat, shook off its dusting of snow, and put out his free hand to Lorena.

"I am pleased to make your acquaintance, sir," Lorena said as she got to her feet to accept his outstretched hand. "I hope we've not intruded on you. You have a lovely home."

There was a mischievous glimmer in the man's eyes that made her smile. Surely Ben could not believe this man was crazy, even though he'd said as much to her when they'd arrived. No, there was something else in Ben's manner, a bitterness behind his words, an animosity that she'd never seen in him before.

"I'll see to the horses," Ben said, and left them.

Now the elder man drew closer and spoke to her in a quiet voice that bespoke a patient nature. "Pleased to meet you, miss. I'm Ben's father."

Chapter Thirteen

✦✦✦✦

BEN MANAGED TO occupy himself for quite some time in the stables, and his absence gave Lorena and his father the time to become acquainted without the somber atmosphere that had pervaded the room while he was in it. Martin Thorne was an easy man to talk to, and she soon found herself relating to him all her adventures in the West. He was very much interested in her life with the Cheyenne and how she'd managed to escape them unharmed.

"Such a thing is all but unheard of," he told her while Lorena sat in his kitchen and he brewed some strong coffee for them.

"And yet you've lived here for—how long is it?" she asked.

Martin's brow furrowed. "I brought my family out in forty-nine," he replied. "'Tis close to twenty years now."

"You've lived here for all that time without

any trouble from the Indians. Why does it surprise you, then, to find that I was not ill-treated?"

"The Sioux in these parts are a superstitious lot. They think I'm a crazy old man, and so they let me be. But when it comes to a lovely young lady like yourself—well, it's more like a miracle," he said, shaking his head.

Martin Thorne did not elaborate as to what it was exactly that gave the Sioux such a notion about him, and Lorena did not press the matter. He handed her a china cup, and she inhaled the aroma of the steaming brew before she sipped at it and felt its warmth run through her. China teacups, Turkish carpets, mantel clocks . . . Lorena wondered at all this finery in the midst of the wilderness, and because this was the home in which she assumed Ben had grown up, it only made her wonder more.

"Where did you come from, Mr. Thorne?" she asked. "Originally, I mean."

"Pennsylvania," he told her. "When we heard the news of the gold strikes in California and of the opportunities just waiting for those willing to make the trip, we packed all we could into a wagon and headed west." Staring over the top of his cup, his eyes glazed over, and Lorena could tell that he was caught up in the memories. "It's not that we were poor, you understand. My brother owned an ironworks, and we lived comfortably enough on the salary I earned as manager, but I wanted more . . . for my family . . . for myself."

"But you settled here, in the midst of the wilderness, instead of going on to California," Lorena noted.

Ben had come in by way of the back door and must have been listening to at least the last bit of their conversation, for he now shut the door behind him with a shuddering slam.

"Shall I explain it to her, Father?" he asked in a derisive tone, but proceeded with his own version of the story before Martin had the chance to reply. "It was greed, pure and simple, that made Martin Thorne uproot his little family and set them on a grueling cross-country trek in search of gold. Heedless of the fact that his wife was a fragile creature, too delicate for such a trip, he pressed on . . . and on . . . and on . . . driven by his visions of wealth and power—because he thought that once he'd built himself a great Western empire, he could finally prove to his elder brother and all the rest of his family that he was not the failure they'd marked him as. But it takes more than gold to make a man, doesn't it, Father?"

Ben stood with arms folded across his broad chest, waiting for a reply. Martin only stared into his cup without speaking, without registering any reaction at all to his son's tirade. Lorena was speechless to see this side of the man she thought she knew so well.

Seeing that his father was not about to answer, Ben continued in the same vein. "In reply to your question, Lorena—we never made it to California because, after having been dragged halfway across the continent, my mother's strength finally gave out. We'd only just reached Independence Rock when she took ill. There was no medicine to be had, no doctor for miles, and so she lay on a blanket in the wagon bed, surrounded by the few of her precious possessions that hadn't yet been cast off along the trail . . . and we watched her die."

His head bent over the table, Martin Thorne shut his eyes as if to stave off the painful remembrances.

Ben quit the house then and headed back out to the barn, upset that he had let his emotions carry him so far. Picking up his saddle blanket, he crawled up the ladder into the loft, as he had so many times when he was a boy. Tossing the blanket onto the haystack, he sat down upon it. At once he felt something hard beneath him and rolled over to pull from the hay one of his father's half-empty flasks of whiskey.

His hands were shaking and his mouth dry as cotton. He very nearly pulled out the stopper, but as he held up the bottle, he saw his reflection in the glass, and Broken Hand's words came back to haunt him. "I look at you, but I see your father."

He flung the bottle at the far wall of the barn, where it struck and shattered, causing a moment of commotion amongst the livestock. Why had he come here at all? Ben wondered. He thought he'd purged himself of this hatred long ago, but now, with both his father and Lorena in the same house, the combined assault on his emotions was more than he could bear.

Martin Thorne lifted the kettle from the woodstove, and Lorena stole a glance out the window at the barn before she followed him into the bedroom. He poured a generous amount of the boiling water into the washbasin and then disappeared, only to return in a few minutes carrying a trunk, which he set at her feet.

"You can't go back to civilization dressed like that.There ought to be something more suitable for you in this trunk," he told her, then added quietly, "it belonged to my wife. Go on and wash up now, and I'll warm us some stew for our supper."

"Let me help with that, Mr. Thorne," Lorena offered.

"I wouldn't hear of it. Now you go on and dress for dinner."

He shut the door as he left, and Lorena did as he bade her, kneeling down on the floor before the trunk. She ran her hand lightly over the brass nails arranged to form the initials V.T., and lifted up the lid. Drawing out the first few garments, she soon became aware that the room was full of the scent of roses. It was, of course, due to the lace sachets secreted between the folds of the clothes, but still, the perfumed air gave her an uneasy feeling. She wondered if the dead woman might resent her rummaging through her things, but quickly put aside such fanciful thoughts.

Lorena found that she was extremely curious about the woman who had been Ben's mother, and so she carefully examined each of the garments as she pulled them out and held them up. True, they were more than twenty years out of date, but she could tell by the cut of the fabrics and the expensive trims that these things had once been quite fashionable. Many of them were far too frivolous for life in the wilderness, and seeing them led her to conclude that Mrs. Thorne had found the West to be a rougher place than she'd anticipated. Lorena wished the woman could have been alive now. How many of the mysteries that plagued her thoughts, of the enigmatic Ben and his somber father, might be explained by just one conversation with the woman that the two of them had loved so much?

At last she came upon a riding skirt of a deep blue, corded fabric and a cambric basque, decorated with lace, which she decided would be as suitable as she'd find. When she drew out the skirt and shook it, though, something hidden in the folds tumbled out and onto the floor. She bent over and picked up a book, its red leather covers tied together with a ribbon.

Lorena's interest was piqued at the discovery. She untied the ribbon and opened the book to the first page. It was a journal, by the looks of it, and the inside cover was inscribed with the name "Virginia Ann Thorne." Her hands were trembling as she turned to the first entry and read.

March 6, 1849—Today the long-awaited day of departure came at last. We have left the bosom of our family, intending to find a better life in a new land, and though our hearts are heavy with sadness, our expectations are high. I shall keep this journal as a record of our westward travels in the hope that years hence, when we are comfortably settled in our new home in California, we will be able to relive our adventures through the words I shall pen on these pages. May the Lord protect us on our journey.

Lorena riffled through the journal; page upon page of entries followed, penned in a neat hand, and the last entry was entered a scant five months after the first, presumably just before the woman's death. There would be no home in California; the adventure had ended in tragedy.

This journal was, Lorena reasoned, as close as she could ever come to a conversation with Virginia Thorne. She was intrigued by this discovery and wondered if Ben or his father were even aware of the journal's existence. She would show it to them, of course, but she decided that first she would read it herself.

She put the journal back into the trunk for the moment and washed and dressed herself in the riding skirt and basque she'd set aside. She brushed out her hair, tying it behind her with a grosgrain ribbon, and as an after-thought she pulled out a plaid, woolen shawl and tossed it over her shoulders to ward off the evening's chill.

When she went looking for him, Lorena found Martin Thorne in his rocking chair, clutching an oval-framed daguerreotype and staring hard at it.

"Mr. Thorne?" she called, to get his atten-tion.

He was startled to see her standing there, as if she might be the ghost of the woman whose picture he'd been musing over. And she might well have been, for as she approached him, Lorena could see more clearly the likeness of a fair-haired young woman, not much older than herself, within the oval of the frame. Lorena assumed that the woman must be Vir-ginia Thorne, and approaching him slowly, she took the picture and examined it. Virginia Thorne had been tall, with proud bearing and a serene expression, and she was dressed in elegant simplicity.

"How did she die?" Lorena asked after a long while.

He cleared the lump in his throat. "Mountain fever," he said. "It was Ben who took sick first. There was no doctor, and so Virginia nursed him as best she could. He was always her favorite, her darling boy. She worried so about him, but Ben's always been a hardy sort, and sure enough, after a time he'd shaken it. By then, though, she was stricken. Fate wasn't so kind the second time."

"I'm sorry," Lorena told him.

"It was a long time ago, but my son can't seem to forget . . . or forgive. He blames me, as you've heard."

With that, Martin Thorne pulled himself from the chair and took his wife's picture from Lorena's hands, putting it back in its place on the mantel.

Lorena followed him into the kitchen and watched as he spooned the stew from the kettle he'd taken from the stove onto two of the plates set at the table. The third plate was set for Ben, who'd not returned, and he left it empty. Lorena could see how this pointed absence distressed him. She went to fetch the coffeepot from the stove and filled both their cups before seating herself at the table across from him.

"He didn't mean all of what he said," Lorena said, trying to soothe him. "Those hurtful words were spoken in anger, and I'm certain that after he considers—"

Martin met her eyes, looking very forlorn. "Don't judge Ben too harshly. He has reason enough to hate me." He dropped his head and listlessly pushed the food around the plate with his fork. "After Virginia died, I went crazy with grief. California no longer seemed a paradise to me, and I hadn't the strength to continue on. So I settled here at Wind River. I tried to make a home for Ben and his younger sister, Mary, but the years taught me that I wasn't meant to be a farmer, Miss Mackenzie. I am ashamed to say that I took to drink, and somehow I got it into my head that if I went up to the goldfields and made a strike, all my troubles would be over. So I went off in search of gold and . . . well, Ben was left with more responsibility than a young boy ought to be made to bear. Over the years I came and went as the whim would take me, searching for the elusive mother lode, but I never found it, and one day when I returned, both my children were gone, gone back East to live with their uncle."

Lorena looked across the table, sympathy welling in her for Martin Thorne, in spite of all he'd told her of himself. She saw him as a tragic figure of a man whom Fate had dealt harshly with, and while he may well have wronged his children, he had spent many lonely years doing penance for it.

"I think," Lorena said, after a long while spent in contemplation, "that even though Ben strikes out at you, it is himself he truly blames for his mother's death."

Martin looked at her in a perplexed fashion,

as though this were the first time he'd considered the possibility. "But he could not be held accountable for his illness," he protested.

"Just as you could not know, when you decided to move your family west, that circumstance would intervene with such tragic results, but you blame yourself nonetheless."

There was a look of gratitude in his eyes. "You are wise beyond your years, Miss Mackenzie."

"I'll admit that I may be able to see things more clearly now," she replied, "but tis you who've given me this new perspective, Mr. Thorne."

Lorena thought about it. She had, indeed, learned a great deal from Martin Thorne, which in turn had given her insights to his son she might not otherwise have had. Since they first met, Ben had tried to convince her to go back to New York, and now Lorena thought she could see the reason why. To his way of thinking, a sheltered young lady coming to this land could only meet with misfortune. He had watched it happen to his mother, and now he must have thought Lorena headed down that same path. If her supposition were true, it would explain much about Ben's actions thus far and even more about his feelings for her.

The conversation took a lighter turn for the remainder of the meal, and after she'd helped him clear the dishes, Lorena excused herself, pleading exhaustion. Her true intent, however, was to settle beneath the quilt in the comfortable bed that Martin Thorne insisted upon giving over to her, to read Virginia's journal, for now she was more intrigued than ever.

There was a creak of hinges as the barn door swung open. Ben roused himself from his sleep and leaned down from his spot in the loft in time to see his father step in. In one hand he carried a tray of food with a napkin thrown over it, and in the other a lantern. Another time Ben might have turned over and pretended to be asleep, but much as he hated to admit it, the sadness in the old man's eyes touched him. He preferred to think, though, it was the hunger gnawing at his stomach that sent him down the ladder from the loft to meet him.

His father set the lantern on its peg, and after a long silence took the steaming cup of coffee from the tray and held it out to his son. "You've made quite clear your feelings for me," he said, "and I can't say as I blame you. But you needn't hide yourself away out here."

"I'm not so hypocritical as to defame you to your face and then expect your hospitality. All I ask is a comfortable place for Lorena to rest."

"You are my son. You helped to build this place. It is as much yours as it is mine, and you have every right to call it home."

Finally, after considering these words, Ben

accepted the cup his father offered, and the tray of food as well. He sat down cross-legged on the floor, balancing the tray on his lap as he blew away the steam rising from the cup and sipped at the liquid.

"I must go to Fort Casper for supplies in the morning," the elder Thorne said as he bent down to sit beside his son. "Stay here as long as you like, though. The girl needs to rest after her ordeal."

"It'll be a few days more before she's ready to return to Laramie," Ben agreed. "She can't ride in looking like a squaw, that's for certain. I thought she might borrow some of Mary's old things . . . or mother's."

"I've already taken care of that. You'll be pleased, I think, at the change that's come over her already."

Ben was surprised to hear himself engaged in a civil conversation with his father; it was a relief—after so many years of rancor. Afraid to tempt the fates, he said nothing more, concentrating instead upon his meal.

"She's quite a remarkable young woman," Martin observed after a long silence. "I wonder how many others in her place would have fared as well."

Having finished his meal, Ben set aside the tray and rose up, dusting off his breeches with his hand as he went to peer out of the open barn door. He could see yellow lamplight spilling out of the window of the room where Lorena was likely readying herself for bed.

"I've not yet met a woman to compare with her," he admitted, finding himself possessed by a pensive air.

Martin got to his feet and drew up behind Ben. "And yet you'd send her back East and risk never seeing her again?"

"Is that what I have in mind for her?" Ben asked, unable to contain the sarcasm that crept into his voice as he wondered how the old man could have known.

"That's what she believes," Martin replied, "and I've found her to be quite perceptive. She cares a great deal for you. That's plain enough to see. If you have any affection at all for her, son, you ought to speak up for yourself."

Ben whirled back to face his father. "I ought to—" He stopped himself short and closed his eyes, determined to keep his calm. "You couldn't possibly understand. There comes a time when, if you truly care for someone, you must put aside what you want, and consider instead what's best for them. . . ."

Those words hung on the air for a very long time. Martin Thorne was well aware of their double-edged meaning. By his son's way of thinking, he had never been able to put aside his own needs and that had destroyed their family. There was some truth in it, but there was also so much more that Ben did not understand. Martin heaved a long sigh, doubtful that he had the strength to battle his son on this. "And you presume to know what's best for Miss Mackenzie? Without ever even discussing it with her?" he said, sounding tired. "Isn't that unfair?"

"I know that there is precious little chance for a gentle-mannered young woman in this land. If she survives the journey, she has yet to face the elements, disease, and the Indians. Life itself out here is a daily trial, devoid of the comforts she's learned to expect. Look at what Lorena has been subjected to already. You, better than anyone, ought to understand, Father. This land kills people, and I won't bear such a responsibility, not ever again!"

Martin was astonished that Lorena Mackenzie had the ability to read his son so well. "Again? Then it is true. You do blame yourself for your mother's death."

He watched as the color drained from Ben's face. "If I hadn't taken sick—" he started. "If she hadn't cared for me, she would never have come down with the sickness herself."

Martin edged closer and laid a hand on his son's shoulder. "You can't blame yourself for that. She was your mother and she loved you dearly. How could she do less than care for her own child? What happened was God's will."

"That doesn't change the fact that I was the cause of her death," Ben said, wrenching himself away, then pacing back and forth before the barn doors. "She died and I was the one to live. Time and time again I wished it could have been the other way around. You all could have gotten by without me, but her death destroyed the family. It left you only a shell of the man you once were and poor little Mary to cry herself to sleep every night."

"That's not so. It was a shock to lose her, and we all grieved at first, but time has healed us. Little Mary is doing quite well living back home. She writes to me once a month. In fact, her last letter mentions that she has a beau and that they intend to marry in the spring."

Martin could see that Ben was listening to him, though there was no hint of expression on his face. "And while you might not think so, I'm doing well myself. I came back from the goldfields with a tidy sum—not a fortune, mind you, but enough to buy some horses and a few head of cattle. I intend to turn a profit here at Wind River, and I'm going to Fort Casper in the morning to see if I can hire a few hands to help me do it.

"I'll be off early, so I've got to get some sleep," he said finally, as he walked past Ben. "I hope you'll reconsider your decision to stay out here in the barn. If that north wind picks up, it'll whistle right through these timbers, and you'll think you were sleeping out on the open prairie."

He put his hand on the door that stood ajar, and Ben called out to him, "Father?"

Martin turned back to meet his son's eyes,

and was encouraged by what he saw in
them.

"Thank you."

Chapter Fourteen

✦✦✦✦

*April 29, 1849—Only one day out of Inde-
pendence and our captain, Jim Stewart, entreated those in our company to lighten the load.
The wagons pulled out, and all of us were saddened, I think, as we looked back upon those
precious possessions which had to be left behind,
scattered now like refuse over the ground. We
parted with a trunkful of clothing, convinced
that we should all make do with what remained,
but when Martin said we must leave behind a
good many of our books, I was truly heartsick.
He has promised me, though, that I may keep my
rocking chair, and for that I am grateful. . . ."*

*May 11, 1849—What a beauteous land is
this! The sun shone warm upon us for all of the
day as our little band cut a path through the
waving fields of lush, green grass. Mary and I
gathered up armfuls of wildflowers as we walked
beside the wagon. There were more blossoms than
can be imagined: tall spires of white indigo and
goldenrod and delicate blue prairie irises.*

Martin asked once again if I resented all we'd had to leave behind, and my answer was the same as when he'd first come to me with this idea of moving West. My home was with him, no matter where that might be. We both knew that there could be no happy future for us with Martin in servitude to his autocratic brother. Whatever the future holds in store for us, at least we would be free. . . .

June 18, 1849—Today the men made time for a buffalo hunt, and Martin took Ben with him. I thought the boy would burst with pride when his father told him he was man enough to go along with the rest. They hadn't much luck, though. I must confess I was relieved, for while these past months have seen me become quite the hard-bitten traveler, I shouldn't have relished the task of carving up the great beast.

July 2, 1849—Ben was taken ill early yesterday morning with chills and fever. He lies upon a bed of blankets in the bottom of the wagon, scarcely able to move at all. I find, to my distress, that I can do naught for him but wipe his brow and pray. Martin frets so that I fear he will jeopardize his own health. He made inquiries with every wagon that passed us today, hoping to find a doctor or someone with medical skills, but with no success. He put on a brave face for me, though, and reminded me that our Ben is a strong young man and will no doubt be recov-

ered in a day or two. "Sooner than you think,"
he told me, "we'll be on our way to catch up to
the others." I pray God that it may be so. . . .

Lorena woke suddenly just before dawn to
find herself still clutching Virginia's journal.
Not surprisingly, her dreams that night had
been of the trip West: a fevered blending of
her own memories and what she'd read of
Ben's mother's experiences. It had all seemed
so very real, and that made it all the more
ominous, for instead of detailing the unfortunate demise of Virginia Thorne, this particular
dream had culminated in Lorena's own death.

Shaken by her vivid imaginings, she could
not settle herself back to sleep, and as the first
rosy light of dawn appeared on the eastern
horizon, Lorena dragged herself out from beneath the warm quilts. Bracing herself against
the morning chill, she dressed hurriedly and
went out to the kitchen to start a fire in the
woodstove.

There were sounds of stirring from behind
the door of the room occupied by Martin
Thorne, and as she passed the parlor, she saw
Ben stretched out on the rug before the hearth,
though the embers of last night's fire had by
now turned to ash. So he'd decided to come in
after all. His father would be glad to see it.
Lorena wished she could somehow help mend
the rift between them. After reading Virginia's

journal, she felt a kinship with the woman and knew that the splintering of her family would have upset her greatly. And then she was struck with an idea. She would let Virginia mend the rift.

After going back to fetch the journal, she went into the parlor. Ben seemed to sense her approach, for he pulled himself upright, hugging his knees. "Good morning," Lorena said to him as she sat down in Virginia's rocking chair.

"Good morning," he replied with a wry smile.

It appeared his manner had improved considerably after a good night's sleep. Whatever words she might have said then were lost when she looked into his eyes and saw him staring at her in an intimate fashion.

"What are your plans for me?" she asked when she had found her voice again.

"I made a promise to see you safely home," he reminded her.

"You—you . . . cannot truly intend—" she sputtered. "Not after—But I don't belong there, Ben, I never did. People grow soft there and stagnate."

"People *die* out here," he retorted.

"The way your mother died, you mean? She, more than anyone, would understand what I'm trying to say. She lived her life the way she wanted."

"How could you know that?" he demanded.

Lorena held up the journal, which had been resting in her lap. "I found this in with her things. You ought to read it. It'll rid you of some of the ridiculous notions you've been clinging to."

She tossed it down to him and went out to the kitchen to busy herself in making breakfast, so she wouldn't have to think about their conversation or that he was still determined to be rid of her.

Martin Thorne could smell bacon frying in the skillet and made sure he was dressed and ready in time for breakfast. He was pleased to see his son camped out in the parlor, but as he sat down to breakfast across the table from Lorena, he wore a perplexed look, wondering what sort of book could be so engrossing as to make Ben miss a hot meal.

Lorena offered no explanation, only kept up her end of their polite little chat. But Martin sensed she was behind whatever it was that had captured his son's attention in the parlor, for every now and again she'd look up from her plate to peer around the corner at him.

Martin didn't have time for guessing games this morning, though, no matter how mysterious. As soon as he'd finished his meal, he picked up the portmanteau he'd packed for his journey, said his good-byes to Lorena, and joined his son in the parlor.

Ben cross-legged on the carpet. He hadn't moved from the spot in all the time his father had been watching him, and he was still concentrating on the pages of that peculiar book. When he heard him, though, he looked up, and Martin wondered about the confused look he wore.

"What is it, son?" he asked.

Ben pressed the covers of the book together and clung to it. "Did you know that Mother kept a journal?"

"No," Martin said, after considering. "Well, yes, I suppose I did notice her scribbling into some sort of book from time to time."

Ben got to his feet and held out the book he'd been perusing so intently.

Martin's heavy brows knit together as he studied the red leather cover. He was almost afraid to take it from his son's hand, but he did, and when he opened it, his eyes blurred with tears as soon as he recognized Virginia's neat handwriting.

"I've just been reliving the past," Ben explained, "through my mother's eyes. It's not the same as I remember it, not at all."

"You were only a child," Martin told him, pulling the book close to his chest so that his son might not see how badly his hands were shaking, "still too young to understand all of what happened that summer."

"All along I blamed you for dragging her out here, but she *wanted* to make the trip, perhaps even more than you did yourself . . . yet you never explained. You let me go on hating you for all those years."

Martin let go a sigh that vibrated with emotion. "Because I blamed myself. I knew the risks in making such a journey, but I let Virginia convince me that what we stood to gain was worth any risk." There was a drawn-out silence before he went on. "It wasn't worth her life, though, and there isn't a day goes by that I don't wish I could go back and do things differently."

Martin's eyes were pressed shut to stem his tears, but he could feel his son's arms go around him, and the both of them stood there for a while without speaking. "I'm sorry," Ben said at last, "sorry that I was too selfish to see that you were hurting too. Take the journal with you on your trip," he suggested then, "I think it'll help you make your peace. It's helped me."

Martin nodded and embraced his son one last time. "Take care of yourself," he told him. "I hope to see you again soon." Then he whispered into Ben's ear, "Both of you."

Lorena did not venture into the parlor, but she knew just the same that Ben had made peace with his father, and as she cleared away the breakfast dishes, he appeared in the doorway, sporting a grin that confirmed it.

"Is it something in your nature, Miss Mackenzie," Ben began, folding his arms across his chest as he leaned against the jamb, "that makes you go about so intent on mending anything broken that crosses your path . . . including people's lives?"

She turned to him, raising one brow as she wiped her hands on her apron. "Your father's on his way, then?" she asked, deciding to ignore the question.

"He's only just now gone," he said as he watched her clear the table. "Wait. Don't throw away those biscuits or the bacon. I'm famished."

Ben got a clean plate for himself and heaped upon it all of what remained of the breakfast. Lorena thought the change in him was no less than a miracle. When she brought him a cup of coffee, he bade her sit beside him.

"Today is my day for apologies, it seems," he began. "It was unfair of me, I'll admit, to presume to know what's best for you, when there is so much yet that I don't know about your life. But I plan to remedy that presently."

Once again she was surprised. Ben attacked his meal with relish, leaving her to guess at what this remark signified. Virginia Thorne's journal had proved a more effective cathartic than even Lorena could have imagined. Quite suddenly the cautious and stoical Ben Thorne she'd come to know was gone, and in his place was a carefree soul, full of zestful enthusiasm.

"Where do you want to go from here?" he asked her.

It was an ambiguous question that could

have called for any number of answers, but Lorena chose the most obvious reply. "California."

"What?"

"I intend to go on to California. I told you that my father lived there for many years, and he wrote me such marvelous letters that I want to see it all for myself."

"I'd expected you to insist I take you to Montana so you might fulfill your wish to be a schoolmarm. California is no place for a woman on her own," he told her, sounding more like himself.

"I won't be alone. My father's partner, Tyler Sanderson, has a home in San Francisco. I know that I would be welcome there. And . . ." She looked at him, deciding to test the waters. "You could come along."

His fork wavered in midair. "California? Me?" He laughed, but Lorena could see just the same that he was considering it.

Before Ben could speak again, there was a pounding on the door. He met Lorena's puzzled look and went to investigate.

"Edgington?" she heard him say. "What the hell—"

Lorena peered out from the kitchen, unable to believe her eyes. There in the center of the parlor stood Henry Edgington, her uncle's stepson.

"You will excuse me, Thorne, but when your man brought the good news, I had to come at once. Lorena? Lorena, are you here?"

With a look of astonishment upon her face, Lorena came out and saw that she'd not been mistaken. It was, indeed, Henry Edgington. He rushed forward to take up her hands, and before she knew what to think, he was embracing her. "Thank God, you're safe, my dear! We were all concerned for you when we heard that poor Ackerman had been killed and then to find that you'd been kidnapped by savages. It's a miracle to find you here and unharmed."

"Did my uncle send you after me?" Lorena asked, though she could scarcely credit that Edgington would do anything without his own motives.

He took the fur cap from his head and stared at the floor in a sober mien. "I'm sorry to tell you, Lorena, that your uncle died six months ago. But I took it upon myself to come out here and bring you back home where you belong. Mother has been sick with worry over you."

While Lorena digested his news, Edgington turned to Ben. "You're as good as they say you are, Thorne, and I haven't forgotten our bargain. Name your fee; you've earned it."

"I'm afraid," Ben said to him, "that Lorena's decided not to return home."

Lorena didn't hear his words, though. With the revelation that Edgington had hired Ben to find her, she fled to the bedroom to hide her disillusionment. She would not shed a tear, yet she could not help but be hurt to realize that it hadn't been the deathbed promise to Charles that kept Ben Thorne searching for her all those months, nor affection for her. It had been the money.

She had to face the truth now. She'd only been building castles in the air to convince herself that she could make a man like Ben Thorne care for her. His heart was too callous. Her instincts had been right all along. How pleased he must have been to realize that he could have what he wanted from her and make a profit in the bargain!

But she did not intend to return to New York with Edgington, no matter what it might cost Ben Thorne. Fueled by anger, she grabbed the bundle of Indian clothing she'd been wearing when she arrived, and slipping out of the cabin by way of the kitchen door, headed for the barn.

In the parlor Henry Edgington's voice was strained and his pasty skin mottled with color as he strode back and forth across the carpet impatiently. "If you think I've come all the way out here only to return home empty-handed, Mr. Thorne, you're sadly mistaken. My cousin is a simpleminded girl; she cannot possibly be left to decide what is in her best interest."

Ben folded his arms across his chest and watched the overanimated peacock as he nervously trod the same stretch of carpet over and over. He shook his head. "Nevertheless, sir, she *has* decided."

Henry Edgington abruptly stopped pacing and turned on Ben, eyes narrowed. "I see what your game is, Thorne," he said in a low voice. "You've discovered somehow that the girl is an heiress, and you think if you keep her here, you can have her, and her fortune as well, all for yourself."

Ben was taken aback by this revelation, but did not let Edgington see it, for he could see that the cunning, New York City lawyer was already sizing him up in order to formulate his plan of attack.

"I'll admit your crude charms might have an effect on some women," Edgington began, "they might even attract Lorena . . . for a time. Remember this, though, before you embark upon such a scheme: Lorena Mackenzie's father made a fortune in the goldfields, and there's a handsome annuity left her by her uncle as well. She can surround herself with anything or anyone she wishes. What is there here to entice her to stay with a man like you?"

"I don't give a damn about the money," Ben snarled. All of Edgington's actions were beginning to make much more sense to him now. "But I can see that you do. You must be in dire straits," he guessed, "to have traveled so many miles after Lorena and her fortune."

Edgington ignored the accusation, turning his back on Ben as he pondered his next move.

"Could it be," the lawyer said, taking a new tack, "that you're in love with her? Ah yes, now there's an amusing possibility. 'Marry me, Lorena, and all of this will be yours.'" He spread out his hands in a dramatic gesture. "Exactly what is it that you have to offer her, Thorne? Or perhaps you plan to live high on her inheritance? I can see that you're the type who prides himself on his manhood, on earning his keep by the sweat of his brow. Just how long do you imagine you'd be able to tolerate the thought that everything you have you have because of her?"

But Ben did not get the chance to reflect nor reply, for at that moment the front door crashed open and one of Edgington's men broke in. He was dragging Lorena with him, one burly arm coiled about her waist, and she was putting up one hell of a fight.

"Let go of me!" she screeched, her arms flailing wickedly about the big man's head.

He obliged, tossing her into the room as easily as he might a bundle of sticks. She landed in an unladylike sprawl on the floor.

"Caught her in the stable, trying to sneak off," he explained to his employer.

Before any of them could react, Lorena sprang up like a wildcat and pounced on the man, raking her nails across his face. Enraged, he grabbed her by the sleeve and pulled back his arm to strike her.

"Hendricks, no!" Edgington cried.

The giant of a man seemed bent on punishing her, though, and Ben rushed to put himself between them. He shoved Lorena aside, taking Hendricks's ham-fisted blows upon himself. Soon he, too, was tossed across the room. His head struck against a low table and he fell dazed upon the floor.

The second of Edgington's men came in by way of the kitchen door then, his pistol drawn and pointed in Ben's direction. Ben decided to lay there a while longer.

Lorena, though, picked herself up, and rubbing her bottom, turned on Edgington. "What's all of this about? You have no right to keep me here."

"I am your cousin," he protested, "and I've come to take you home, where you belong."

"Don't pretend concern for me, you—you pompous ass. You're no cousin of mine. Our only connection is through an accident of marriage, as you well know, and I have no intention of going back to New York with you."

"You're right. I'd thought to take a delicate approach, but let's be quite honest, shall we? You were always a rebellious brat who gave my poor mother no end of trouble when she was left with the unfortunate task of raising you, and as you've just now demonstrated, you've grown into an unmanageable hellion. For my part I would gladly leave you here in the wilds. It's clearly where you belong. But unfortunately for us both, my dear, I have a pressing need for cash, and you are the only key to a vast treasure chest just waiting to be unlocked."

As Edgington went on with his discourse, Ben lifted his throbbing head. His interest was piqued by the hoot of an owl that seemed to be just outside the window. It was a very distinctive call, which he recognized at once, and a smile crooked on his lips.

"Your father's will states that his partner, Tyler Sanderson, shall retain control of his estate until such time as you come into your majority," Edgington explained to Lorena, "or upon the occasion of your marriage."

"You can't be entertaining the notion that I'd consent to marry you?" she said, astounded by his conceit.

But the malevolent glare in his deep-set eyes sent a shiver through her. "Consent implies that you have a choice, my dear. You do not."

Chapter Fifteen

✦ ✦ ✦ ✦ ✦

FOR THE FIRST time since she'd been dragged back into the house, Lorena turned her full attention on Ben Thorne. He had picked himself up and was standing, head in hand, by the rough-bearded man barring the entry to the kitchen. Though he'd come to her aid earlier, she was crestfallen to discover that now he seemed wholly uninterested in what was transpiring. Even if he did not care for her at all, she reasoned, even if he'd come after her only because of the money, he could not be so heartless as to allow Edgington to get away with such a scheme. Yet Ben made no move to stop him.

"And once you've got your hands on the money, you'll have no need of me," Lorena surmised, speaking to Edgington but hoping to prompt Ben into action.

"Your father was nothing if not a clever man," Edgington replied. "The will stipulates that if you should marry and any misfortune befall you before the time of your second wedding anniversary, the entire estate reverts to his partner. So, you see, you have nothing to fear from me . . . for two years, at least." Edgington punctuated the statement with a throaty chuckle. "And by then you'll likely have grown quite fond of me."

"And if I refuse to cooperate with this scheme of yours?"

Edgington pointed to the man standing in the doorway beside Ben. "This is Dr. Morton. Despite a rather rough exterior, he's a physician of particular talents. We met on the docks in St. Louis, where he had been doing a brisk business tending to the peculiar needs of the local soiled doves. It was, I believe, an unfortunate surgical 'accident' which precipitated his hasty departure. But then, I digress . . .

"I was fascinated to learn," Edgington continued, "that the good doctor has an intimate knowledge of pharmaceuticals. He tells me that with a simple injection, a person can be made to appear to be suffering from the most unusual ailments . . . and through carefully administered doses, can be rendered incapacitated for an indefinite amount of time. Interesting, no?"

Lorena felt her strength waning, and she looked to Ben one last time. His jaw was bruised purple from Hendricks's assault and he was still cradling his head with his hands. Perhaps she was expecting too much of him. What more could even he do in face of these odds?

At that moment the air was rent by a series of bloodcurdling shrieks and whoops that could only have been Indian war cries. Hendricks and Edgington went out onto the porch to investigate and were met by a hail of gunfire. In that instant Ben sprang to life, delivering a blow to Dr. Morton that doubled him over and knocked the pistol from his hand, then another under the chin that felled him.

"This way, quickly!" Ben shouted to Lorena, and ushered her out of the kitchen door to where their horses were waiting for them.

They mounted at once. Only then could Lorena see Broken Hand, who, from his hiding place behind the barn, had constituted the whole of the invading Indian force. He had Hendricks and Edgington pinned down on the front porch. Ben, astride his pony, drew his own rifle from the case hanging on his saddle and began shooting in the direction of the cabin to cover Broken Hand's retreat. By now, though, the trio within had discovered the ruse and were returning the fire.

Broken Hand rode by at a gallop. "Follow him!" Ben shouted to Lorena, and slapped her white horse on the rump.

Lorena leaned forward, clinging to her mount as a keen wind whistled in her ears and her long hair waved out behind her. Broken Hand was riding hard, but she somehow managed to keep pace with him. The crack of gunfire cut the still, winter air again and again as their adversaries took to their horses and pursued them. Lorena, fearing for Ben, turned and breathed a long sigh of relief. He was not far behind her.

At least the rough terrain ahead was in their

favor, she thought. Edgington and his men could not possibly know the lay of this land as well as Ben Thorne and Broken Hand.

Their pace was slowed as the ground beneath them grew more treacherous. Following the twisting paths that wound through the rock-cut ravines, they climbed high into the foothills, putting some distance between themselves and their pursuers. Finally, after more than an hour's ride, they had reached the shelter of the pine forest.

Broken Hand dismounted. "I knew even as I rode into Laramie with Thorne's message that there would be trouble," he said.

"It's fortunate for us that you followed them," Lorena replied. "Thank you."

"We will rest here for a time," he said and with rifle in hand, went off to scout the area.

Lorena dismounted as Ben rode up. He seemed to be resting on the saddlehorn and favoring one side. She thought he was exhausted from their ordeal, until he drew nearer and she spotted a wide circle of blood staining a shoulder of his buckskin jacket.

"Ben, you're hurt!" she cried, running to him.

His skin was ashen and his eyes glazed as he battled for the strength to maintain his seat. When she reached out to him, he let her help him down from the saddle. Leaning on her for support, he took a few steps then collapsed into a snowbank.

"Broken Hand!" Lorena called. "Come quickly!"

Ben lay unmoving, facedown, in the snow. With her heart beating a frenzied rhythm, Lorena struggled with his heavy limbs to remove his jacket so she might examine the wound. Using his knife, she cut away a section of the bloodied flannel shirt from his back, then used a clean piece of fabric torn from the hem of her petticoat to wipe the wound clean.

Her hands were shaking as she probed the torn flesh. He'd lost so much blood that she wondered how he'd found the strength to ride at all.

"He was hit behind the left shoulder," she explained to Broken Hand, who'd returned and was resting on his haunches opposite Ben. "The bullet's lodged there, I can feel it. It's likely glanced the bone, and he's lost a lot of blood."

The Indian nodded solemnly. "We cannot stay here," he told her. "The big man with them is a tracker; they are not far behind us even now."

Lorena's eyes misted, and she fought to hold back the tears. It was her fault that Ben was hurt, she thought. If she'd only agreed to go back with Edgington, Ben would not be lying there so pale and still, his blood making a red pool beneath him in the snow. "But we must do something about that bullet," she protested, "and I doubt that he can even ride."

Ben's eyelids fluttered. It was the first indication that he was still conscious. "Just bandage me up," he said. "I can ride."

Gathering together what remained of her own strength, Lorena took a breath and turned to Broken Hand. "We'll be ready to go in ten minutes. Keep an eye out for Edgington."

When he was gone once more, Lorena stepped out of her petticoat, proceeding to tear what remained of it into long strips, using them to staunch the flow of blood and to bind Ben's arm close to his body.

"I'm sorry," she said to him over and over again, "so sorry."

Ben did not reply. He needed to concentrate all of his energies, it seemed, upon the task ahead. When she had finished, Lorena managed to raise him up a bit in order to slip his buckskin jacket over one arm, and using the long rawhide fringes that hung from it, she tied the empty sleeve firmly across his body. She was just helping him to his feet when Broken Hand rejoined them.

"Are you certain that you can do this, my friend?" he asked Ben. "We can stay and fight them here."

"No," Ben replied, perspiration beading his brow. "I can't shoot if I can't see straight. Let's get out of here while we've still got the chance. Just find a place for me to rest—for a few hours, at least—and I'll be fine."

But he needed more than rest—Lorena could see that. He needed a doctor, and as she well knew, there wasn't a doctor to be had within a hundred miles.

As she and the Indian helped Ben into his saddle, Lorena said, "There is a place, not far from here—the Cheyenne call it their sacred medicine spring. The waters there have the most amazing healing properties."

"That's only superstition," Ben said impatiently, his harsh breathing evidence of his pain.

"I have heard of such a place," Broken Hand replied, ignoring Ben's comment, "but where it might be in these mountains, I cannot say."

"I have been there, and I can find it again," Lorena insisted. "I know I can. We must first ride past the old Cheyenne hunting camp and through the canyon that twists back upon itself like a snake. Even Edgington's tracker won't be able to follow us through that maze."

Broken Hand nodded his assent and mounted his pony, while Lorena put Ben's reins in his one good hand and then rummaged through his saddlebag, finally drawing out the pistol she knew he carried. As she checked the chambers for bullets, the Indian's eyes went wide. "There is no need—" he said to her anxiously, as though he thought it unwise for her to be armed.

"Don't worry about her," Ben told him.

"She may look harmless enough, but she's a crack shot. I can vouch for that."

They set out for the medicine spring with Lorena leading the way and Broken Hand watching the trail behind them for any sign of Edgington.

They rode hard across the rough terrain for much of that afternoon, and by evening's approach Lorena was confident that they had lost their pursuers. Ben was slumped low in the saddle, though, and she was relieved to at last see the wispy wreath of fog that told her their destination was at hand.

Broken Hand decided that they should camp that night in a shallow cave he'd discovered at the edge of the secluded glade near the spring Lorena had spoken about. They settled in for the night, and while Ben lay on a bed of blankets, tossing feverishly, the Indian built a fire near the mouth of the cave and Lorena went after the parfleches Blue Elk had sent her along with her horse. She was pleased to find that one of them was a medicine bag containing many of the Indian remedies he'd taught her to use. But she also took the flask of whiskey she'd seen earlier in Ben's saddlebag, for it would come in handy as an anesthetic.

When she returned to the cave, Broken Hand went out, anxious to see for himself the mysterious spring. Lorena began at once to minister to Ben.

"Lorena?" he said as she bent over him. His voice was barely a whisper.

"Drink this," she instructed, offering him a sip from the whiskey flask.

Ben obliged, and Lorena began at once to remove the bandages and the remains of his blood-soaked shirt. Too much time had been wasted already; he was perilously weak. She worked with efficiency, but also with a gentle hand, for each time he winced, it was as if she could feel the pain herself.

"You'll have to turn over, if you can manage," she told him. "That bullet's got to come out."

The deep creases in Ben's brow eased after he'd had a few more sips from the flask. Then Lorena carefully helped him to roll onto his stomach. Removing the remainder of the bandages, she could see the jagged hole where the bullet had pierced his flesh, near the left shoulder blade.

Lorena cleaned the wound as best she could and then probed with a cautious touch, feeling for the bullet. It had not worked itself much deeper, where it might have done more damage; she was thankful for that at least. She reached then for Ben's knife, but only when she held it in her hand did she stop to consider that although she'd heard this procedure described, she had never seen it done.

She knew that she had no choice but to try—Ben's life depended upon it—and so she doused the sharp blade with some of the whiskey and struggled to ignore the whirling in her brain that threatened to render her useless. She was angry with herself for her weakness. She had seen worse than this when she'd worked in the hospital during the war, and never once lost her calm. But then, she reasoned, she'd never before been in love with the patient.

"Not that I doubt your talents as a surgeon, Lorena," Ben said, seeming to have regained some of his vigor, "but hand me the bottle, will you?"

Lorena obliged him. The pressure of a hand on her shoulder made her gasp, but she discovered soon enough that it was only Broken Hand.

"You have done well, Miss Mackenzie," he said as he took the knife from her, "but it is better that I should do this."

Lorena had to admit that she was relieved. Her hands were still trembling as she used water from the canteen to wet one of the clean rags she'd torn from her petticoat and began to mop Ben's brow.

Broken Hand, meanwhile, had bent on one knee by the campfire and passed the knife blade through the flame. When he returned, he gave Lorena a short, sturdy stick from which the bark had been stripped.

She guessed what it was for and held it out to Ben, instructing him to clench it between his teeth. He reached up and gently touched her face before taking it from her. "Go and sit by the fire, Lorena," he said, "or take a walk."

But she shook her head, determined not to leave him, and took up his hand as Broken Hand set to work. Sitting astride Ben's broad back to keep him still, the Indian proceeded, with great care, to dig out the bullet.

There was nothing quite so distressing, Lorena soon discovered, as standing by helplessly while someone for whom you cared deeply was suffering. As the Indian probed the wound, Ben squeezed Lorena's hand so tightly she feared her bones would break, yet this very strength in him was a comfort to her somehow. Ben's face contorted in agony and a slick sheen of sweat glistened on each taut muscle. Even the thick cords in his neck stood out as though they'd been fashioned in stone.

He must not die, Lorena told herself. It was the first time she'd even allowed the thought of death to surface, but as she looked now upon the man she'd come to think of as impervious to pain, she saw that he was as human as any other and just as vulnerable. Dear God, he *must* not die!

A grunt from Broken Hand indicated that he'd found the bullet at last, and Lorena, who'd been holding her breath, said a silent prayer of thanks.

She was still shaking as she dressed the wound with an ointment made from powdered crowfoot and bandaged it carefully. Mercifully, Ben had fallen unconscious. He needed rest more than anything now.

*   *   *

Days were hard to reckon when one slipped in and out of consciousness. You could open your eyes and see the twilight about you, yet still not know if it were a herald of the morning or portent of the night. And the dreams that haunted these twilights were such vivid things that soon they became indistinguishable from reality. But this, Ben told himself, was surely a dream.

It combined, as dreams were wont to do, elements that had been snatched up from his memories: Lorena, standing there with her hair unbound, wearing that same white doeskin dress she'd worn on the night they'd spent alone in the mountain cabin. And just as before, she was undressing before him.

Ben fancied himself resting on the smooth rocks in the shallows of the medicine spring, with its warm waters churning and bubbling around him, soothing away his pains. All about, wisps of fog hung on the air, obscuring the landscape. But he could see Lorena quite clearly on the opposite side of the pool. She stretched out one long leg and stepped in, moving as gracefully through the water as she had on that day on the trail when he'd come upon her bathing. Foam resting on the surface of the water like fine white lace swirled about Lorena's slender waist as she waded across to him. Rising steam dampened the tendrils of hair framing her face, and crystal beads of

moisture collected on her skin, strung out like
shiny jewels about her throat, across her white
shoulders, between the soft swell of her
breasts. Yes, this was a dream but, oh, such a
pleasant one!

Lorena came near, then, to bathe him with
the healing waters. The tender ministrations
eased the painful throbbing in his shoulder,
but served as well to inflame his desire for her
as her soft hands slid over his charged flesh,
leaving a pleasant trail of warmth wherever
they touched. When Ben could stand no more,
a low groan broke from his parted lips.
"Lorena, please—"

"Hush now, you need to rest," she whispered.

"What I need," he countered, as he reached
out to encircle her waist with his hands, "is
here before me."

He drew her close, and a surge of pleasure
rushed over him as her smooth body twisted
against him in a half-hearted attempt to break
free. But he saw his victory reflected in her
eyes, and when he'd captured her generous
mouth in a kiss that dared her to deny him,
her soft arms wound themselves about his
neck in reply.

He led her to the shallows then, and settling
her upon the wide ledge of rock where he'd
been resting, he proceeded to pay her back in
kind, his callused hands boldly exploring her
silken skin as he bathed her with the healing
waters.

As the clouds of steam enveloped them, their bodies met and melted together, and when Ben could hold back no longer, he spilled himself deep within her. It was the most pleasant of dreams.

After having sheltered for more than three weeks in an abandoned adobe ranch house on the banks of the Sweetwater River, Henry Edgington's patience was worn thin. He paced the dirt floor of the building that was, by his standards, little more than a filthy hovel, and wondered at his ill fortune. What had seemed at the start an easy solution to his financial woes had turned into a debacle of grand proportion, and here he was trapped in the middle, having gone too far to turn back. Damn Lorena Mackenzie! He swore he'd make her pay for all the trouble she'd caused him, and the fierce hatred burgeoning in him only served to fuel his determination to find her and carry out the threat.

The door flew open and the brisk wind swept into the far corners of the room as Hendricks and Morton came in. Without a word they went to the hearth to warm their hands. Hendricks produced a wooden taper which he held in the flame and used to light his pipe.

"Well?" Edgington demanded impatiently.

"It's a big country," the burly man replied, unruffled.

"I take it that's meant to signify that you've not found them, then."

Hendricks took a long draw on his pipe and shook his head, but it was Morton who replied. "They could be anywhere in the whole of the territory by now. Maybe they ran across a tribe of hostiles and lost their scalps, or got themselves lost in the high country."

"Not likely," Edgington replied. "Thorne and the Indian are familiar with the land hereabouts."

"Well then," Hendricks put in, "maybe they decided to cut and run for Californy and help themselves to that fortune you been tellin' us so much about."

Edgington considered this. It was a likely possibility, he had to admit, even if it had been proposed by the otherwise thick-witted Hendricks. Undoubtedly, from Lorena Mackenzie's point of view, it would be the wisest move. If she went to San Francisco, she could seek out Tyler Sanderson and expose Edgington as an unscrupulous schemer before he could plot against her again.

"Likely as not, though, they'd find the mountain passes still drifted deep in snow," Hendricks went on to say.

Morton spoke up next. "We know that one of them is wounded. We found bloodstains on the snow. I'd be willing to wager that they're holed up somewhere, to let their companion heal while they wait for the thaw."

Edgington was pleased to hear this. "Well, boys," he said as he shrugged on his overcoat, "that's decided it. If you've a mind to remain in my employ, gather together your belongings and let's be on our way."

"And where exactly are we bound?" Morton inquired.

"The nearest stage station," Edgington replied, "to buy ourselves a seat on the first westbound coach. We've business to tend in San Francisco."

Chapter Sixteen

✦✦✦✦

WHEN THE MILD days of spring arrived at last, the crystal waters began to flow down from the mountains, swelling the many rivulets that cut through the valleys below. In no time at all they'd overflowed their banks and inundated the land, leaving a swath of green in their wake.

The change in seasons was not well-received, however, by Ben Thorne. He knelt to pick up a pebble in his free hand, then tossed it into the churning waters of the medicine spring, staring after it long after it had drifted downward and disappeared. The smell of sulfur hung heavy in the air, and as the peculiar odor assailed his nostrils, it conjured vivid remembrances in him. Ben had always considered himself a pragmatic sort, but he believed that this was a magical place, for in the delirium that had gripped him while he was recovering from his wound, he'd dreamed he made love to Lorena here.

"You are well enough to walk today, my friend?" Broken Hand called to him as he approached, carrying his rifle in one hand and the carcass of a fat sage hen in the other.

"I am," Ben replied.

"See what I have brought for our dinner," the Indian said, holding up his prize.

"Lorena will be pleased."

When he'd recovered sufficiently from his injury, Ben had at last been able to see for himself just how well Lorena could adapt to a life in the wilderness. She nursed him tirelessly, while making a comfortable nest for them in the shelter of the cave and improvising meals with whatever meager game Broken Hand was able to scare up, and what was more, she seemed to thrive. Her eyes were bright, her complexion flush with color, and sitting by the campfire each evening, she would talk with Broken Hand and fill the air with her laughter as if she thought this the most idyllic existence. Still, none of it could change what Ben felt he must do.

"The snows have melted," Broken Hand said to him then, as if he'd been reading his thoughts. "You are well enough to travel. What will you do now?"

Again Ben stared into the waters of the spring. "What I must do. Take Lorena to her father's friend in San Francisco."

"And then?"

"She'll have little need for me after that," he told the Indian. "Her father's left her a fortune. She can go anywhere, do anything she likes."

"But if you love her, why do you not ask her to stay? She is happy here, caring for you. Surely even you can see this."

"I will not live off of her money, and I cannot ask her to live without it," Ben retorted, his bitterness plain.

Broken Hand was silent. He could not comprehend Ben's dilemma nor, indeed, how any man could allow such a thing as money to stand in the way of his happiness.

"And you, my friend?" Ben asked him, in such a way as to apologize for his previous tone. "Will you go with us to California?"

Broken Hand shook his head. "I have drifted for too long like a leaf upon the waters. The time has come for me to make a place for myself . . . among my own people."

"Even if it means you must fight alongside your people against the Army?"

Broken Hand nodded solemnly. "I have learned many things in the years I have spent among the white man, but it is you, Ben Thorne, and this woman of yours, who have made me see that the man who wanders will come to nothing. Perhaps one day you will see that for yourself."

"I wish you well, my friend," Ben told him, ignoring the Indian's final remark.

"Come," Broken Hand said. "We will enjoy one last meal together."

Lorena resettled herself into her allotted fifteen inches of space on the upholstered seat of the stagecoach and shut her eyes in a futile attempt at sleep. She found herself jostled against her fellow passengers time and again as the driver, anxious to keep to his schedule, set his team of fractious mustangs a breakneck pace across the unfriendly terrain.

Nearly twelve hours before, in front of the ticket office in Salt Lake City, Lorena and seven of the other passengers had climbed into the Concord coach—painted bright red, WELLS FARGO & CO. OVERLAND STAGE embossed in gold leaf above the door. Once they'd settled in and introductions were made, they'd chatted excitedly about the journey ahead. For most, it was their first trip to California.

Hannah Wakeford the pretty young woman who occupied the seat beside Lorena, was traveling with her two children: Annabelle, an impish five-year-old, and Jacob, who was eight. They were going to join Hannah's husband, the Reverend Elias Wakeford, who'd been sent by his ministry to establish a church in the small, northern California town of Redmond.

There were two downy-faced young gentlemen from Ohio, who were just out of school by the looks of them. They had dressed for the occasion in woolen shirts, canvas trousers, and wide-brimmed felt hats, and it was apparent that much of their knowledge of the West had been gotten out of dime novels. By their own admission they had come out in search of adventure, with no particular destination in mind.

And lastly, seated on the opposite side of the coach, was Mr. Horace Acton, a portly, elderly gentleman with long, white sidewhiskers, who'd explained that he was traveling to Sacramento on business. Beside him sat his associate, a fidgety, bespectacled little man.

Only one of the passengers had chosen to take his seat on the roof, and Lorena thought this particularly significant. It was Ben Thorne, who seemed determined to deep his distance from her.

All the while he'd been on the mend, she had hoped he would declare himself. But he had not, and she was too proud to beg for his favor. From his recent behavior, she'd concluded that his only interest now was in seeing her safely into the hands of her father's partner, and it was a bitter pill for her to swallow, especially now that she knew for certain she was carrying his child.

On the seat beside her mother, little Annabelle began to fuss and then set up a wail, jarring the already-rattled nerves of those poor souls within the coach. They'd been pressed tightly together for hours, shoulder-to-shoulder, knee-to-knee, their feet resting upon the sacks of mail that had been crammed into any available space, and exhaustion had come to replace their initial excitement.

"Hush, dear," Hannah told her daughter. "You must try and get some sleep."

"Can't sleep," came the child's reply. "Injuns will get me. Jacob says so."

Yet in his space upon the middle bench, Jacob had sidled up next to one of the Ohio boys and was fast asleep himself, presenting a deceptively angelic picture.

Hannah Wakeford wore an exasperated expression, for try as she might, she was unable to persuade her daughter to stop whimpering. Though Lorena was tired herself, she realized that with the jouncing of the coach and the thoughts preying on her mind, she was not likely to be able to sleep, and so she called to the child. "Come sit on my knee, Annabelle."

Anxious for change of any sort, the child obliged. Lorena stroked her chestnut curls. "Here now," she said, "I'll move aside the curtain. You can look out and tell me if you see any Indians."

The waxing moon spilt its bright blue light over the desolate landscape, casting long shadows that made each rock and shrub take on an ominous shape. Perhaps this was not such a wise idea, after all, Lorena decided, and let the curtain drop back.

"I'll tell you what," she said to the child, taking another tack. "You rest a bit, and I'll watch for Indians."

Annabelle settled her head against Lorena's shoulder, but then seemed to reconsider. "You must keep a careful watch, miss. They're all sneaky devils, Jacob says."

"That just isn't so," Lorena retorted, then lowered her voice when she noticed that most of her companions had drifted off to sleep. "There are good and bad Indians, just the same as any other folk. There are not only warriors among them. They have families . . . children . . ."

"Children?" Annabelle echoed, then quietly considered this as Lorena moved aside the curtain to stare out of the window.

"Do you see those stars up there?" she asked the little girl as she pointed upward.

"Yes," she replied. "It's the Big Dipper. Papa showed them to me once."

"That's right, but did you know that the Indians have a special story they tell their children to explain how those stars got up there?"

"Would you tell it to me, please? It could be like a bedtime story. Papa told me a bedtime story every night back home."

"I suppose I could . . . if I had your promise that you'd try and sleep afterward."

"I promise," Annabelle said at once, "I do."

"Well, it's all about an Indian squaw who could do the most beautiful quillwork—that's sort of like embroidery, you know. She had seven sons, and she made each one of them a suit of white buckskin, decorated with marvelous, colorful designs.

"An enemy nation heard about this talented woman and they wanted her to come and live with them, and one day a band of their warriors came after her. The woman and her sons were very much afraid, all except for the youngest of the brothers, for he had special powers.

"The family ran off to the mountains, to the very top of Cloud Peak, but the enemy braves followed, and soon they caught up with them. With only the cliff's edge before them, the woman and her sons saw that they had nowhere left to run. It was a long way down. If they fell from this spot, they would surely be killed.

"The smallest boy, though, did not tremble like his older brothers. He called for his mother to give him her shawl and when she did, he tossed it into the air and shot it clean through with one of his arrows. This magic arrow made the shawl stretch out until it hung in the sky like an endless blue blanket. Then the youngest brother told them to step off the cliff's edge onto the shawl. They were not afraid now. They did exactly as he told them, and one by one they were all turned into stars, and there they remained. At night you can see them in the sky. Those seven stars are the seven brothers, and the mother is there, too, filling the sky with her beautiful quillwork."

"I like that story," Annabelle said when Lorena's words had died away.

"You must try and sleep now," she said in a soothing voice. "You've promised."

"But how did you learn such an Indian story, miss?"

"I lived with them for a time," Lorena whispered against her ear, a note of wistfulness in her voice.

Lorena noticed too late that Hannah, who sat beside her, was not resting, as she'd thought, but had been listening all the while. Her eyes went wide at Lorena's revelation, but she was too polite to question. Annabelle, however, was intrigued.

"Did you live in a tepee?" she asked.

"Yes," Lorena told her, "I did."

From his place across from them, young Jacob sprung suddenly upright. Somehow Lorena had suspected that he hadn't been asleep.

"Did you hunt buffalo with bow and arrows? And wear feathers in your hair? And put on war paint?"

She laughed at his enthusiasm. "You've been listening to those two, haven't you?" she guessed, tossing her head in the direction of the dozing gentlemen who flanked young Jacob like a pair of bookends.

The boy bowed his head to affirm his guilt. "I'm afraid my life was more tame than all of that," she said. Sensing his disappointment, she added, "If it's adventure you're after, you might talk to Mr. Thorne. He's a proper Westerner."

And so her thoughts had come around to Ben Thorne again. Why she'd come to care so much for him, she could not say. He was brusque and unpolished, a puzzle of a man who never spoke his mind—not at all the sort she'd imagined herself falling in love with. Yet he was exactly what she needed, and there were times she believed he needed her just as much. In the end, though, he'd always pushed her away, and now, at last, she was beginning to accept the fact that she would have to live without him. At least she would have his child, she told herself. It was the one good thing that had come of all this. Closing her eyes in an attempt to erase the memories that flashed unbidden through her mind, she put her arms around the little girl resting on her lap and breathed a long, tremulous sigh.

Chapter Seventeen

✦✦✦✦✦

IT WAS WELL past ten o'clock when the stage pulled into a way station in the midst of the Utah badlands. Ben had passed most of the journey in the seat behind the driver—a bristly-bearded jehu of indistinguishable age— and the Wells Fargo express messenger, a lank young fellow called Jackson, who carried a shotgun across his lap and two revolvers stuck in his belt. There'd been only a modicum of conversation between them, but that suited Ben just fine, since the landscape was new and unfamiliar and his attention had been full upon it.

He took stock of the station as they approached. It was made up of a few meager buildings of rude construction, including the barns where a fresh team of horses resided that would carry them on the next leg of their journey, and a long, low structure where the passengers might find a meal.

When the coach had rocked to a halt, Ben jumped down from his perch, swept the hat from his head and began to beat it against his weathered buckskins, sending up a flurry of dust. Next he stripped the kerchief from his neck and used it to wipe the layer of road dust from his face. This was a God-awful way to travel, but still better by far than cramming himself into the coach with the others and subjecting himself to Lorena's accusing eyes for the whole of the journey.

It was difficult enough for him to let her go, but to have spent these last days at close quarters would have sorely tested his resolve. More than once he'd questioned his own sanity; Lorena Mackenzie was the only woman he'd ever considered sharing a life with, and he was sending her away. It would have been so easy to ask her to stay, but then he was reminded of the fortune awaiting her in San Francisco and of the suitors she would doubtless attract, any one of them more worthy than he. She was still young enough to rebound from this hurt he'd caused her. And, too, he remembered what he'd once said to his father. "There comes a time when, if you truly care for someone, you must put aside what you want to consider what's best for them."

Surely Lorena had come to hate him by now. He'd taken the love she gave to him yet offered nothing in return, and her eyes told him clearly what was in her thoughts: that Ben Thorne only had one use for women. But no matter what the truth might be, no matter what was in his heart, it would be easier for her to leave him in the end, he reckoned, if she went on believing that.

The coach door swung open, and one by one the bleary-eyed travelers stepped out to stretch their legs. When Lorena had still not yet emerged after several minutes, Ben stuck his head into the darkened interior.

She was sitting in the far corner, cradling the little Wakeford girl in her arms and staring blankly into the darkness, her liquid, silver eyes reflecting the moonlight.

"How are you faring?" Ben asked her.

"Well enough," she replied, no hint of emotion in her voice.

"You ought to come out and stretch your legs a bit and get something to eat while you have the chance," he said.

"Hush," Lorena admonished, "you'll wake the child."

Ben was insistent, though, and lifting little Annabelle off of Lorena's lap, he carried her into the waiting arms of her mother, then held out his hand to aid Lorena in alighting. She refused at first, then hesitantly let him help her. But as soon as her feet touched the ground, she left him standing there alone and followed the others into the station house.

Later, as he lingered over his meal of salt pork, cornbread, and coffee, Ben found his eyes drawn again and again across the room, to the opposite end of the long table, where Lorena had situated herself. There was something markedly different about her of late. She looked almost fragile in the lamplight, with dust smudging her pale, translucent skin, and wisps of hair escaping the knot at the nape of her neck.

Little Annabelle had awakened and left her mother's arms to crawl up onto the bench beside Lorena, whom she seemed quite fond of. Lorena smiled and handed her cornbread to the child, smoothing her tousled hair with a gentle hand. "Here's something I've saved just for you," she said.

His fork poised in midair, Ben's eyes shifted from Lorena to the child and back again.

"You must eat," he heard Lorena say, "for we'll soon be on our way again."

Annabelle obliged finally, prompting her mother to shake her head in amazement. "You've a way with the child, Miss Mackenzie," she said. "You'll make a fine mother someday."

These words had an immediate effect on Lorena, whose hand began to shake. The coffee in the tin cup she was holding sloshed over, dousing her dinner plate. Setting down the cup, she rose unsteadily from her place and fled the building, leaving a host of confused souls in her wake and Ben Thorne trailing after.

He followed her across the yard, where the hostlers were hitching the fresh team, and past the stables. When she'd reached the rough-hewn split-rail fence that bordered the station, she suddenly halted in her flight and clung to the rail, her back to him.

"What's wrong, Lorena?" he called to her, walking until he'd closed the distance between them. Taking a firm hold of her shoulders, he turned her to face him and saw that her eyes were filled with tears. "You're crying," he said, as if it surprised him. "What is it? What's wrong?"

Lorena wrenched away and swiped at the tears with the back of her hand. "Leave me alone!" she wailed in halting breaths.

"I want to help," he told her as he turned her to face him once more. He'd never seen her look so vulnerable. Overwhelmed by the need to protect her, he put his arms around her and pressed a kiss against her soft lips.

If Ben had thought somehow that the kiss would soothe her, he was wrong. It had exactly the opposite effect. Lorena dragged herself away from him, and crossing her arms tightly over her chest to control the tremors that now coursed through her, she turned on him. "I don't want your pity. I don't want anything from you. I can get on fine by myself, do you hear!"

Her voice rose, ending on a shrill note. There was something troubling her, that was apparent, but it was something that she did not wish to share, and especially not, it seemed, with him.

Ben stood there, helpless. Lorena was determined to make a stranger out of him, and he could scarcely blame her. He was beginning to see exactly how cold his life would be when she was gone.

After a few minutes she composed herself.

"Please," she entreated, "just leave me alone."

He turned and did as she asked. There was nothing else he could do.

Ben Thorne recalled later that the day had begun with a wicked thunderstorm. It ought to have been warning of things to come. As it was, though, the stagecoach passengers found the chilling wind and rain a welcome change from all they'd suffered the day before, when they'd crossed that part of the Utah desert called the Devil's Playground. Early on, their coach had become mired in the desert sands and they'd had to walk for several miles in order to lighten the load. And for all of the day they'd been plagued by the heat and the sand gnats and enveloped in clouds of choking alkali dust kicked up by the unchecked winds. A rainstorm, by comparison, was a pleasant diversion.

Though he well might have, Thorne did not seek shelter within the coach, even when the storm was at its height. Bundled in his gutta-percha cape, with a wide-brimmed hat pulled low across his face, he weathered what the elements had to offer, just barely managing to keep his seat behind the driver's box as the coach careened at high speed through tortuous mountain passes and twisted upward by way of unpaved, ungraded roads that in some places were only a narrow shelf cut into the mountainside.

Ben had nothing but admiration for the drivers of these rigs, who would each work a twelve-hour shift and then bed down at the next home station, where a new driver came on. Each one seemed as adept as his predecessor at communicating his wishes to the team of six barely-broken mustangs through only the three pairs of reins wrapped in the fingers of his left hand. And it was due to the skills of this particular driver, a wizened old cuss named Bishop, that they had traveled through the storm thus far without mishap.

At last the heavens relented. Just before sundown the weather cleared, leaving the western sky bathed in brilliant orange light, the portent of a pleasant morrow. The coach rumbled on through the twilight, heading for the next station, which was the only haven for miles in the Nevada wilderness.

All of the passengers had settled themselves into a dazed sort of half sleep which was the most that could be hoped for under the circumstances, and so they were doubly startled when the horses took a precipitous slope at full gallop, jerking them awake. Near the bottom of the incline one of the wheels struck a boulder, half buried in the mud and the coach rocked sharply. Teetering on two wheels, it hung in the air for what seemed a long while before gravity finally seized it and it crashed upon its side.

From his seat atop the coach, Ben had seen the disaster in the making and was able to jump free. A bank of soft mud cushioned his fall, and he dragged himself to his feet at once, feeling the pull of bruised muscles but, as far as he could ascertain, nothing more serious than that. Then he remembered Lorena, who was trapped inside with the others, and he cried out to her as he rushed back to the road.

"Lorena!"

There was no reply.

Despite the jarring accident the driver, Mr. Bishop, had not lost his grip on the reins. He'd set about collecting his panicked team, which was protesting noisily and pulling at the traces. Jackson, the express messenger, had narrowly escaped being crushed when the vehicle overturned. He'd been stunned for a moment but picked himself up now, shaking his head in amazement, and went to join Ben, who was frantically attempting to lift up the door of the coach.

"Is anyone hurt?" Jackson called to the passengers.

There was upheaval within. The children were crying, and it was difficult to see what was what because of the tangle of blankets and cushions. From where he stood, Ben could not not see Lorena at all. One by one he and Jackson helped the dazed and bleeding passengers as they emerged, and Ben tried to contain his growing anxiety. Jacob and little Annabelle climbed out of the wreckage, fright-

ened but uninjured. Mr. Acton, the banker
had a gash on his forehead, which his com
panion was attempting to bandage with a
handkerchief, and one of the Ohio boys ap
peared to have broken his leg. When they'd
carried him out, Jackson gave directions for
making a splint.

"We'll need some help down here," Han
nah Wakeford called, still inside the coach

A sudden fear crept over Ben as he re
sponded cautiously. "What is it?"

"I can't seem to rouse Miss Mackenzie. She
may have struck her head."

After handing Mrs. Wakeford up, Ben wen
in after Lorena. Darkness had settled in now
but he could see well enough in the moon
light. His hands were shaking as he reached
out to her. She lay unconscious amid the
wreckage—pale and still. There were no
bruises, no blood. It looked as if she migh
only be sleeping. Ben knelt beside her, check
ing her limbs carefully for broken bones
There did not appear to be any.

"Lorena?" he said to her in a choked voice
"Lorena, can you hear me?"

Ben dared not breathe. His heart hammered
painfully against his chest as the minutes
passed with no response. And then she
stirred. The dark fan of her lashes fluttered
against her white skin, and all at once Ben
found himself looking down into her silver
eyes.

"Ben? What happened?"

"There was an accident. The coach over-turned . . ."

As Lorena tried to raise herself up, she winced in pain and touched a hand to the back of her head. "I struck my head, I think."

"Most likely," Ben replied, breathing a re-lieved sigh. "How are you otherwise?"

"Just fine," she said, leaning on him for support as she got up. "If you could just help me out of here—"

"Easy now," Ben warned. "You're likely to be unsteady on your feet for a while. Let me go up first, and I'll hand you out."

The driver had managed to calm his nervous team, and after all of the passengers and their baggage were settled by the side of the road, those gentlemen who were able set about righting the coach. When this had been ac-complished at last, Mr. Bishop carefully in-spected the damage and then told his passengers that he figured they could "limp along well enough" for a mile or so to the next station, where repairs could be made.

Lorena had ignored her small aches at first, in order to help Hannah tend the two injured men, and she was still not terribly out of sorts as they were all reinstalled in the coach. But as the vehicle lurched forward and swayed into motion, she felt her head reel, and an awful uneasiness possessed her. The knot of pain that had begun in the small of her back now

radiated outward and would no longer be denied. She suspected what was happening to
her, but with a childish sort of logic, she decided that if she shut her eyes and pretended
that nothing was wrong, it would somehow
be so.

It took another half hour to reach the way
station at Jacobsville. When Ben jumped down
and opened the coach door, he could see the
strain written upon the faces of all those
within. The station keeper and a pair of hostlers appeared on the scene in minutes, and
on instructions from the driver, they carried
out the young man with the broken leg. The
others stumbled out, one at a time, and only
then did Ben hear a soft moan from inside the
coach. His attention went at once to Lorena.
She was doubled over, her head resting in the
lap of Mrs. Wakeford, who spoke to her in
soothing tones as she wiped her brow with a
handkerchief.

"Mr. Thorne," Mrs. Wakeford said when
she saw him there, "carry her inside at once."

"What is it?" Ben asked. "What's wrong?
Shall I ride for a doctor?"

"There's no time for that. Be careful now."
It was all she would say.

"Can't you tell me what's wrong with her?"
Ben pleaded as he bundled Lorena into his
arms.

Mrs. Wakeford hurried into the station, as if

she were anxious to avoid his questions. The night air was cool, and Ben was distressed to see the beads of perspiration dotting Lorena's brow. Her skin had an ominous ashen pallor, and he had to admit to himself that she must have suffered some internal injuries that had not been immediately apparent. All of the apprehension he'd felt in the first moments of the accident returned to him in a rush. As he carried her into the station, she was seized by a pain that increased in intensity until each muscle of her slim form was rigid. It abated at last, only to leave her limp and gasping against him.

Once he'd brought her inside, the station keeper's wife directed him to a private bedroom, where she and Mrs. Wakeford took charge, tending Lorena behind a closed door and leaving Ben to pace outside, helpless.

He tried to avail himself of the meal that was offered, but could only manage a cup of coffee. Some of the others had bedded down on the dirt floor of the cabin, wrapping themselves up in blankets, but for Ben sleep was out of the question. He took himself outside, where the sounds of the station crew making repairs on the coach drowned out the faint cries emanating from behind that closed door.

Seated outside on the ground with his back propped against the rough wall and his head resting on his bent knees, Ben slept for a time. It was nearly sunrise when the cabin door opened, awakening him. Mrs. Wakeford, wearing an apron, and with her sleeves rolled to the elbow, swept past him. He dragged himself to his feet, watching as she tossed a basin of dirty water into the bushes and then started back. When she did not acknowledge his presence, he put himself in front of the door.

"Can you tell me what's happened to Miss Mackenzie?" he asked, swiping a hand across his weary brow. "She seemed to be fine, and then all at once . . ."

Hannah Wakeford shuffled her feet like a shy maid and bit down on her lip. She would not meet his eyes, would not reply.

"Tell me how she's faring, at least," Ben pleaded.

"Well . . . You are her friend, aren't you?" she said, as if she'd decided to confide in him, though her gaze was still focused on the toes of her shoes. "She's resting now. It is, I suppose, for the best."

"What?"

Ben could not understand Mrs. Wakeford's peculiar behavior.

"I can understand, after hearing that she'd been captured and was living among the Indians, how such an unfortunate circumstance might have come about—" she went on.

Ben's patience was stretched to the limit. "What is it, exactly, that you're trying to say, ma'am?"

"She's lost a baby," Mrs. Wakeford replied, then turned and went back into the cabin.

Ben stared after her, stunned. Now he could

see why Hannah Wakeford had had such difficulty. She assumed that since Lorena had been a prisoner of the Indians, the child she was carrying was a product of an awful violation. Ben knew otherwise, though. He suddenly realized that the beautiful dream he thought he'd had while recovering at the medicine spring had been much more than a dream, and the child Lorena was carrying and had evidently meant to keep secret from him . . . had been his.

Ben wanted to go to her, to comfort her and set things right, but he knew he must not. Regardless of what he wanted, he was now even more convinced that a better life awaited Lorena with her guardian in San Francisco. Frustration welled in him and he slammed his fist again and again against the log wall of the cabin.

Chapter Eighteen
♦ ♦ ♦ ♦

TWO DECADES HAD passed since the great gold rush that turned the quiet coastal town of San Francisco into the Babylon of the West. Will Mackenzie's missives of that time had called the city "an exhilarating town, wild and unbridled, full of the frenzied activity and people whose dreams stretch as high as the stars."

Little wonder that Lorena should be disappointed to find, upon her arrival in the spring of 1868, a sedate metropolis with broad avenues and square buildings that was home to nearly 150,000 people. The harbor was a forest of bare masts, and there were massive warehouses laid out along the docks to service the many ships at anchor. On higher ground were residences of fine construction, similar to those east of the Mississippi. In fact, the only thing that made this city different from any of those Lorena had known back East was that it seemed to have been constructed on its spot in spite of the geography. Regardless of the steep hills in their path, the streets of the city climbed upward past houses clinging to the hillside in neat rows. It was picturesque, but still not enough to lift Lorena's spirits.

She sat in silence beside Ben Thorne in the cab, clutching the wilted yellow spike of a wildflower that little Annabelle had presented to her yesterday when they'd said their goodbyes at the stage station in Sacramento. The Reverend Wakeford had been there to meet his family, his eyes bright with tears, and the sight of their joyful reunion had affected Lorena more than she could have imagined it would. She had begun to feel a great emptiness within herself these past few days and swore that, if she could, she would gladly trade every penny of her father's fortune for such happiness as the Wakefords enjoyed. It was a childish wish, Lorena well knew, and one that could never come true, for the man whom she loved did not love her. He'd all but admitted as much.

Since the night of the stage accident nearly two weeks ago, Lorena had spoken nary a word to Ben. He'd been solicitous enough as she was recovering, it was true, but even after he'd learned about her miscarriage, he hadn't said a word to her about it, though he must surely have realized that the child had been his. He was, it seemed, as determined as ever to take her to San Francisco, where he could be rid of her for good.

It was pride that finally decided Lorena's course. She would not become a pathetic, pining creature, not on account of any man, and so for the remainder of the journey she was determined to harden her heart against him. She directed all of the hurt and anger that she felt at Ben. She even came to hold him responsible for the loss of her child, reasoning that it was he who insisted that she make this trip. Soon, she told herself, very soon, she would come to hate him, and then it would be so much easier to watch him leave.

The home belonging to Tyler Sanderson was on Harrison Street, a prestigious Rincon Hill address. It was a brownstone building of Italianate design, with large windows and an ornate pediment over the door. Ben let out a low whistle as he helped Lorena alight from the cab.

"Mighty fancy digs," the cabbie called down. "You sure you got the right address, mister?"

Lorena could see how he might imagine they'd made some mistake. With Ben in his buckskins and her wearing a faded, rose-colored calico she'd borrowed from Virginia's trunk, the pair did not seem at all suited to this particular neighborhood. Nevertheless, Ben paid the man off, and offering Lorena his arm, escorted her up the stairs.

"Would you like me to wait?" he asked her as they stood before the door.

There was a lump in Lorena's throat that threatened to choke her. She shook her head vigorously as she fought to find her voice, and then the angry words tumbled out. "Unless you're expecting payment for my safe delivery."

But he paid her no mind. "I'll be staying at the Fulton Hotel for a day or so . . . if you should need anything."

Before she realized what he was about, he'd bent over her and pressed a warm kiss against her lips. "Have a good life, Lorena," he said softly.

She turned away so that he would not see her tears, and drew a ragged breath as she knocked on the door. Almost at once, a red-haired maid in a starched white cap and apron appeared.

"Might I help you?" the girl asked warily as she spied the carpetbag at Lorena's feet.

Lorena knew that she was being unfavorably assessed, but she drew herself up nonetheless with a proud tilt to her head. She fully intended to act like a lady, even if she no longer looked the part.

"This is the home of Mr. Tyler Sanderson?"

"It is," the girl replied, and Lorena detected the hint of a brogue, "but I'm afraid we're not hirin' at the moment."

The corners of Lorena's mouth turned up and dimpled. She could not fault the girl for assuming she'd come in search of a position. Indeed, she must have looked a sight in her worn calico, with her hair escaping its pins and her face smudged with dust from her travels. "I am Lorena Mackenzie," she explained. "Mr. Sanderson will be acquainted with the name, if you would be kind enough to tell him that I'm here."

After thinking on it, the girl swung wide the door, allowing Lorena into the foyer. She instructed her to wait for a moment and then disappeared down the corridor that cut through the center of the house.

Lorena dropped her carpetbag at her feet and turned anxiously to push aside the draperies and peer out of one of the tall windows that flanked the door, hoping, though she would never admit to it, that she might catch a final glimpse of Ben Thorne. But he was already gone.

With a sigh, she looked up to admire the chandelier of crystal teardrops hanging from the ceiling high above. There was a wide stairway to her right that curved around again and again, winding upward for at least two flights more. Will Mackenzie's partner had done well for himself, it seemed.

The maid returned promptly with an elegant woman trailing behind her. She was dressed in a fashionable gown of crimson faille, her black hair pinned up in a neat coil. Lorena guessed by her features that she was of Spanish blood, and her accent confirmed this.

"You are Miss Mackenzie?" she asked, wearing a pleasant expression, as though she had not even noticed Lorena's bedraggled appearance.

"I am."

The woman put out her hand and smiled warmly. "What a surprise this is! I am Mariella Sanderson. My husband is away on business, I'm afraid. Of course, he has mentioned you. He and your father were very good friends. If he had known that you were coming to visit us, I am certain he would have postponed this trip."

"I'm sorry that I did not send word, but I have been . . . traveling, and my decision to come to San Francisco was rather sudden."

Lorena was disappointed. Only now did she realize how much she had looked forward to this meeting with Sanderson. There was a longing within her to find a place for herself, and she'd thought that by talking with Sanderson and discovering what had made her father come to love this city, perhaps she, too, would feel the desire to make a home here. She had hoped that Tyler Sanderson would be a garrulous sort who'd enjoy reminiscing with her about his wilder days. He was the only one who could fill in the details of those lost years of her father's life, years she knew of only through the few letters he'd sent. "If you can tell me when he is expected to return," she said, "I can make arrangements to come back."

"No, my dear. You will stay here with us until he returns," Mrs. Sanderson told her, laying a graceful hand upon Lorena's arm. "My husband would never forgive me if I did not insist that you stay." She turned then to her maid. "Emily, take Miss Mackenzie's bag upstairs and see that one of the guest rooms is made ready, and then tell Rose that she may serve tea in the breakfast room."

Lorena was overwhelmed by her generosity. Staring down at the creases in her skirt, she wished now that she'd thought to take a room for the night somewhere and cleaned up a bit before she'd appeared on Sanderson's doorstep, looking like a kitchen maid. But it was too late for that.

"I should like to tidy up first, if I could," she requested.

"Ah, si. I forget that you have been traveling," Mrs. Sanderson replied, and after some consideration added, "Perhaps you would like to rest for a while after your journey?"

Lorena nodded, feeling grateful toward her hostess.

"Emily?" Mrs. Sanderson called to the maid, who had already climbed halfway up the stairs. "Please take Miss Mackenzie up with you. See that a bath is drawn for her, and help her with whatever else she might need. I shall speak to Rose myself about the luncheon arrangements."

"Yes, ma'am," the girl replied.

"Go along now," Mrs. Sanderson told Lorena, "rest for a while, and I shall send for you when our meal has been prepared."

Lorena leaned back in the tub, which had been set up near the hearth, closed her eyes and let the warm water wash over her. Stagecoach travel had not allowed her the luxury of a bath, and she intended to fully enjoy every minute of this one. As she relaxed, she found herself concentrating on the rhythmic sound of Emily's footsteps as she scurried back and forth across the room, pouring another pitcher of hot water into the tub, fetching a cake of scented soap and towels, unpacking the carpetbag that contained all of Lorena's things—

and grumbling all the while under her breath about the extra work she'd likely have and all on account of an unexpected houseguest. When the room grew suddenly quiet, Lorena lifted one eyelid, consumed by curiosity.

The girl had laid out Lorena's only change of clothes—a blue riding skirt and plain cambric basque—in neat fashion across the bed and was standing there, with Lorena's doeskin Indian dress clutched in her hands.

"This is yours, miss?" she asked when she found her voice.

Lorena nodded as she made a grab for the sponge bobbing on the water at the far end of the tub.

"Shall I . . . dispose of it for you?"

"No," Lorena decided. "I'll keep it, I think, as a souvenir of my Western adventures."

Emily's eyes went wide as she reflected on exactly what sort of adventures her employer's unusual houseguest might have experienced. Lorena knew that keeping the dress was, perhaps, not the wisest decision she could have made, but she was determined to do so regardless. As she settled back in the tub, a smile twisted on her lips as she realized that by tomorrow morning she would doubtless be the object of intense speculation among those residing belowstairs in the Sanderson household. Once, perhaps, she might have been concerned. Now she was only amused.

"If you need anything, miss," Emily said, "you need only to ring."

Lorena nodded, and as the warm water relaxed her, she let her eyelids slip down again. The sound of Emily's retreating footsteps filled the room, followed by the sound of the door being pulled closed. A few seconds later, though, that same door creaked open.

Lorena imagined that Emily must have returned, but when she looked up, there on the threshold was a small boy, no more than five years old. He was dressed in a jacket of dark blue, with matching knee pants and white linen stockings, and he seemed fully as surprised to see Lorena as she was to see him. "And who might you be?" she called to him.

The boy laid a finger across his lips, pulled the door closed behind him, and went to hide himself behind the window hangings, apparently unimpressed by Lorena's deshabille. After a time he poked out his head and said in a whisper, "I am Edouardo Luis Sanderson. Are you a friend of Mama's?"

He was a dark-haired little moppet with expressive dark eyes fringed by long lashes, and Lorena was enchanted with him at once. "Actually, it is your father and mine who were friends. My name is Lorena Mackenzie. Please forgive me for not rising to greet you, Señorito Sanderson."

"You may call me Luis," he said to her, then ducked back behind the draperies.

There was a commotion somewhere down the hall; frenzied footsteps and the slamming of doors. A woman shouted the boy's name, and this was followed by a flurry of excited phrases, all in Spanish. Apparently someone had detected the young master's escape from the nursery.

"Luis?" Lorena called to him.

He peered out from his hiding place, eyes wide. "You won't tell on me, will you?"

"I don't wish to spoil your game, but you can't stay in here hiding forever, you know, or I'll catch my death sitting here in this tub."

Luis came out then, sheepishly scuffing the toe of his shoe on the carpet. "I borrowed Mama's china bowl to share my milk with the cat, but it fell off the table and broke. I hid the pieces at the bottom of my bureau drawer. Anna must have found them, I think."

"Anna is your nurse?" Lorena guessed.

Luis nodded and expelled a long sigh. "I suppose I must do as Papa says and take my punishment like a man."

Lorena agreed, then covered her mouth to hide her amusement at the child's sober mien.

"Adios, Señorita Mackenzie."

Drawing himself up, his little chin held high, Edouardo Luis Sanderson crossed the room and marched back out into the hall to meet his fate.

Lorena noticed, as she followed the maid into the dining room, that the long table had three places set upon it. She half expected to see Luis lurking somewhere about, but there was instead a tall blond gentleman standing near the sideboard who, Lorena surmised, must be the other luncheon guest.

Mariella swept forward and took her by the arm. "You look well rested, my dear. Come and sit."

She took her place at the head of the table and motioned Lorena to sit on her right. The gentleman took the chair opposite, after the ladies were seated, and there was an awkward silence before Mariella had settled herself finally and rung the bell on the table to signal the servants.

"This is Mr. Peter Davis," she said to Lorena at last. "He is my husband's attorney and a close friend of our family. And, Mr. Davis, this is Miss Lorena Mackenzie. You were acquainted with her father, I believe."

The statement caught Lorena's attention at once. "You knew my father, Mr. Davis?"

The man pulled on one corner of his moustache. "I did," he replied.

"I am pleased to hear it," she replied, and before she realized it, she was chattering on. No doubt it was nerves. "So much of my father's life in California remains a mystery to me. I have his letters, of course, but Papa never was one to go on about himself. I'm sure that his first years here must have been exciting ones, though, and I'd appreciate anything you could tell me about him."

Just then a maid brought in a large tureen of soup, and it served to effectively distract them

all before Davis could reply. Lorena did not
miss, though, the meaningful looks passed
between him and Mariella. She had begun to
suspect that there was far more going on in
the Sanderson household than was plain to
the eye.

Though there was a surprising dearth of
conversation to accompany the meal, Lorena
did not mind, for she had not been served
such elegant fare in a very long time and she
was able to concentrate fully upon her plate.
After lunch Mariella excused herself so she
might have a visit with her son, and Mr. Davis
offered to show Lorena the garden.

Past the pair of French windows at the rear
of the house there was a flagstoned courtyard
with a fountain at its center, and this was
flanked by a pair of wrought-iron benches.
Beyond, the garden was a luxuriant tangle of
boughs, hung heavy with fragrant and exotic
blossoms. It was hemmed in on either side by
a high stone wall, and a mass of thorny brambles defended its outer reaches to the rear.

Lorena sat herself down upon one of the
benches, staring at her hands as she smoothed
the wrinkles from the blue riding skirt. She
knew that Mr. Davis was studying her, wondering at this plain, young miss who claimed
to be Will Mackenzie's daughter. She had
sensed the uneasiness in the house from the
first. Could that be the reason? Could it be
that these people doubted her identity?

Lorena could tell at once that Peter Davis

was a cautious man. "What brings you to San Francisco, Miss Mackenzie?" he began, as he paced a length of the flagstone walk.

She knew that he was trying to draw her out, but she had not the patience to play games. "What is it, exactly, that you wish to hear, Mr. Davis?" she asked.

"Shall we be frank? I handled Will Mackenzie's legal matters for him," Davis admitted, "drew up all of his papers—I corresponded with Harrison Gilmore for many years. Shortly before his death he wrote me that his niece had run off to Montana to teach school."

Lorena sighed. "I never made it quite that far. I stopped at Fort Reno to visit my friend, Brevet Major Charles Ackerman," she explained, "and was taken hostage by the Cheyenne. Is that the story you wished to hear, Mr. Davis? I decided that I wasn't meant to teach school, after all, and as there was nothing for me in New York, and I could scarcely remain where I was . . . Tyler Sanderson was my father's partner, and my father trusted him enough to leave my inheritance in his hands. I suppose I thought that I could trust him as well."

"And so you can, Miss Mackenzie," Davis said as he sat down beside her. "Forgive me if my manner has offended you, but I had to be certain that you were truly who you purport to be. Your reply confirms it."

"Then Mr. Sanderson has known of my whereabouts all along?" Lorena asked, incredulous.

"As soon as he received word from your uncle that you'd left New York, he sent one of his men to Virginia City. The man discovered that you'd never arrived and went on to investigate. When Mr. Sanderson learned that you'd been abducted by Indians, he instructed his man to continue with the search, but we've heard nothing since.

"Rest assured, Miss Mackenzie, word of your arrival will be sent to him before the day is out," he went on to explain, "but I have full authority to act on his behalf in his absence. You will, of course, remain as a guest in this house. I understand that you arrived with very little in the way of personal belongings. Arrangements will be made at once to have a seamstress at your disposal, and a personal maid will be engaged as soon as it can be done. If there is anything else you require, you have only to ask. I shall authorize the staff to see to all of your needs."

Lorena was left speechless. As Mr. Davis went through each item, detailing the secure and pampered existence she could now expect, it was as if Lorena could feel the cocoon that was her old way of life folding around her once more. Rather than be comforted by this, though, it left her fearful and full of the sick feeling that she was being smothered.

Chapter Nineteen

✦ ✦ ✦ ✦ ✦

"Good morning, miss!" a cheery voice called.

Lorena opened her eyes just as the draperies were opened. The brilliant sunlight blinded her for a moment, and raising herself up on one elbow, she found that she had to think hard to remember where she was.

She'd been dreaming again of Wind River . . . and Ben Thorne, and so even when Jane opened the windows to let in the sweet, spring breeze, Lorena still could not shake her melancholy air.

"I thought you'd like to have a breakfast tray this morning," the maid said, smoothing out the bedclothes then arranging the pillows behind Lorena's back. "Seein' as how the seamstress will be here bright and early this morning for your final fittings."

"Thank you, Jane," Lorena replied as the girl set the meal before her.

There was a veritable feast crowded onto the tray: poached eggs and bacon, oatmeal, toast with marmalade, sliced oranges, strawberries in cream . . . but Lorena reached only for the cup of black coffee as she unfolded the newspaper. she scanned the pages in an absent manner, and was blowing at the curl of steam hovering over her cup when an item caught her eye.

In order to negotiate a peaceful settlement to the recent hostilities initiated against the United States Army by the combined forces of the Sioux and Cheyenne tribes under Chief Red Cloud, the United States government has decided to immediately abandon those outposts situated along the Bozeman Trail in the newly established Wyoming Territory. . . .

As she read the news, Lorena was stunned. She would never have imagined the day would come when the U.S. Government would yield to Indian demands, yet that was exactly what this action signified. For the first time in many months she thought about Blue Elk, and she smiled. He and his people had their victory at last, it seemed; the white men had been driven from the Black Hills and the Powder River country.

Lorena thought, too, of her friend Sarah Rawlins, who'd come to make a home at Fort Reno with her husband, Jed. This news meant they, and countless other families, would be uprooted, packed up and transferred to yet another Army outpost in yet another God-forsaken spot, and no doubt more pieces of Sarah's precious china service would be sacrificed in these travels.

It was hard to think on all of this and not be struck by the bitter realization that Charles Ackerman had made the ultimate sacrifice, and all for naught. The Army had taken a kind, sweet young boy and made of him a hard-bitten soldier who obeyed every order without question and who had, in the end, defended with his very life a parcel of land the government would now relinquish with the stroke of a pen.

Disquieted, Lorena tossed the newspaper onto the quilt and set down her empty cup. "Take all of this away, please, Jane," she said, waving her hand at the tray. "I can't eat this morning."

"My, but you're fretful, Miss Lorena," Jane observed, and did as she was bade. "It's all on account of the party the missus has planned for this evening, I'll wager. It would have been better if you'd had a mite more time to settle in before they begin paradin' you before the neighbors."

"I've been here more than a week now," Lorena admonished the girl, "and Mr. Davis tells me that tonight's party is a celebration of Mr. Sanderson's latest business success. Though I don't know all of the details, it was planned some time ago and was certainly not meant as a means of 'parading me before the neighbors.' "

"Still and all, you'll be the center of attention. You mark my words, miss."

On that prophetic note Jane returned to the kitchen with the breakfast tray. Lorena disentangled herself from the bedclothes and began to pace before the windows, hoping it might help to expend some of her restless energy.

For days now she'd been confined to this house, and she was growing more fretful. Her every need was anticipated, her every wish indulged, it was true, but she still felt a prisoner here. And her uneasiness was compounded by the fact that she had yet to meet her father's partner, Tyler Sanderson. Each day she woke expecting to find that he'd returned, only to be disappointed. Surely, she told herself, he would endeavor to return for this evening's celebration, and at the very first opportunity, she would speak to him.

Lorena had had time in these past days to reflect upon a good many things, and there was one thing that she had come to see quite clearly. The life she had been raised to was no longer the life that she wanted for herself. Now she had only to consider how she would explain this to Tyler Sanderson, to make him understand that the experiences she'd had in coming West had changed her irrevocably. She was not a child, and regardless of what her father's will might stipulate, she could no longer live the sheltered and stultifying existence that was expected of a privileged young lady. She wanted her freedom.

As she thought on it, Lorena decided that she'd been feeling far too sorry for herself. She was as much responsible for the state her life was in as anyone. She had shown up on the Sanderson doorstep looking like an orphaned waif; was it any wonder she was treated as one? She could see now that she had *allowed* herself to be overwhelmed by all of this luxury, thinking that somehow it would heal the pain she'd been living with since the day Ben Thorne went out of her life. It had not.

Lorena determined to put control of her life back into her own hands. With a firm set to her jaw, she decided that today she was going to walk the streets of San Francisco and see the sights. She shed her nightgown and fetched the clean linen Jane had laid out for her, but she'd done no more than pull on her chemise and drawers before her maid reappeared to chastise her.

"Here now, let me help you with that, Miss Lorena. You'll have an awful time of it fastening them ribbons, and how'd you ever expect to lace that corset all on your own?"

"Really, Jane, I'm not completely helpless. I thought I'd hurry and dress so that I could go out for a walk—"

The girl's brow furrowed. "Oh no, miss, that'll never do. There's no time for such things today, and whatever would we do if you should freckle in the sun . . . on the day of your party? Besides, the seamstress has just come in downstairs; she'll want to make all the final fittings on your new dresses. You must have a special milk bath, and I shall need time to fix your hair just so . . ."

With Jane's voice humming in her ears, Lorena shook her head and gave in.

*   *   *

It was early afternoon before the seamstress was at last finished poking pins into Lorena and Jane was done with her curl papers, lotions, and creams. They left the room one at a time, each promising to return before long, but Lorena decided to make her escape before they did. Throwing on a silk wrapper, and with her hair still done up in curl papers, she peered around her door to be sure the hall was clear and then went out. Just a few moments alone was all she asked, away from the incessant chattering of the women who'd been entrusted with making her over into a fashionable young miss, just a few moments to contemplate all that was going on around her.

Lorena swept along the halls, trying to avoid being seen by the servants, and decided to take refuge in Tyler Sanderson's study. As he was not in residence, surely that would be as safe a hiding place as any.

The draperies were drawn, but some light filtered into the room still, and as Lorena went to seat herself in Sanderson's massive leather chair, she noticed some of his things on the desk. There was a photograph, set on an easel, of Mariella and Luis, just recently taken by the looks of it, and a letter opener fashioned to resemble a miniature saber. There was a stone, just big enough to fit in the palm of Lorena's hand, with a yellow vein running through it which sparkled when the light caught it. On the opposite corner of the desk, beneath a stack of papers, she saw another, smaller photograph in an ornate brass frame, lying face down on the desktop. Curious, Lorena pulled it out to examine it and was startled to see that it was a picture of her when she'd been only about eight years old, dressed in white and sitting on the lawn of her uncle's house in New York.

She imagined that Sanderson must have gotten this from her father, then wondered if it was possible that he might have more of her father's things. She'd have to be sure and ask him about it. Such mementos meant a great deal to her now.

In the stillness that surrounded her, Lorena suddenly was aware of what she took to be the sound of someone humming softly—here, in this very room. With her heart keeping a staccato beat in her breast, she strained to hear the melody. It was "Oh, Susannah." And then the still-invisible intruder began to sing in a soft voice, "Oh, I come from New York City with my washbowl on my knee, and I'm bound for California, the gold dust for to see."

Uneasiness crept upon her as she scanned the room, but she dared not leave the safety of the enveloping leather chair. That song was as familiar to her as an old friend. Her father had taught it to her when he'd come back from the goldfields, before he'd gone away again and left her behind.

"It rained all night the day I left, the weather it was dry, the sun so hot I froze to death, oh, brothers, don't you cry. Oh, California! That's the life for me! I'm going to Sacramento with my washbowl on my knee."

Now Lorena recognized the voice and looked over the edge of the desk to see Luis, sitting on the hearth rug, playing with a whole company of painted, tin soldiers.

"Oh Luis, it's only you," she said, relieved.

The boy looked up at her in surprise. "Lorena, how did you get in here? And why do you look so funny?"

"Hush!" she whispered. "I came in to hide from my maid, and you frightened me half to death!"

Lorena realized then that the boy was staring at her head. "Are you surprised by my hair?" she asked. "Jane is curling it for the party tonight. It may look funny now, but she assures me I'll be quite beautiful by this evening. What do you think about that?"

"I think I'm tired of playing soldiers. I'm hungry. Let's go out to the kitchen and ask Rose for some of those pretty, pink-frosted cakes she was making yesterday."

"I don't think I ought to be running around the house like this," Lorena told him, "and those cakes are for the party."

Luis pouted. "Then I shan't have one at all. I must go to bed before the guests arrive."

"I'll put one aside for you," Lorena said. "I promise."

"You will?"

"If you'll promise not to tell Jane you think I'm funny-looking. She's liable to try and remedy the situation with more fussing, and I'm afraid I can't bear any more of it."

"You have my word as a gentleman," he said, picking himself up and straightening the tie of his sailor's blouse, like a proper young man. "And, Lorena, I really didn't mean it when I said you were funny-looking."

"I know you didn't," she told him as he turned to go. "Luis?"

He looked back at her. "Yes?"

"Where did you learn that song you were singing just now?"

"Papa taught it to me. He said that all the forty-niners sang it when they came out to look for gold."

As the twilight faded, Ben Thorne made his way down Montgomery Street, through the very heart of San Francisco. The buildings that rose up on either side of him were of recent construction, brick with granite sills and iron shutters, and they housed some of the city's most prosperous commercial establishments. There was the smell of money everywhere one went in this city, Ben thought: from the boisterous gambling tables of the saloons on the Barbary Coast to the ostentatious palaces that were just now being built on the California Street hill by men who'd made their fortunes in Nevada silver. But what struck him more as he roamed the darkened streets, past row upon row of houses, was the uneasy feeling of being hemmed in by civilization.

Ben had not been in a city of this size, with so many people all in one place, for more years than he could recall, and rather than enjoy the excitement, it made him edgy. San Francisco was a fine place for those raised to that sort of life, but he'd be happy to return to Wind River once more.

Each morning he had woken bright and early, intending that it would be the day he'd leave. Yet by day's end something always made him change his plans. It was the same something that drew him out now. He wandered, restless, trying to deny where his steps were leading him. It was not wise, and he knew it, but he had to be certain that Lorena was happy before he could contemplate leaving for good.

He crossed south of Market Street, heading for Rincon Hill, and found his way as though he'd traveled the route a hundred times before. Sanderson's house was on a large lot, and as he came around, Ben heard the lilting strains of an orchestra carried on the breeze, then noticed the host of fancy carriages lining the street. There was a party within.

He knew at once that he could not show himself. Though he'd shed his buckskins in favor of the remnants of his old Army uniform, it was still not acceptable attire for this sort of function. Still, perhaps he could catch a glimpse of her. . . .

The house was ablaze with light, and yet from his vantage point at the corner of the lot, Ben had a poor view. He paced for a moment, then followed along the decorative stone wall that sheltered the yard toward the rear of the house. With the row of French doors that edged the ballroom opened out, he could hear music and laughter and snatches of conversation well enough. The view, however, was no better. He nearly turned away, but knowing Lorena was somewhere within strengthened his resolve. As quickly as the thought occurred to him, he scaled the stone fence and perched himself on top, where he was hidden by the overgrown tangle of shrubbery.

Yes, now he could see quite clearly—the lush garden beneath him, the courtyard in the distance. Just inside the house couples began to dance as the musicians struck up a waltz. Ben watched for a long while, without interest, until at last he saw her. In a dress of pale lavender edged in lace, with her soft shoulders bared and a small bunch of violets tucked in her bosom, Lorena whirled by the opened windows in the arms of a stranger and then promptly disappeared again.

Rubbing salt in his own wounds, that's what he was doing here, Ben told himself. Yet he stayed, and before too much more time had passed, she came out to the courtyard to rest on one of the wrought-iron benches beside the fountain. Staring into its waters, she fanned herself with a pensive air. She looked so gentle and refined, so like she had on that very first day—when he'd seen her crossing the parade ground at Fort Kearney in Nebraska—that it was hard to believe anything of consequence had happened to her since. At length her companion returned with a glass of champagne, and setting aside her fan, she took it.

"Hallo up there, Captain. Doing sentry duty, are we?"

Ben was startled by the voice and looked down on the outside of the wall to see an older gentleman regarding him. He was wearing a rumpled frock coat and a dusty, silk hat, but had a disarming smile.

"No sir," he said, embarrassed by having been discovered in such a position. "I, well, that is to say—"

"What's that? I can't hear you. Hold on, I'll come up."

Ben thought he hadn't heard right, but true to his word, the older gentleman scrambled up the face of the wall and staked out a place for himself just beside Ben.

"Well," he began, with a merry twinkle in his eye, "you don't appear to be armed, so I imagine you don't mean anyone harm. Do you now, Captain?"

"Of course not," Ben retorted, feeling ridiculous to be sitting atop this fence and carrying on a conversation with a stranger.

"Good. Let me see now. A meal? Is that what you're after? Do you suppose they've one for a dusty, old traveler like me as well?"

Ben shook his head and smiled at this most unusual character, who looked to be a gentleman, but must have fallen on hard times. "I wouldn't count on it, sir. I doubt you'll find much charity in this neighborhood."

The vagrant seemed disappointed. "Oh . . . that is too bad."

"I've been lucky at the faro tables today, though," Ben said, and reaching into the pocket of his waistcoat, he drew out a gold eagle and tossed it to the man. "Have your supper on me tonight."

As Ben watched him, the man's brows knit together, perplexed at Ben's generosity. "Thank you kindly, Captain," he said and pocketed the coin. "Now, if you don't mind my asking, what *are* you doing perched up here on this fence like a tomcat stalking his supper?"

Ben was amused at the analogy, but wondered how to reply to the old gentleman's question without appearing to have lost his reason. Ben knew well enough that if he hadn't spent the afternoon looking for direction in the bottom of a whiskey bottle, he'd not be sitting up here now. Still the old man had a face that invited honesty, and Ben couldn't see the harm in confiding in him.

"Can you see the young lady there?" he began. "The one sitting beside the fountain?"

The gentleman craned his neck in that direction but was silent for a very long time.

"Do you see her?" Ben asked again.

"Yes," he replied at last, his voice only a whisper now, "indeed, I do. What's she done?"

"Done? She's upset my life so much that it can never be the same. She's invaded my thoughts, waking and sleeping . . ."

Ben regretted his outburst at once. His whiskey-loosened tongue had got the better of him and made him sound like a lovesick fool.

"Well then, Captain," the old man said at length, "I suggest that you jump down off this wall at once and tell her so before that fancy whelp she's conversing with manages to turn her pretty head."

Ben was certain now that he'd lost his reason. How could he have imagined that confiding in the old man about his problem might somehow change things? "I can't do that, sir," he replied.

"And why, in heaven's name, not . . . if you love her? You do love her, don't you?"

"Yes," Ben said, turning his sights to the ground beneath him in order to mask his frustration, "but I have nothing to offer her. I've only come here tonight to make certain . . . to see that she's well and happy."

"Without you?" the old gentleman put in.

"If that's how it must be."

The gentleman doffed his hat, and staring

hard at it, brushed off the dust and began to toy with its brim. "I found myself in such a situation once . . . a very long time ago," he said. "The woman I loved was born of a wealthy and aristocratic family. And I? I had nothing."

Ben looked up in surprise, then considered that this garrulous old vagrant likely fancied himself the philosopher and was inventing fairy tales. Yes, he did look the type. "What did you do?" Ben asked, encouraging him to continue nonetheless.

"I've always believed that it's what a man is that matters, not what he has. I asked the young lady to marry me, and she accepted."

"And so you snatched her out of the lap of luxury?" Ben said, unable to contain his irritation. "Or did you make the difficult decision to live on her fortune instead?"

The gentleman looked tired. He threaded a hand through his thick shock of gray hair and replaced his hat before he replied. "We lived with her family for a time," he admitted. "I gave all my attentions to proving myself to her, and not many more years had gone by before I'd amassed for myself a fortune that surpassed even that of my wife's family's."

"And so you lived together, happily ever after," Ben guessed.

The old man shook his head. "She died before we could enjoy so much as a penny of my wealth."

At this the strength seemed to go out of him

and the rumpled old gentleman slid back down to earth and doffed his hat once more. "Good luck to you, Captain," he said with a wistful sigh, "whatever road you choose." And then he was gone.

Ben put a hand to his brow to rub out the creases. He turned his attention to the courtyard once more, but Lorena was gone. He sprang down from his perch, more confused than he'd been at the outset. "Damn!" he exclaimed, and walked away.

Chapter Twenty
✦✦–✦✦

TYLER SANDERSON DID not return in time to enjoy his own celebration. It was more than likely, Mr. Davis explained to the guests, that his business in Sacramento had detained him longer than he'd anticipated. Everyone seemed to understand this and accepted their host's absence in gracious fashion . . . everyone, that is, save Lorena Mackenzie, for her patience was wearing thin.

But Sanderson could afford to be eccentric, she learned soon enough as she caught bits of conversation here and there around the room. He had such an incredible knack for making money, and some avowed quite plainly that it was sinful. That fact did not discourage their attendance at his parties, however, nor did the fact that he'd married a Spanish woman, and one nearly half his age at that. He had dazzled them with his success, turning a profit from all he set his sights on: shipping, mining, railroads. The shrewd among them realized that there would certainly come a time when their connection with Tyler Sanderson would prove a lucrative one.

And as his newly-arrived ward, Lorena Mackenzie basked in his glory. Her company was sought by a score of young sycophants and, as well, by the sons of the nouveau riche, whose snobbery began and ended solely with the size of a man's bank balance.

Though she had not yet met Sanderson, her father had always considered him a sharp hand, and as the night wore on, Lorena began to form the impression that he organized such functions as these not so much out of a social obligation but rather as an amusement for himself. These guests he'd gathered together were, by and large, a pompous lot, and he might well have found amusement in their petty machinations. Lorena, however, did not.

She had danced more than her share, her poor satin slippers scuffed where they'd been trod upon by clumsy feet. She'd found herself engaged that night in so many inconsequential and inane conversations that she feared just one more would surely cause her to run screaming from the room, tearing at her perfectly coiffed hair like a madwoman.

And so, as soon as she was able, Lorena slipped away from the crowd, looking for a quiet place in which to hide. The foyer seemed a likely spot, and she settled herself upon the steps, halfway up the curve of the first landing. She tossed off her shoes, massaging her sore feet and wondering if it were too early yet to retire.

"Lorena?" a small voice called to her, and then again, "Lorena?"

She tried to ascertain from where it had come. The foyer below was empty. Across the way and through a pair of double doors the orchestra played on and the guests continued to enjoy their evening. Perplexed, Lorena looked overhead through the open stairwell. There, two floors up, standing in his nightclothes, his small head poking through the balusters, was Luis.

"You ought to be asleep," Lorena said in a loud whisper that echoed up the stairwell.

"You have forgotten your promise," he called to her, his eyes downcast.

"Not at all. Rose has put aside some of the pastries, just as I asked her to. You shall have them tomorrow. Now go to bed."

"But I'm not the least bit tired, and I want to

have one now—a pretty one with candied sugars on it."

Lorena considered this and breathed a long sigh. It was not difficult to decide that she'd much rather share her dessert with Luis than return to the party.

"All right, then. I'll be right up. But if Anna finds out you've escaped, we'll both catch it for sure."

Lorena made a quick foray to the buffet tables and mounted the stairs to the third-floor landing, a plate in each hand.

The pair could scarcely see any of the goings-on from this spot, but then again, they could not be seen themselves, and that, Lorena decided, was exactly as she wished it. Luis asked her about the party, and for half an hour she made up fanciful stories for him. The truth was too dull by far. She danced with him for a bit then, and as she wiped a smudge of icing off his nose, she noticed his eyelids were growing heavy.

"Off to bed now," she told him, as she gathered up their empty plates, and started toward the stairs.

He turned to go and then, on impulse, ran to her, threw his arms around her waist and hugged her. "Will you stay with us forever, Lorena?"

She brushed the dark strands of hair from his brow, and her eyes filled with tears as she felt his small body clinging to hers. How foolishly sentimental she was becoming! But she knew that the tears were not so much for this little boy she'd befriended as the babe she had lost and was still mourning . . . Ben Thorne's babe.

"I—I don't know, Luis," she told him, "I just don't know. Run along to bed now."

"*Hasta mañana*," he said as he left her.

She was shaken. Intending to find Mariella and plead exhaustion so that she might retire, Lorena returned to the party, setting the empty plates on the table just inside the door. Abruptly, someone caught her arm and squired her in the direction of the dance floor.

"How lovely you look this evening, Miss Mackenzie" he said. "May I have the pleasure of this dance?"

By the time she saw that it was Henry Edgington, it was too late to protest. They were out on the floor and he had pulled her close, too close for her liking. "Precocious little lad," he told her, indicating that he'd seen her with Luis. "Sanderson's son, is he?"

Lorena's wrist burned under his painful grip. "Release me at once," she said through clenched teeth, "or else I shall scream loud enough to wake the dead."

Edgington only smiled. He had about him the look of a cat toying with a small bird. "I don't think that you will, my dear. You don't wish to be an embarrassment to our hostess, the charming Mrs. Sanderson, now do you?"

"How did you get into this house?"

"It was not difficult to procure an invitation.

I'm a respectable attorney who has come to San Francisco on business. So you see what a fine husband I shall make you, Lorena."

He was sporting a lighthearted smile that contrasted with his calculating words, and as he whirled Lorena across the floor in the dance, he would nod now and then to those with whom he was acquainted. He was, by his manner, making them all think that he and Lorena were the best of friends, and when Lorena realized what his game was, she was furious.

"I will expose your little scheme to Mr. Sanderson," she shot back, "the very moment he returns."

Edgington appeared unimpressed. He was so cool that Lorena feared she didn't have the strength to fight him. "And do you suppose any of it will matter to him?" he retorted. "Sanderson has a family of his own to worry about and a reputation to uphold in this community. So remember, Lorena, that before you shout out your accusations, I shall very likely have the opportunity to answer those charges, and as a lawyer, my dear, I have been trained to, shall we say, put things in their best light. I'll wager that by the time I'm through he'll be as anxious to get you off of his hands as I am to have you—" At this, Lorena dug her nails into the back of his hand to make him loose his grip. "Especially once he discovers you've the temperament of an alleycat . . ."

Lorena's blood had begun to run cold. Was

there nothing this man would not do to achieve his own ends? As fear and frustration gripped her, Edgington delivered the coup de grâce.

"You know, you really must take care with your reputation, Lorena. Everyone here in this room tonight knows by now of the handsome inheritance you're to come into, and that makes you rather a curiosity. Why, there are already rumors flying about your Western adventures and of how you arrived here last week, unchaperoned and filthy as a street urchin.

"No one will think twice when Sanderson gives your hand to me in marriage. They'll say it's doubtless the best thing for such a wild girl—to settle down with a responsible, upstanding young gentleman."

It wasn't so, Lorena thought. He was twisting everything to suit his purposes, and somehow she had to stop him. The music died away at last, and Edgington released her with a curt bow. "We will meet again soon, you and I," he said in warning, and left her standing alone.

"Step on up here, boys, and put your money down! On the red! On the black!"

Ben drained his glass and leaned forward in his chair to push another stack of chips across the wax cloth until they rested on the ace of spades.

Smoke hung like a pall on the air, making it difficult to ascertain whether or not daylight had come. He had no idea how long he'd been sitting at the faro table; winning, then losing, then winning again. And if he sat there long enough, he wondered, could he ever parlay those few chips into a respectable fortune? Damned foolish notion! It was only the whiskey talking, he knew, and so after he'd watched the banker appropriate his chips on the next turn, he picked himself up and headed for the door.

His head was throbbing a painful rhythm that did not serve to improve his disposition, yet he had full command of his senses. He'd gone and drunk himself sober, that's what he'd done. Blinded by the blaze of morning sunlight that met him at the door, he grumbled, pulling the wide brim of his hat down over his eyes.

He stepped immediately into the street and was nearly run over by a delivery wagon. But if he hadn't been, Ben might not have looked up to see the man on the plank walk opposite him—a pale, rawboned man, with a prominent forehead that was crowned by a bowler hat. Ben froze in his tracks and straightened up. It was Henry Edgington.

This was far too convenient to be coincidence. Lorena and that man in the same city, and she the only key to the fortune Edgington lusted after. Ben's uneasiness grew minute by minute as he watched Edgington walk down

Pacific Street and disappear into a ramshackle whorehouse, only one in a block of such buildings. Here, too, there were saloons, gambling dens, and cheap lodging houses. This was the Barbary Coast, purported to be the worst stretch of waterfront in the whole of the country, and no one who'd seen it would argue with the claim. Here anything could be had at a price, a thought that sent a shiver of fear down Ben Thorne's spine and made him change direction and head for Rincon Hill.

Lorena had slept scarcely at all, and dawn found her pacing the length of her room, deep in thought. She contemplated going at once to Mr. Davis and apprising him of Edgington's scheming, but then thought better of it as she remembered Edgington's warnings. What did she know of Sanderson, really? Perhaps, just as Edgington had suggested, he would be only too anxious to get her off his hands and relieve himself of the burden of managing her affairs. Lorena knew she had to tread carefully lest Henry Edgington made her look like a simpering fool.

What was there for her to do, besides wait for the return of Tyler Sanderson, and for Edgington to make his next move?

But no, she told herself and stiffened her spine, she would not allow Edgington to cloud her thinking with his invented threats. Will Mackenzie had had faith enough in his partner to entrust him with the management of all of his assets, and the welfare of his daughter as well, and Will Mackenzie had not been a fool.

Lorena determined then to cast her lot with Sanderson and trust him as her father had. A sense of great relief followed this decision. Later, she would think about how to say all that needed to be said to her guardian, but for now she wanted only to relax and enjoy the day.

Going to the window, she threw open the draperies. The sun was brilliant, even as it burned through the morning fog that had settled like a vaporous carpet on the landscape. Below in the garden the mists muted the vivid magentas, oranges, and golds of the blossoms and lent to them a magical quality that intrigued her. She still felt restless, but had tired of pacing her room, and so, donning the embroidered muslin wrapper laid out at the foot of her bed, she went downstairs, intending to explore the jungle that bloomed just beneath her window before the magical mists had faded.

It was inevitable, at this time of the morning, that her path should cross that of at least one of the servants as they went about their morning duties. She met Emily in the hall just outside the kitchen. "Good morning to you, Miss Lorena," the girl said. It was plain by her expression that she had not missed the fact that Lorena was wandering about in her nightdress and wrapper. "Something I might help you with?"

"I'm only going out to the garden to sit for a while," Lorena explained.

Emily raised a disapproving brow. "You ought to take care, miss. While it might look warm enough from your window, there's a chill on the air at this time o' day."

"There's no one else about, and I'll not tarry long."

The girl shook her head and turned to go about her work. "As you say, miss."

It was like walking in a dream. The cool, still air raised gooseflesh on Lorena's arms but was exhilarating. Sounds, like the chatter of a bird hiding somewhere behind her in the brambles and the splashing of the fountain, were amplified and echoed. Here and there, where sunlight had cut through the fog, it reflected on dewdrops scattered over the foliage and set them to sparkling, as if each leaf were set with diamonds, and the smell of damp earth and the exotic perfumes of rare blossoms blended in a way that pleased the senses.

Lorena dropped onto the bench, closed her eyes and drank in the air. It was this, she realized, that she missed most of all—this closeness with the elements that made one feel truly alive. She knew then that she could never be happy in this house, in this city. There was only one place for her, and when

Sanderson returned, she would tell him so.

Lorena was loathe to lose this feeling, and so she remained where she was. She knew that Jane would come looking for her soon enough and scold her for wandering, but for now there was peace.

A callused hand closed over her mouth all at once, and Lorena's eyes opened wide to see that it was Edgington's man, Hendricks. Beside him stood Dr. Morton. She began to struggle.

"Don't raise a fuss now," the doctor warned with an evil hiss. "We've orders to take the little boy as well, if it looks like you'll give us trouble."

Lorena had learned well enough that Edgington would not hesitate to use any means he could to get what he wanted, even something so cruel as doing harm to an innocent child. And so she sat there, unmoving, as Hendricks straightened out her arm and the sallow-faced doctor reached into his jacket and drew out a small pouch.

Lorena felt the prick of the needle, and as the syringe was emptied into her vein, the world began to spin. She looked up at the windows of the upper floors of the house then and thought she saw Luis, waving to her . . .

Curiously enough, at that moment Lorena heard a voice, Ben Thorne's voice, and he was shouting. She knew it must be the effects of the drug as it muddled her brain.

"You listen to me, woman! I must speak to

Mr. Sanderson. No, I will not return at a more seemly hour. I need to see him at once!''

Lorena would have run to him if she could. There was so much she needed to say, but her limbs were leaden and useless and the fog was rolling in once more, thick and black. She tried to gather the strength to form his name on her lips, but the drug had reached her brain by now and held her in its grip. The fog settled in and covered her.

Chapter Twenty-One
✦✦✦✦

BEN THORNE COULD see the maid's fear increasing as he spoke, and he could not blame her for thinking him a madman. His eyes were wild, his clothes looked as though they'd been slept in, and he reeked of whiskey and stale cigar smoke, but somehow he had to make her understand.

''Miss Mackenzie is in danger,'' he repeated slowly, making a last effort to keep his calm.

Somewhere upstairs a child began to wail, calling out for his mother. *''Mama, Mama! Venga aquí, Mama, por favor!''*

''Now see what you've gone and done. You've frightened the poor child.''

"I'm sorry," Ben said, "but I can assure you I'm neither drunk nor crazy. Won't you please tell Mr. Sanderson that I'm here? He can decide whether or not to believe my story."

The girl shook her head. "He's been traveling and didn't come home till late last night. I daren't disturb him."

"Will you at least tell me then if Miss Mackenzie is at home. She hasn't gone out with anyone or had any visitors?"

The maid cast him a sidelong glance. "At this time in the mornin'? Are ye daft?"

"So she *is* here, then," he said, somewhat relieved.

From inside the house Ben heard a voice. "What's going on, Emily?"

"Oh, sir. I'm dreadful sorry if we've disturbed you, sir, but this 'gentleman' insists upon speakin' to you. I've told him tisn't a convenient time, but he won't take no for his answer."

The girl stepped back, and in her place at the door appeared a man wearing a dressing gown of Chinese silk, scratching his gray head in bewilderment. Ben recognized him at once.

"Well, Captain. When I heard all of the commotion, I certainly didn't expect to find you here knocking at my door."

"Mr. Sanderson? Tyler Sanderson?" Ben queried.

"Just don't stand there gaping, son, come on in. Emily, fetch a pot of coffee." He shot another look at Ben. "Black coffee, and bring it into my study."

Ben was speechless as he followed the man along the spacious hall and into a large room, with bookshelves that stretched from floor to ceiling along the rear wall, and a carved mahogany desk at its center. It was still hard to credit that the rumpled, old stranger that Ben had taken to be a vagrant and conversed so freely with the night before could possibly be Tyler Sanderson.

He waved Ben into the chair before the desk and then seated himself behind it. "First off, Captain, it might help if I knew your name."

Ben swept off his hat and found himself nervously drumming his fingers on the arm of the chair. Sanderson had certainly put him in a spot. "Thorne," he replied at once, "Ben Thorne, and I'm sorry to have upset your household, sir . . ."

Though he struggled to keep an even temper, Ben's irritation grew steadily as the minutes ticked by. He had, he felt, been made to look like a fool. "Why didn't you tell me who you were when we met last night?" he blurted out finally, in spite of himself.

"Sometimes, Mr. Thorne, a man can learn a great deal more about a situation by keeping his mouth shut."

That was certainly the truth. When the maid arrived with the coffee, Sanderson stood up, took the tray, and dismissed her. As he poured a cup and handed it to Ben, he continued. "I'd been traveling for three days, and when finally I arrived home, what did I see but a man spying into my garden. You can imagine that I'd be curious to discover the reason why."

Ben nodded, feeling foolish.

"Now, Mr. Thorne, perhaps you'd best explain how you came to know my . . . ward, Miss Mackenzie, and what brings you here at such an hour and in such an anxious state."

Ben emptied his cup. Sanderson promptly poured him another, then set down the pot, crossed his arms over his chest, and leaned back against the edge of the desk.

"Well, sir," Ben began, "I earn my living as a scout for the U.S. Army. I met Lorena—Miss Mackenzie, that is—when she came West."

"We'd had word that she'd run off to Montana," Sanderson admitted, "with the notion of becoming a schoolmarm."

Ben regarded the older man carefully. He had no idea how much of the story Sanderson knew, but he was determined to tell him the whole of it. "It wasn't that, exactly, which made her run off, sir," Ben explained. "It was fear. Miss Mackenzie's friend, Charles Ackerman, showed me a letter that she had written to him in which she explained that she was coming West rather than be forced by her uncle to marry his stepson, a man named Henry Edgington. It seems that the two were scheming to gain control of the fortune her father had left her."

Sanderson's knuckles whitened as he gripped the corner of the desk he leaned against, and he was silent for a very long time. "I can see now that I put my trust in the wrong man. But how could I have known? Harrison Gilmore was her uncle, her blood kin."

"You're not to blame, sir," Ben assured him, "and it may be that Gilmore truly believed that he was doing what was best for Lorena, that a young woman could not possibly manage such a fortune all on her own."

Sanderson seemed to ponder this awhile, and then went on to question Ben further. "When I'd heard she left home, I sent one of my men out to find her. He learned that she'd been taken hostage by the Cheyenne, but precious little else."

"The situation with the Indians in the area had gone from bad to worse, sir. Ackerman was killed fighting them—"

At this Sanderson went around to his chair, slumped into it and buried his head in his hands. "What a mess I've made of things. I'm to blame for this, all of it. She was my responsibility. I should have brought her here to live from the first. You must understand, though, Mr. Thorne. All those years ago, San Francisco was not the settled community that it is now, and by no means a suitable place to raise a child. I assumed that she would be better off living in New York with her uncle."

Ben was struck by Sanderson's deep sense of responsibility for Lorena. Certainly Will

Mackenzie had chosen the right man as her guardian. "Mr. Sanderson, please. The Cheyenne did not harm Lorena, I can vouch for that. When I brought her back from their camp, though, she very nearly fell into the hands of Henry Edgington, who had come West after her. I have never before met a man of such overwhelming greed and devilish motives, sir, and it is precisely that which brings me here this morning. Edgington is in San Francisco; I have seen him."

Sanderson blanched. "But what mischief can he intend now, with Lorena living here safely under my roof?"

"If he knew you were away for all of this time, perhaps he believed he could still get to her before you'd returned," Ben suggested. "He has a hypnotic sort of charm, an ability to make the most hideous lie sound plausible. I'm ashamed to say I fell prey to it myself at first."

"Well, he's run out of time," Sanderson said. "If he returns for her now, I'll be waiting."

Ben ought to have felt relieved. He'd turned over responsibility for Lorena Mackenzie's well-being to her guardian, a most capable man. Now she could have the sort of life she deserved, and he could go back where he belonged. He rose.

Sanderson rang for the maid. "Emily, tell Miss Mackenzie that I should like to speak with her at once," he said when she appeared, and then turned to Ben. "There are some things that must be explained to Lorena, Mr. Thorne, and I'd be obliged if you could stay and hear them too."

"I can't, sir," Ben protested. "I only came to warn you about Edgington."

Sanderson captured him with an accusing look that fairly pinned him to the wall. "You're running out, then?"

"There's nothing more that I can do for her, except stand in her way. She's convinced that I'm irresponsible and unfeeling, and it will be a damned sight better for her if she goes on believing it."

Sanderson said nothing, but his eyes accused Ben all the more.

"What would you have me do?" Ben said in retort.

"Tell her what you told me last night," the old man replied.

"Excuse me, sir," Emily said upon entering the room, "but it appears Miss Mackenzie is not in the house."

Lorena awoke with a start at a shriek of female laughter and the discordant chiming of piano keys somewhere far beneath her. She had to blink her eyes to adjust them to the yellow light that alternately flickered and glowed through the greasy globe of an oil lamp set atop a battered chest of drawers. There was one small window, covered by hangings of faded crimson damask, and a tall, cheval glass, with a crack running through it, which stood in one corner. What was this place?

Her head throbbed painfully and her mouth was dry as cotton. She tried to ease herself up on one elbow but didn't have the strength and so fell back onto the mattress, the springs of the iron bedstead squeaking in protest. And then she remembered. Edgington!

With her heart pounding a frantic rhythm, Lorena struggled with her torpid limbs, thinking only of escape. She edged one long leg, an inch at a time, till it swung off the end of the bed, then, when she'd moved her other leg the same way, she reached over, straining with all her might, to grasp at the bedpost.

Again and again Lorena tried and failed, her breathing punctuated by raspy sobs that gave voice to her frustration. But she would not give in, and at last, concentrating all of her strength into one arm, she caught hold of the bedknob.

Using it for support, she dragged herself upright and shook her head firmly to stop the room from spinning. Her mind was clearer now than it had been before. She could feel the blood as it coursed through her veins, restoring her vigor. The effects of the drug were subsiding.

She got to her feet ever so slowly, and supporting herself on the furniture, managed to cross to the door. A wave of nausea swept over her, and she fought it back. She reasoned that if she could somehow get down to the street, a good scream would get all the attention she needed.

Resting her hand on the doorknob, Lorena whispered a silent prayer. If it were locked, then her efforts had been for naught, and she feared she might cry out in frustration. It was only too easy for her now to imagine how someone could be driven mad through the administration of this evil drug, which, by his own admission, was precisely what Henry Edgington had planned for her.

With a twist of the knob the lock clicked and Lorena pulled open the door, breathing a long sigh of relief.

Before her, though, in the dark recesses of the hall, floated a gaunt, skull-like face. Edgington's face.

"Ah, good afternoon, my dear, I see that you've awakened at last. If it's our wedding you're anxious for, you haven't long to wait. Just a few more hours and I shall have both a license and the judge."

Lorena crumpled in a heap on the floor at his feet.

Ben was startled as an elegant, dark-haired woman swept into the study and shut the doors behind her. She stood silent for a moment, folding her graceful white hands as she waited to be acknowledged.

"This is my wife," Sanderson said. "Mariella, this is Mr. Thorne, who is a friend of Lorena's."

"A pleasure, ma'am."

Mariella Sanderson inclined her head in response and promptly addressed her husband. "We have searched the whole of the house," she said. "She is not to be found."

"Might she have gone out without anyone knowing?" Ben wondered. "For a walk, perhaps?"

"It is possible, I suppose," the woman replied.

In a soft rustle of skirts she moved to stand beside her husband, seated at his desk, and put a hand on his arm. "Mr. Davis has been sent for, as you requested. He is waiting in the foyer. You look worried, my dear. What is it?"

"I fear that some mishap may have befallen . . . Miss Mackenzie. Mr. Thorne has told me that there is a man who means to do her harm, a man named Henry Edgington."

"*Madre de dios!*" Mariella exclaimed, and put a hand to her mouth.

"What is it?" Sanderson asked.

"This man, this Edgington—he is a thin man, with a sharp face and dark eyes, si?"

"He is," Ben supplied.

"He was here," Mariella explained, "in this house, only last night, as one of our guests."

Ben felt a numbness spread over him. There was no doubt now. Edgington was in San

Francisco because of Lorena. "Could he have spirited her out of the house last night?" he inquired.

Mariella shook her head. "Her maid helped her to undress and put her to bed, señor."

"It's still possible she decided to go out on her own this morning," Sanderson put in hopefully.

"Possible, yes," Ben replied, "but not probable."

A hand caressed Lorena's arm through the sleeve of her muslin wrapper, then reached to unfasten the tiny pearl buttons one at a time, slowly baring the soft, white skin of her throat, hesitating as restless fingers toyed with the ribbons of the nightgown beneath.

"Ben," she sighed. "Oh, Ben, I had such an awful nightmare."

Lorena opened her eyes and looked up to see Henry Edgington leering down at her. Horrified, she pressed her back deep into the mattress to avoid his touch and would have screamed if he hadn't clamped a hand across her mouth.

"Hush now," he said, putting his face close to hers. "It's time to dress for our wedding."

Again he reached for her. Lorena could not escape him, bent over her as he was, but she squirmed against him as his splayed hand lingered over her breast then inched lower, groping for her thigh beneath the thin fabric of her nightgown. She squeezed her eyelids shut and a tear trickled out.

"You'll come to enjoy this soon enough, my dear," he said, and pressed his flaccid lips on hers.

Lorena felt as if she'd suffocate, trapped there beneath him. Even after he'd loosed her mouth she could not draw breath, but only lay there, shuddering in revulsion.

"We've no time for this now, though," Edgington said, picking himself up and straightening his tasteful cravat. "Our guests are waiting. I've just planned a quick ceremony for today; I hope you won't be too disappointed, and tomorrow we shall sail for New York. Once we're safe at home, we can do it all again, if you like, in a cathedral, and be feted with flowers and champagne in proper fashion, and you can write to your guardian, Mr. Sanderson, and tell him how we ran across one another at a party in his own home and renewed our old friendship. I swept you off your feet, and overwhelmed by youthful enthusiasm, we decided to elope."

Lorena tried to turn away but could not. It was as if she'd been hypnotized. Henry Edgington was no mere man. He was a hideous creature who pleasured himself by the torture of others. He stood there, wearing a cruel smile, and she could see that he was heady with the feeling of absolute power, for his tentacles had already entwined themselves around his next victim—Lorena Mackenzie. There must be a way to escape from this fate, she thought to herself. There must be!

Edgington reached for her once more, drawing his thin fingers lightly across her cheek. Her distress was plain to see, and it pleased him all the more. "You needn't worry, Lorena, my dear, there'll be plenty of time later on for you to learn how to please me."

He went to open the door, then, and turned to send her one last, triumphant look. "Yes, plenty of time."

A young girl entered as he was going out, and Edgington gave her an order: "Ruby, see to it that she's dressed and ready in five minutes."

As soon as he was gone, Lorena picked herself up and retched into the washbasin, wracked by spasms that left her doubled over and clutching at her middle.

"Oh, poor miss," the girl said as she swept into the room. She tossed the bundle of clothes that she carried onto the bed, and fetching a cloth from the washstand, dipped it into the ewer, wrung it out and handed it to Lorena, who received it gratefully. After mopping her brow and recovering somewhat, Lorena looked up at the girl, now engaged in sorting through the clothes on the bed.

Edgington had called her Ruby. She had red hair, in perhaps too vivid a shade to have been natural, and it was piled high upon her head. Lorena could see when she drew nearer that her face was painted, and in the lamp-light it did give the illusion of youth, though she was certainly not the young miss Lorena had imagined at first. She was clad in only a chemise and drawers, and over these she had thrown on a silk wrapper in a Chinese print of black and emerald green. Such was not the fashionable attire of a proper young lady. This fact, along with the raucous laughter that drifted up to her through the floorboards, told Lorena that Edgington had most likely brought her to a brothel or a gambling house somewhere near the docks. It was a neighbor-hood not frequented by polite folk. And so, she realized regretfully, even if she were somehow to effect an escape, she could expect no aid from friendly passersby.

"Come along now, missy. We've got to get you dressed," Ruby said, and as if she were a lady's maid, began to help Lorena out of her nightclothes and into the things she'd brought for her. "None of us girls has the fine things you're likely accustomed to, but the man says dress you up for a wedding, and so we'll oblige him as best we can."

Lorena, still suffering from the effects of the drug, was unsteady on her feet. She leaned for support against the bureau and kneaded her brow as Ruby laced her stays.

"You've got to help me," she pleaded. "Edgington is a madman, and I have to get away from here at once. Please, Ruby!"

The girl only shook her head as she bundled

Lorena into her dress and fastened the hooks at the back. "I'd like to help you, miss, truly I would, but those fellows your friend has with him wouldn't think twice 'bout cutting my throat."

Lorena studied the fingers on both of her hands, then reached to her neck, looking for a piece of jewelry to offer in payment, but she'd been taken this morning from the house in her nightclothes, and she hadn't been wearing any. Desperate, she met the girl's faded blue eyes, begging her to understand. "Please!"

"It won't be so awful for you, miss," Ruby explained. "That Edgington fellow's not bad to look at, leastwise not bad as some I've had, and he does have a gentleman's airs. What you got to do when he aims to touch you is just to close your eyes and think about somethin' else."

It was hopeless. Lorena could hardly expect sympathy from a girl who made a living in giving herself to strangers. Lorena thought that she might, indeed, have been able to steel herself against Edgington, to accept what indignities he would surely inflict—until her heart had grown calloused and cold—if she had never before known what pleasure there was in giving her body to a man that she loved.

Memories of Ben Thorne rushed in and swept over her like a warm surf, filling up the emptiness for a time. Yes, she had loved him, and he had loved her, though she had only come to realize it now, when it was much too late. Ben had never hesitated to put her needs before his own, he'd even offered up his life for her, and yet because he never said the words, she'd let him slip away without a fight.

It was her memories of him that left Lorena reviled by Edgington's touch and why she promised herself now that she would die rather than let him touch her again. If there was no pleasure greater than giving oneself as an act of love, then there was no sin so grievous as allowing oneself to be taken by a soul bereft of it. Ruby, even with all her experience, could never know this.

Chapter Twenty-Two

✦✦✦✦

BEN SOMEHOW KNEW, even before he'd crossed the threshold of Sanderson's study and seen their anxious faces, that the two men had been unsuccessful. Peter Davis, using all of the resources at his disposal, had spent the day making polite inquiries about the missing heiress. Sanderson had taken another tack, trying to pick up Edgington's trail and even managing a search of the man's fashionable downtown hotel room, but he did not uncover even a clue as to his whereabouts.

It was left to Ben to make a search of the waterfront and Pacific Street, where he'd seen Edgington earlier that morning. But questions of any kind were not welcome in that section of the city. The Barbary Coast stretched for eight long blocks and contained a countless number of saloons, lodging houses, and gambling dens where a man like Edgington might find safe haven. As Ben had anticipated, he could find no one who'd admit to seeing or even hearing of either Henry Edgington or Lorena Mackenzie.

"Sit down and have a drink, Mr. Thorne," Sanderson offered.

Ben took a chair but refused the glass that Davis poured. "I'm going out again, sir," he said. "I only wanted to stop by and see if either of you had had any success."

Sanderson shook his head and had just begun to speak when a small boy burst into the room.

"Papa, Papa," the child cried as he rushed toward Sanderson's desk. He froze in his tracks, though, his dark eyes wide, as he caught sight of Ben sitting nearby, wearing his buckskins and sporting a revolver and a long-handled knife on his belt. "They wouldn't let me come and see you," the boy continued in a cautious voice, "and I've been so frightened—"

"I've been busy today, Luis. I'm sorry. Come and sit on my knee now and tell me. What is it that's got you so upset?"

Just then the maid rushed in through the open door. "Master Luis, so there you are. You frightened Anna and your mother half to death, runnin' off like that. We've been looking all over the house for you. Come away now. Can't you see your father's busy?"

"It's all right, Emily," Sanderson told her, and motioned for Luis to come closer.

Thorne watched Sanderson's expression soften as the boy came to sit on his knee. "Now tell me, Luis. *Que hay?* What's frightened you?"

"I tried to tell Anna, but she wouldn't listen. She said I was only telling tales and made me drink my milk and take a nap. But I did see them, Papa, the two men. Their clothes were dirty. One had spectacles and one of them was tall like a giant."

"That sounds like Edgington's men," Ben put in.

Sanderson nodded, still regarding the boy. "Where did you see them, Luis?"

"In the garden . . . this morning. I was watching from my window. They took Lorena away, Papa, and I'm afraid they've hurt her."

Luis buried his face in his father's jacket, and Sanderson stroked his hair. "You mustn't worry. Lorena will be just fine. Now you're certain it was in the garden that you saw them?"

The boy bobbed his head in reply. "Lorena was sitting by the fountain when they came."

"That's right, sir," Emily echoed, trepidation in her voice. "Miss Lorena did go out into the garden early this mornin'. I didn't see her come in again, leastwise not with me own eyes. But she was dressed in her nightclothes, and I figured she'd only stepped out to take the air then come right back. I never saw no men, and I swear to you, sir, it never crossed me mind that such a thing had happened or I'd have spoke out at once—"

Her voice broke off, and leaning upon the doorjamb, she covered her mouth with her hand. "Calm yourself, Emily," Sanderson told her. "Take my son upstairs to his mother and explain to her what's happened."

"Yes, sir. Right away, sir."

After she'd gone out with Luis under her wing, Peter Davis, who'd been silent thus far, spoke up. "What's to be done now?"

Sanderson rested his head on his hand and stared at the carpet. "It's certain that Edgington has her, but there's no way to tell where he's taken her or what his plans are."

Ben pulled himself out of his chair and crossed the room, pausing to stand on the threshold and point down the hall. "Is this the way to the garden?" he asked.

Suddenly the boy rushed past him, with Emily close on his heels. "Papa," he said, "I'd almost forgotten. After my nap I went out into the garden to see if I'd only been dreaming about the bad men, like Anna said, and I saw this lying in the brambles. It was shiny, so I picked it up. Is it real gold, Papa?"

He put something into his father's hand, and Sanderson shook his head. "No, Luis. Go on upstairs now."

As quickly as he had come in, the child was gone again. "What is it?" Davis wanted to know.

Tyler Sanderson lifted up the token his son had given him, and the lamplight caught it and reflected on it. Ben Thorne knew as he approached that he'd seen its like before. It was a two-dollar brass check, the kind given out to patrons at some of the establishments on the Barbary Coast. He took it from Sanderson and read the legend stamped upon its face: *Silver Dollar Saloon. Eat, drink, and go to bed, or get out!*

"There now, don't you look pretty?"

Ruby stepped back and pointed to the cheval glass in the corner. Lorena studied her reflection. She was aghast. Her skin was pallid, her liquid eyes darkened and opaque with shadowy crescents in the hollows beneath them. Her blond hair hung long and loose, and Ruby had fastened a garish brooch on a ribbon tied around her neck.

The dress was of black velvet, the nap worn

smooth in spots, and the full skirt was short enough to allow more than a modest glimpse of stocking and layered red petticoats of crisp taffeta beneath. The cut, of course, was far too low, leaving the swell of her breasts to nearly spill over the top of the tight-fitted bodice. To complete the ensemble, Ruby provided her with a pair of red satin dancing slippers, two sizes too small. It was truly a costume to match the occasion, Lorena thought, overtaken by a fit of gallows humor.

When she turned back into the room, it was to see that Dr. Morton had come in. He was readying another syringe.

"Oh, no," Lorena groaned, edging back against the wall.

"Just enough to settle you down a bit," Morton said, adjusting his spectacles as he measured out the dosage.

Ruby caught her arm. "Don't fret, miss," she whispered, "you'll be grateful for it later on."

With her back pressed against the wall, Lorena felt again the bite of the needle as it pierced her vein. A rush of warmth coursed through her, followed by a brief spell of vertigo, and then there was only the feeling of being at ease.

Leaning heavily on Morton's arm, Lorena followed where he led—floating, as if it were all a dream, across the faded, floral carpets in the upstairs hall and out onto the wide landing that looked down on the gambling floor below. There Morton paused, and Lorena peered over the railing.

The back bar had a sign that read SILVER DOLLAR and mirrors of fine-cut glass reflecting the whole of the room, with its chandeliers, green baize tables, velvet hangings, and walnut bar—elegant from a distance, but up close, tawdry and threadbare.

A horde of unwashed clientele thronged the floor below, intent on their games of poker and faro, keno and roulette. There were women as well, in careless attire, only too anxious to heap their affections upon the winners. And at the far end of the room, standing upon a long, raised platform beside the piano player, was Henry Edgington.

At his signal the man put his hands to the keyboard and began to play a tune that, between the missed chords, sounded vaguely like a wedding march. Benumbed, Lorena took in the whole scene impassively. It was more like a circus than a wedding, really.

She stumbled several times upon the stairs, garnering the attention of a good many patrons of the establishment, who called out lewd suggestions as she passed among them, thinking she was part of the evening's entertainment.

Morton led her to stand at Edgington's side before a besotted old judge who was dozing in a chair, and as Edgington slipped his arm through hers, he sent a twisted smile her way that told her that this whole sordid scene had been staged to punish her for the times she'd spurned him.

The pianist finished his selection, and as the room quietened somewhat, Edgington cleared his throat to rouse the judge.

"Hmmm? Oh, yes," the florid-faced man said as he got to his feet and fumbled through the pages of his leatherbound book. "Now, let me see—"

"Just get on with it," Edgington ordered, irritation plain in his voice.

He had meant to shame her by this spectacle, Lorena thought, but if that was his game, he'd lost, because she was far too giddy to be truly affected. The drug had heightened all of her senses, and now her concentration was centered on the myriad sounds in the room, amplified in her head to a deafening cacophony: a chinking of glasses, the call of the dealers, the click of the roulette wheels, and laughter and murmuring voices . . .

The old judge dropped his book and it slammed to the floor. As he bent to retrieve it, a voice called out, above the din. "Lorena!"

Her heart leapt at the call, though she knew at once she could only have imagined it. The drug was affecting her mind again. It could not have been Ben Thorne who'd called out to her, for he had gone back to Wind River. And yet Edgington must have heard it, too, for he suddenly stiffened and whirled around, leaving Lorena standing there, her head reeling as she tried to maintain her balance on her own.

Some of the onlookers had broken off gambling and were watching now, intrigued at the strange events unfolding before them.

"It's too late, Edgington," the voice cried out, and the room became surprisingly quiet. "Sanderson knows all about your little scheme. You'll never see a cent of Mackenzie's money!"

This voice was too real to be only imagined, Lorena decided, and she cautiously turned to see for herself. There, before the shuttered doors, the spectators had cleared a space for the stranger who'd only just come in. It was, indeed, Ben Thorne.

Her eyes were rheumy as they met Ben's for a brief instant, and she was still not quite able to believe that it was truly him. Then Edgington captured her roughly by the arm again.

"Damn you, Edgington! Let her go!" Ben shouted.

Too late Lorena saw Hendricks cut through the crowd, bent upon putting a quick end to the interruption.

"Ben, no!" she cried, fear cutting through the numbness that had gripped her.

Lorena struggled against her captor in a vain attempt to free herself, but it would not have helped if she could have, for Ben had already been felled by a blow and lay on the floor, apparently unconscious.

Some of the onlookers grumbled, then most went back to their game. Hendricks turned away, triumphant, not reckoning that his victim had only been feigning in order to gain the advantage. Ben sprang on him with startling swiftness, like a wildcat turns upon its prey. Fighting Indian fashion, he used all his limbs to strike with wicked accuracy, until he'd felled the bigger man like a giant redwood tree.

A mixed reaction of cheers and catcalls went up from the crowd. It did not take much provocation to set the Silver Dollar's half-drunk patrons to arguing amongst themselves, and soon more fights had broken out on the floor, and Ben had to wade through the melee in his attempt to reach Lorena.

A bullet whizzed by his head, and his attention turned to the opposite corner of the room, where Dr. Morton stood with pistol in hand. But before Morton could take aim again, he was dispatched by a shot from behind, courtesy of Peter Davis, who'd come in through the back room by way of the alley door. Davis waved an all-clear sign, then was promptly felled himself by a bullet that struck his shoulder. This had been fired by Edgington.

Ben drew nearer to the raised platform at the far end of the saloon. Desperate now, Edgington turned on him, brandishing the revolver he'd drawn from his frock coat. Then thinking better of it, he hooked one arm around Lorena's waist and aimed the barrel of the gun at her temple, keeping Ben at bay as he edged toward the back room and the alley-way.

Lorena considered resisting Edgington as he dragged her along, in order to slow him down. But with his just-fired revolver pointed so perilously near, and the air full of the acrid smell of gunpowder to remind her of the immediate threat, she hesitated to put up too much of a struggle.

Edgington dropped his guard, though, after they'd stepped into the darkened alley, when Ben was no longer in sight.

"He thinks he's won, does he?" Edgington hissed into her ear. "Well, we shall see about that. I can still turn a profit on you yet. It's no less than you deserve, after all the grief you've given me, damned troublesome bitch. There are plenty of places hereabouts that will pay a handsome price for a woman like you—"

Where was Ben? she wondered. As Edgington scanned the alley in either direction, seeking an avenue of escape, she gathered her wits about her. She'd been weakened by her ordeal: nausea threatened to overwhelm her, and she was still plagued by moments of vertigo from the drug she'd been given. But she could wait no longer to be rescued, and so with all her might she thrust her elbow back into Edgington's midsection. It knocked the breath from him, and he doubled over in surprise. Without a moment's hesitation, Lorena turned and drove her knee upward into his groin.

The effect was immediate. Edgington loosed his hold on her and dropped to his knees, moaning in agony. The gun slipped from his grasp, and by the time he was able to pull himself to his feet once more, she held it and was backing away from him.

Edgington stretched out his hand. "Give it to me, you little fool!"

Lorena had backed to a wall and now stood there trying to stave off the spinning in her brain.

"I doubt you've got the skill to use it," he said, "and even if you had, you haven't the nerve."

Edgington fairly spat out the words, then slowly got to his feet and took deliberate steps toward her, closing the distance between them.

Lorena had never killed a man before. Her hands were shaking, but as she lifted the revolver and aligned her sight, she swore she could hear her father's voice reassuring her—speaking the same words he had so many years before, when he'd taught her to use a gun. "Steady, Lorena! Don't be afraid now. Take aim—"

"Lorena!" Ben shouted, appearing at the far end of the alley.

It drew her attention for a split second, and Edgington charged, thinking to overpower her. But again he'd underestimated her. Lorena fired.

Edgington's eyes widened as the small hole

in his shirtfront flooded crimson, and he dropped facedown in the mud.

Ben rushed to her then and caught her up in his arms, and Lorena collapsed, twilight fading to black.

Chapter Twenty-Three

✦✦✦✦

LORENA AWOKE IN her room in Sanderson's home, convinced that it had all been an awful nightmare. No trace remained of the evening before: not the squalid room where she'd been kept, nor the painted, red-haired woman, the shameless black dress, the saloon, the alley, nor Henry Edgington. . . .

She lay in the center of her bed, propped up with pillows and covered in a quilted counterpane, a nightdress of delicate, embroidered muslin buttoned demurely to the hollow of her throat. If it had been a nightmare, then she'd only dreamt that Ben Thorne had come to her rescue . . . and held her in his arms.

She lay still for a very long time, pondering, and then a thought struck her and she rolled up one sleeve to study the inside of her arm. Yes, they were there, the two needle marks . . . and as the realization rushed over her, she cried out and sprang upright in the bed.

Mariella, who she now noticed sitting in the chair beside her, laid out a hand on her arm. "Hush, dear. It's all over now."

Lorena, her brow deeply creased, regarded the elegant woman. "I've killed him, then, haven't I?"

Mariella nodded. "But you had no other choice. And if I understand all that he's done, a man never needed killing more than this Edgington fellow."

"Mr. Davis . . . he tried to help me. Is he—"

"Recovering nicely. The doctor tells us his arm will be healed in only a few weeks' time."

Lorena was careful now, guarding her feelings lest she be disappointed. "And Ben Thorne?"

"He is downstairs, talking to my husband, and preparing to go, I believe."

"No, he can't. I have to speak to him!"

Lorena tossed off the quilt and got to her feet. If Thorne was in this house, she would make him listen, tell him and her father's friend, Sanderson, that she had made up her mind. There was only one place that would ever be home to her, and inheritance or not, she was going back there.

Lorena quit the room and padded down the hall to the staircase. "The doctor says you must rest," Mariella called after her.

But she would not listen, and stopped only when she'd reached the second-floor landing. Gripping the banister, she peered over. Ben

was there, in the foyer, and talking to someone Lorena could not see but supposed was
Tyler Sanderson.

"This is not a rash decision, sir," he said,
"as you well know by now. It doesn't matter
that I love her, it doesn't matter what I want,
only that I can never hope to give her the sort
of life she deserves. She'll be better off, in the
end, without me."

"Damn you for your arrogance, Ben
Thorne!" Lorena called down, her voice echo-
ing sharply off the walls. "Doesn't it matter
what I want?"

She paused at the head of the staircase and
looked down on him. "Do you think I'm the
sort who'd enjoy a life where I'd be coddled
and catered to . . . and caged?

"Well, I've had my fill of it, I can tell you
that, and if gaining my inheritance means I
must live like a pampered child, then I'll give
it all up and good riddance to it. I've made my
decision. With or without you, I'm going back
to Wind River. Your father needs someone to
help him build his dream, and I'm just the
woman who can do it."

He stared up at her, speechless.

"You've figured your own worth far too
low, Ben Thorne," she went on. "As my own
father told me a long time ago—"

From somewhere below, a disembodied
voice finished for her. ". . . It's what a man *is*
that matters, not what he *has*."

Lorena's face paled. She grasped the railing

for support, descending slowly, one step at a time. "Papa?" she called, her voice thin and tremulous.

When at last she could see the man to whom Thorne had been speaking, she threw herself into his arms. "Papa! Oh, Papa, then it *was* you I heard speaking to me in the alley last night."

"I was hiding not far away, but I couldn't get a clear shot at that devil, so I thought to calm you down—"

"But how?"

"I don't understand," Ben said, watching Lorena embrace the man he knew as Tyler Sanderson. "Do you mean to tell me, Lorena, that this man is your father?"

Lorena could not find a voice, but bobbed her head in reply.

"It's true. I am Will Mackenzie," the man Ben had thought to be Sanderson told him now. He put an arm around his daughter and gestured for Ben to follow. "Come into my study, my boy, and I'll explain it all to you."

Behind the closed doors of the study Mackenzie seated himself at his desk and motioned Ben and Lorena into the two chairs opposite. "Only two other people know the truth of things," he began. "Mariella, of course, and Peter Davis, who has handled my legal affairs from the first."

"But why, Papa?" Lorena put in. "Why have everyone think you were dead?"

"I never intended for it to be that way . . . at first," he explained to her, then turned to Ben. "As I explained to you before, Mr. Thorne, my first wife, Lorena's mother, came of a wealthy family, but I had no money of my own. I came out here in 'forty-nine with all of the other argonauts, hoping to make my fortune so I could return to New York with my head held high.

"It didn't take long to discover that I wasn't cut out for prospecting, but I learned that I could make a tidy profit selling supplies to the miners, and so I formed a partnership with another New Yorker I'd met; his name was Tyler Sanderson. We set up a tent store in the Placerville gold camp and then another at Spanish Flat and still another at Indian Bar. Needless to say, in a few years' time our little venture had prospered considerably, and I had something to write home about. By then, though, my wife had taken ill, and I returned to New York, leaving everything in Sanderson's hands.

"When I got there, I struck up a relationship with a young daughter I scarcely knew. She'd been only a babe when I left her, but now she was a vibrant child. She tagged along behind me wherever I went, and I taught her how to ride and shoot. She couldn't get enough of my stories about the West.

"When her mother died, I knew I had to come back here; I'd grown accustomed to the life. New York wasn't my home anymore. I knew, too, that I couldn't take Lorena with me. California was a wild place in those early days, not at all suitable for raising a child, especially a daughter. So I left her in the care of her uncle, promising I'd return for her when she turned sixteen. It was a promise I'd come to regret.

"I arrived back in California to find things greatly changed. A good deal of our fortune had been lost when the businesses we'd invested in in San Francisco burnt to the ground during the plague of fires that hit the city in the 'fifties. Sanderson was taking it well enough. He'd settled to the south, near Monterey, and was living quite comfortably. He'd even fallen in love with a beautiful Spanish girl. When I got there he convinced me to share his home while we searched together for a way to restore our lost riches.

"Tyler Sanderson was a likable fellow with a good heart, and that's how I'll always remember him. One night he came upon me, in frustration, as I tried to compose a letter to Lorena. I was never any good at letter writing, and so he offered to do it for me, and from that time on he drafted a letter to her, once a week faithfully, and signed my name to it."

Lorena looked up at him, eyes wide. "Papa. . . ?"

"I'm sorry to say it, but it's true, my dear. Well, to get on with my story—Sanderson and I decided at last to pool our remaining capital and make an investment in a Nevada silver mine. We traveled out to Carson City and made the deal, but got caught up in a poker game one night with a drunken miner who accused Tyler of cheating him. Before either of us knew what had happened, Tyler lay bleeding to death on the floor. I sat up all that night, thinking as how it would have been better if it had been me who'd been the one to die. Tyler had everything to live for. He'd found happiness at last with that young lady of his, the beautiful Mariella, and she was carrying his child. They were to have been married upon his return.

"And I had worries of my own. I had promised to return for Lorena when she turned sixteen, and the time was fast approaching, only now the empire I'd planned to build for her was naught but a crumbling foundation. The answer struck me as I fumbled through my pockets and came across the last letter Tyler had written for me to Lorena. If, for all this time, he'd pretended he was me, why then could I not now pretend that I was him? On the following morning 'Will Mackenzie' was laid to rest in a cemetery outside of Carson City.

"I came back to explain things to Mariella and offered to marry her and give the child a name, the name it truly deserved—Sanderson's. My friend Peter Davis arranged all of the legal matters. I could afford to send some money to Lorena's uncle, but the fortune that was alluded to in all the documents was left in my—that is to say, Sanderson's—hands until Lorena reached the age of twenty-one. By that time I reckoned I could amass a comfortable enough sum to settle on her, as indeed I have.

"Mariella and I settled in San Francisco, with only we three knowing the truth, and from that moment on, I became Tyler Sanderson. I swear to you, Lorena, if I had known what your uncle was capable of, I'd never have left you in his care, and if I had it to do over again, well—"

"It's all right, Papa," Lorena told him, and reached across the desk to grasp his hand. "Everything's come out all right in the end."

"Then you'll live here with Mariella and me, and I shall make up for all the lost years—"

"No," she said plainly. "Much as I love you, Papa, I can't stay here. I don't belong in San Francisco."

Mackenzie nodded, and a smile touched the corner of his mouth as he looked first at his daughter and then at Ben Thorne. "Well, I've said my piece, and now there are things between the two of you that ought to be said, so I'll leave you alone."

When he was gone, there was silence in the room for a very long time. When Lorena could stand it no more, she pulled herself out of her chair and went to the windows to stare out on the garden.

Ben had been struck hard by Will Mackenzie's story—of the life that he'd led and the mistakes he'd made. He determined that he'd not make the same kind of mistakes.

Following Lorena to the window, he lay his hand on her soft shoulder and turned her around to face him. "Did you mean what you said . . . about going back?"

"You know that I did. I've seen nothing here, nothing in the whole of my life, to compare with Wind River. It's a part of my dreams now."

He stared into her liquid eyes and swore that he could see those dreams too. Maybe Broken Hand had been right; in the end, a wanderer would come to nothing. The only chance at happiness was to find your place and make a stand.

"I'll only say this once, Lorena, and then you can be free of me if that's what you will. I love you. I've loved you from the first time you crossed my path, before it was proper, before it was wise. . . . And if you truly intend to go back and make a place for yourself in the Wyoming wilderness, then you'll be a damned sight better off with me at your side."

"If this is a proposal," Lorena said to him, "then I'd like to hear the words."

Ben reached out and pulled her to him. "Marry me!"

And before another second could pass, Lorena kissed him and he had his answer.

The End?

The end of a book is never really *the end* for a person who reads. He or she can always open another. And another.

Every page holds possibilities.

But millions of kids don't see them. Don't know they're there. Millions of kids can't read, or won't.

That's why there's RIF. Reading is Fundamental (RIF) is a national nonprofit program that works with thousands of community organizations to help young people discover the fun— and the importance—of reading.

RIF motivates kids so that they *want* to read. And RIF works directly with parents to help them encourage their children's reading. RIF gets books to children and children into books, so they grow up reading and become adults who can read. Adults like you.

For more information on how to start a RIF program in your neighborhood, or help your own child grow up reading, write to:

RIF
Dept. BK-1
Box 23444
Washington, D.C.
20026

Founded in 1966, RIF is a national non-profit organization with local projects run by volunteers in every state of the union.

A HISTORICAL ROMANCE
TO CAPTURE YOUR HEART!

KAT MARTIN
MAGNIFICENT PASSAGE

Mandy Ashton is fleeing her stifling existence at
Fort Laramie and is heading toward California. Travis Langley, a white man raised by the
Cheyenne, is hired to escort her, although he
mistakenly believes she is the rebellious daughter
of the governor. This dangerous deception becomes
even more perilous when the two discover they've
become captives of a passion as untamed as the
wilderness of the American West! Will they be able
to overcome their contest of wills and let true love
reign?

ISBN: 0-517-00620-0   Price: $3.95

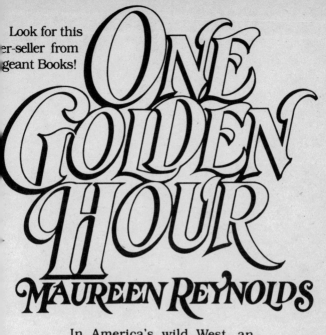